DEMONS AFTER DARK
COVENANT

DEVILISH DEAL

WRITTEN BY

JENNA WOLFHART

JOIN THE GROUP

*To stay up-to-date with **Demons After Dark**, join my Facebook reader group by clicking here. It's full of book discussions, giveaways, cover reveals, and more!*

Today could go straight to hell.

I leaned against the rusted fire escape railing, staring out at the city. As the night deepened, the lights in a thousand windows flared in the darkness like a blanket of stars. The buzz of taxi horns, murmured conversation, and clinking glass swirled around me. A pigeon kept me company, nibbling on the chunks of bread I tossed into the air. I'd named him Hendrix. He visited more days than not, always recognizable by the single black spot above his eye. This place had begun to feel a little like home, even though I'd only moved to New York a few months ago.

Moved. Ha! I'd been living out of my car before this.

My best friend, Serena, joined me on the fire escape and handed me a coffee mug full of white wine—the cheap kind that came in a box. Her midnight hair cascaded around her slim, dark shoulders in perfect waves as she tipped back her head to stare up at the sky. A crescent moon glowed over the buildings. She caught the look on my face and frowned.

"Bad news again?" Serena asked.

I sighed and took a sip. The wine tasted like boiled socks, but it was better than nothing, especially on a night like this. "Rejection. Again. They went with someone else. Surprise, surprise. No one is ever going to give a job to someone who was charged with involuntary manslaughter. The HR guy said I was more than qualified, but they had 'concerns' about me. What a dick."

It was at least the fiftieth job I'd applied to since moving to the city. I'd managed to make it to the interview stage a few times, but it always ended the same. As soon as they Googled my name, it was all over.

"You were acquitted."

"Only because they couldn't prove it. Everyone thinks I'm guilty." I glanced at Serena, who swirled the wine in her mug. "Except for you."

She slung her arm around my shoulder and sighed. "This sucks. I'm so sorry. You know I love the hell out of you, Mia."

"But you still want me out of your very voluptuous hair." I gave her a knowing smile. "Is Noah coming over tonight?"

Serena flushed and downed her drink in one gulp. "I'm supposed to hang out with him tonight, but I'm not going to kick you out of your own apartment just to see a guy."

"*Your* apartment," I corrected. "And this studio is not big enough for the three of us, especially when there's a date involved."

I glanced at the open window that led back into the Brooklyn apartment. It was in the shape of an L. Along with a minuscule kitchen, the longer section was just big enough for a two-seater couch, a small TV, and a few cluttered shelves. The smaller corner fit nothing but a bed. Serena had hung up a beaded curtain between the two spaces, so we could have the illusion of privacy, but we could still hear each other breathe at night. The place was barely big enough for Serena, let alone the two of us, but she'd insisted I crash on her couch until I found a job and a place for myself.

Unfortunately, my past refused to let me move on.

"Doesn't matter," Serena insisted with a fierce smile. "This is your place for as long as you need it to be. Noah and I will go somewhere else. There's a new bar in Bushwick I've been meaning to check out."

"You've been dying for some alone time with him." I ducked through the window and jumped down onto the warped hardwood floor. "I'll make myself scarce for a few hours. No big deal."

Serena followed me inside, frowning. "Mia, I don't want you to feel like you have to do this. Where will you even go?"

I shrugged and grabbed my knee-high boots from the rack beside the door. "Exploring. It's New York City. It's not like I'll be bored."

Before she could object, I tossed her a smile, grabbed the handle, and tugged open the door. I jogged down the three flights of stairs and pushed out into the night. Hordes of people bustled past. The commuters with their backpacks and scuffed sneakers they changed into after a day spent in office shoes. Then there were the 'artistes' with their hipster beards and artisan coffee cups. The harried mothers and the children, the grocery store workers, and the locals who had lived in the neighborhood for decades.

I joined the fray, wandering aimlessly through the streets until a flyer nailed to a telephone pole caught my eye. The big bold letters announced a job opening for a club in Hell's Kitchen, of all places. They needed a dancer, someone to wriggle around in one of the elevated cages while the drunken partiers watched. Auditions were open only on Monday nights when the club was shut to patrons.

There was a strange symbol drawn at the bottom of the flyer. Squiggly lines wrapped around each other, ending in what looked like a devil tail.

Tonight was Monday. I shook my head and stepped back. It was a crazy idea. A dancer at a club? My parents would hate that, not that they would ever hear about it. They hadn't spoken to me in months. Unlike Serena, they believed the lies about me.

But still. Me, a dancer? Sure, I'd taken ballet and jazz in high school, but I doubt I'd be prancing around in a tutu. This was way out of my comfort zone.

There was really only one way to find out.

I was in desperate need of a job. My bank account

was in the negative, and I had nowhere to live. Serena wouldn't kick me out, but I knew she wanted her space. The other day, I'd overheard her and Noah talk about moving in together one day. I'd squatted in her tiny studio for three months. She'd saved my ass when I had nowhere else to go. It was time to repay the favor.

I snatched the flyer off the telephone pole and turned my feet toward the subway station.

***

It took me well over an hour to reach Hell's Kitchen from Clinton Hill. The subway ride was long, stinky, and boring as hell, and it was enough time for me to rethink my hasty plan. I hadn't really come dressed for a dance audition, and I had no routine prepared. My dark skinny jeans and black crop top would constrict my movements, and my boots were clunky and heavy.

Still, I found the club anyway and eyed the door from the opposite side of the street. Fitting for Hell's Kitchen, the owners had dubbed it *Infernal*. The sign was dark, but it looked as though the words glowed with flames when the place was open. Set inside an old, industrial warehouse, it took up half the block. That same strange symbol had been painted onto the single door out front.

Other than that, it was impossible to tell anything about the place. I shifted on my feet and bit my lip. This was probably a terrible idea.

I glanced down the quiet street. Hell's Kitchen had

once been a grungy, crime-infested corner of the city, but the past few decades had transformed it into a bustling, lively, trendy place with popular bars and nightclubs. But this street was as dark and as silent as a tomb, and I swore I felt a pair of eyes on the back of my head. Fear skittered down my spine.

I rolled my eyes at myself. This was ridiculous. All I had to do was walk through that door, put on a good audition, and go back to Brooklyn. By that point, Noah and Serena would have spent several hours alone, and I could crawl onto the couch, cozy into a blanket, and watch Netflix until my eyelids fell shut. Maybe have another few mugs of that shitty wine. Just like I did every night.

Ugh. What a life.

Squaring my shoulders, I strode across the street. My boots clicked on the pavement, the only sound in the strange silence. When I reached the club's entrance, I tried the handle. Locked. I took a deep breath and pushed the buzzer.

A moment later, the door swung open. A blast of heat slammed me square in the chest as a tall, dark-haired man gave me a single glance. Time seemed to slow. My heart flickered beneath my ribs. This guy was *hot*. Broad chest, chiseled cheekbones, and—he slammed the door in my face too fast for me to see anything else.

I scoffed, my mouth dropping open.

How *rude*.

Narrowing my eyes, I knocked again. Immediately, he opened the door, as if he'd known I wouldn't go away that easily. It was all I could do not to stare at the guy. His sweeping cheekbones cut like glass, and his piercing blue eyes were flecks of ice. A fitted black tee draped across his well-muscled chest, and his snug jeans hung low around his hips, showing off just a hint of his washboard abs.

My heart pounded as I glared up at him. Nice to look at, but still *rude*.

"I'm here about the job." I held up the flyer, grateful that my hand didn't shake. "It says auditions are tonight."

He eyed me, a strange expression rippling across his face. "The job is only open to a specific type of dancer. As far as I can tell, that isn't you."

His voice was deeper and smoother than I expected, like a big mouthful of melted dark chocolate.

I narrowed my eyes. "What kind of dancer?"

"One you aren't." He moved to shut the door again, but I stuck out my boot to stop him.

"How can you tell what kind of dancer I am if you don't let me audition?" Honestly, I didn't know why I was fighting so hard for a chance at this job. It wasn't like I really wanted it. Something about this place didn't sit right in my gut, and I had no idea what went on behind these closed doors. So I should take his hesitance—and *total assholery*—as a sign and go home.

The only problem was, I didn't have a home. Not a real one, at least.

He folded his arms and smiled. "Trust me. I can tell just by looking at you."

"And I can tell you're a dick just by looking at

you." The words popped out of my mouth before I could stop them. Whoops. Probably not the *best* way to impress a potential employer. I ground my teeth as I watched another job lead fall through. At least it meant I wouldn't have to look into this asshole's perfectly-sculpted face every day.

His brows winged upward. "I own this place. I can be as much of a dick as I like."

Inwardly, I rolled my eyes. Of course he owned the place. With a deep breath, I bit back my agitation and swallowed a little pride.

"Look, I'm new to the city, it's been a rough few months, and I just really wanted a chance at this job. I have over ten years of dance experience. Unless the gig involves parading around topless, I know I would be good at this. Nothing against it, of course, but it's not for me. The topless thing, I mean. Dancing *is* for me. Clothed dancing. What I'm trying to say is I don't want to show my boobs."

Heat flooded my cheeks, and I cut myself off before I rambled on about my boobs for another five minutes. Hopefully this guy didn't think I was trying to flirt. He might look good, but I'd rather sleep on Serena's couch for the rest of my life than even think about touching him with a ten-foot pole.

"Over ten years?" He regarded me again, and a strange sizzling heat trailed down my spine. I swallowed hard beneath his gaze, my heartbeat flickering like butterfly wings. It almost felt as though he was peeling back the layers of my skin and staring into my soul.

But that was ridiculous.

"I got serious about dance when I was twelve. I'm twenty-three now…although, I haven't done much dancing recently."

"College?"

I nodded. "I graduated two years ago."

"What have you been doing since then?"

I swallowed hard. There it was, the question I wanted to avoid. If he knew about my past, he'd never let me step foot through that door. "Nothing important."

A beat passed in brutal silence. His eyes bored into the very depths of me. At least, that was what it felt like.

"I see. What's your name?"

I frowned. What was with the fifty questions? I didn't want to tell him my full name. He would look me up—they all did. And nothing good ever came of that. But if he decided to hire me, he'd have to know my name for the paperwork. Ugh.

"Mia McNally."

"Hmm." His sharp blue eyes flashed as he took a step toward me. I stiffened, and my breath caught in my throat. He was taller than I'd realized. At least six foot and brimming with pure muscle. I swore I could smell a hint of bonfire rippling off his skin. The tension in my body rocketed up a notch. "I'll give you five minutes for an audition, but only because I can't quite figure you out."

I swallowed hard and laughed awkwardly. That made two of us. Who the hell was this guy? Why was he such an asshole? And did I *really* want to work for him?

He turned and stepped into the shadows of his club. Without another glance in my direction, he held the door open and waited. "Aren't you coming?"

I pulled the night air into my lungs and stepped into *Infernal*.

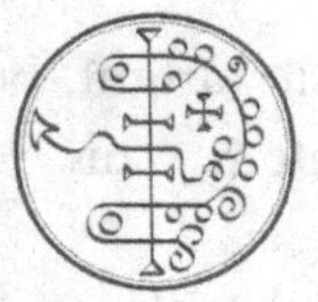

2

"Welcome to my club." The owner, whose name I still didn't know, led me through a dimly-lit corridor. The walls were lined with framed photographs of famous people. Actors and pop singers, politicians and reality stars. My heart thumped as we drew close to a gleaming oak door. Had all of these people been here? What kind of place had I ended up in, and why had I never heard of it before?

This guy's opinion of me was starting to make a little more sense. With my casual, well-worn clothes and flaming red hair, I wasn't exactly a shiny, glamorous kind of girl. I was more at home stomping on a bar top than mingling with women who wore glittering jewels that cost more than my entire life's earnings.

He pushed open the oak door, and I followed him into the main section of his club. The once-gritty warehouse had been transformed. A black marble floor stretched out before us, leading to a small stage with a DJ stand. Intimate booths ran along the walls where leather seats curved around tables stocked with champagne buckets. Above the dance floor, seven human-sized birdcages hung from the lofted ceiling. Diamonds glittered along the bottom of each one.

Infernal was a club alright, but it was unlike any I'd ever been in before. This place was meant for people with money.

"What do you think?" the owner asked.

I jumped at the sound of his deep voice, and then inwardly cursed at myself for the reaction. "It looks expensive."

His lips curved into a wicked smile. "That's because it is."

"So, that's why you didn't want to give me an audition. Because I look like I'm poor." Again, my stupid mouth betrayed me. I really should learn how to keep my thoughts to myself in situations like this. But something about this guy really brought out my snark.

"That's not entirely accurate," he said smoothly before strolling across the floor with his hands slung into his jean pockets. I watched him. I couldn't help myself. His dark hair was the color of night itself, and something about the way he moved reminded me of shadows. Very mesmerizing shadows. Gritting my teeth, I glanced away.

"This is where you'd be dancing." I turned back to find him gazing at me with those sharp blue eyes. Something flashed in the depths of them, something I couldn't read. I followed the line of his arm, and then his finger. He was pointing up at the oversized bird-cages. Just as I'd thought. "Is that a problem?"

"Why would it be?" I strode over to him with all of the bravado I didn't feel. "It's just a platform for dancing as far as I can tell."

He shot me a dark smile. "You'd be trapped. If you wanted to leave, you couldn't. Not until the end of your shift when we lower the cages."

My stomach flipped. Well, that was more than a little unnerving. Plus, shivers coursed down my spine from the *way* he'd said it. Like it was a threat. But I knew he was only trying to get a reaction out of me. Probably. And I wouldn't let him see that he'd gotten one.

"No big deal," I said as breezily as possible. "What kind of hours are we talking about? Are there any breaks?"

"The dancers work from eleven to three. No breaks while you're up there. The guests enjoy the dance floor during those hours, and lowering the cages is a logistical nightmare."

I nodded as if the idea of being trapped inside a cage for four hours was at all reasonable. "Do dancers get any tips?"

The owner motioned at something—or *someone*—hidden in the dark shadows near the ceiling. Were we being watched? A moment later, chains groaned as the nearest cage lowered to the ground. He opened the door and pointed at a small golden bucket. "If someone seems interested in your dancing, you can lower that with a rope. But be sure to pocket anything you receive. If you lower it with cash still inside, the tricksters in the crowd will happily take it."

"Tricksters? Sure." I nodded again. *Who uses the word tricksters?*

"Are you ready to audition now?"

I swallowed hard. "One last question."

He raised a brow.

"What's your name? I don't think I caught it."

He flashed me that wicked smile again. "Because I didn't give it to you."

I gave him a blank stare. Was he really going to have me audition for his club and not tell me his damn name? "And it is…?"

"Asmodeus."

I bit back a laugh. What the hell kind of name was that?

Was he joking? Or was he giving me a fake name for some bizarre, unknowable reason? I met his dark gaze. He looked serious enough. There wasn't even a hint of a smile on his face.

"Nice to meet you, *Asmodeus*," I grumbled. Though…was it really? That sense of *wrong* had only increased since I'd stepped foot inside his club. I didn't belong here with this fancy man and his fancy famous friends. With a deep breath, I stepped inside the cage.

Immediately, the door slammed shut behind me, and the cage tipped beneath my feet. It inched off the ground, swinging lightly on its heavy chain. I bit back the urge to scream and stood stock still until the cage shuddered to a stop. Gritting my teeth, I peered through the glittering bars at the sleek, marble floor far below me. Asmodeus stared up at me with a grin that could only be described as pure evil.

I was going to have to dance in this thing.

My heart took flight as Asmodeus strode over to the stage, rounded a DJ stand, and punched a few buttons. Music blared through hidden speakers, an upbeat, clubby song that bounced against my skin. I swallowed hard and wiped my sweaty palms against my jeans. I knew ballet and jazz but nothing more modern. How the hell was I going to pull this off?

"Whenever you're ready," he called.

Pulling my breath into my lungs, I closed my eyes and listened to the beat. This place, this guy, all of it was unnerving and way out of my comfort zone. But I needed a job, desperately so. I hadn't asked about wages, but I didn't need to. The diamonds and the wall of famous faces said it all. I would be paid well if I got this job. Probably well enough to get my own apartment.

All I had to do was put up with a weird asshole of a boss and dance in a cage for a few hours several times a week. That really wasn't so bad in the grand scheme of things. A lot of people had it way worse than that.

The bass thumped through the club, reverberating through the thick soles of my boots. Slowly, I began to nod, letting the music fill my body. The notes wound into my ears, mixing with my blood. I'd always felt attuned to music, like it was part of me. After a few moments, my body moved. I didn't overthink it. I lost myself in the sound and let my soul take over.

I'd spent years training my body, and it knew

what to do without me asking. My arms twisted in the air as my legs bounced from side to side. I pushed up onto my toes and spun, my fingers skimming the bars, my hair swirling around my shoulders.

The world dropped away as I danced. All my fears were forgotten. My worries and anxieties whispered away. The job didn't matter. My parents didn't matter. The trial and the charges and the social media hate I'd endured were momentarily nothing but a shadow in my mind.

The music cut off. And suddenly, it all came rushing back in. The accusing eyes. The headlines. The sirens. The look on my parents' faces when they shouted at me to get out. Tears flooded my vision, but I quickly blinked them away.

I looked down to find Asmodeus staring up at me with appreciation in his eyes. I swore I even saw the hint of a smile. My chest lifted as hope chased away the fears battling their way back inside my mind. I'd impressed him.

The job was mine. I could see it in his face.

Asmodeus motioned to the ceiling, and the cage cranked down to the gleaming floor. I tried to push the door open, but it didn't budge. My lungs squeezed tight. I was locked inside.

For a moment, Asmodeus stood on the other side of the door and made no move to release me. My heart hammered my ribs, and panic stuck in my throat like a rock, choking my breath away. Darkness swirled across my vision, and a sudden heat pulsed against my skin, as if a nearby radiator had suddenly flared to life.

I'd been an idiot for walking into this club. Alone. No one even knew where I was. All I had was a few borrowed dollars in my pocket. My hands fisted by my sides as the instinct to fight rose within me like a storm. If he didn't let me out of this damn cage, I would scream bloody murder. This might be a quiet street, but *someone* would hear me.

Maybe. How thick were these club walls?

After far too many tense moments, Asmodeus cracked a grin, shoved the key into the lock, and released me from the cage. I stumbled forward with narrowed eyes. "For a minute there, I didn't think you were going to let me out."

"You think I would bother trapping you in a cage?" He turned his back on me and strode over to the empty bar in the far corner. It was a curving wooden thing that had been polished to perfection. Behind it, rows of top bottles glimmered beneath a hidden spotlight. There were champagne bottles that cost more than Serena's monthly rent.

"The way you said that makes it sound like an insult." I stayed beside the cage, watching him grab a bottle of gin from behind the bar.

"Would you like a drink before you go?" he asked, ignoring me. "You look like a gin and tonic kind of girl."

I wasn't sure what that meant, and annoyingly, he was right. Begrudgingly, I trailed over to him. "Sure, I'll have one."

A slight smile lifted the corners of his lips as he mixed the drink. He grabbed a second glass, made another, and then pushed one into my hands. His fingers brushed against mine, and a shot of electricity went down my arm. I stiffened and sucked in a sharp breath, and then scolded myself for being such a goddamn idiot. His eyes darkened as he pulled back his hand, and I swore I saw the reflection of flames deep within the sharp blue.

Obviously, I was imagining things. This guy was really getting under my skin, and I hated him for it.

"So," he said, leaning back against the bar. He looked so calm and in control, so relaxed in who he was. There was a confidence that radiated off him, like nothing in the world could ever tear him down. I couldn't imagine ever having a life like that. "You're not a bad dancer."

"Wow, what a compliment." I took a sip of the drink and fought back the urge to moan. It was the best gin and tonic I'd ever tasted. Sharp yet sweet, with the perfect amount of bitters. It was all I could do not to chug the entire thing and then ask for another.

The right corner of his lips tilted up, dimpling his cheek. I swallowed hard. It was the first time I'd noticed the dimples. They hadn't been there before, had they? Or was this just the first genuine smile? "All right, I'll admit you're good. Your body seemed to suck up the music, and then pour it all out again. Mesmerizing, really."

I fought back a smile, hiding it behind another sip of the gin and tonic. "Thanks. So, does that mean I got the job?"

His expression darkened as he raised the glass to

his lips. "Unfortunately, no. I meant what I said, Mia. You're not right for this establishment."

My hand tightened around the glass as frustration rushed through me. "But you had me audition."

"Because I was curious about you. You're a hard one to figure out." He shrugged. "I told you that before you came in. You're a very good dancer, but it changes nothing. We're looking for someone you're not."

I lowered the glass to the bar top and scowled. "I can't believe you had me come in here and waste my time. If I'd known I had no shot at this, I wouldn't have bothered."

He raised a brow. "Are you sure about that?"

"Very," I shot back. With a frustrated growl, I twisted on my heels and stormed toward the door. Just as I reached it, I cast one last glance over my shoulder. Asmodeus still stood by the bar, a bemused look on his face. "Here's a tip. You might have a fancy bar and famous friends, but being a rude asshole will only get you so far in life. Keep this up, and one day your pretty castle will crumble down on top of your head. Goodbye, Asmodeus. I hope I never see your smug face again."

3

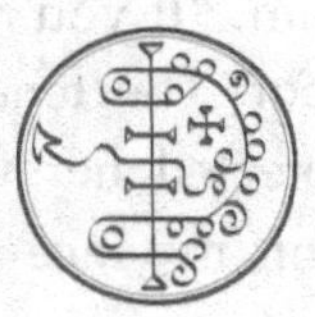

By the time I reached Brooklyn, I still hadn't calmed down. Where did Asmodeus get the idea he could treat people like that? And what was he trying to imply about me? That I wasn't good enough for his stupid, overpriced club? To hell with that.

Serena opened the door before I could knock. Her mussed hair and lazy smile told me everything I needed to know. When she caught the look on my face, she straightened. "Everything okay? Did something happen?"

"I'm fine." I trudged into the apartment and kicked off my boots. "Is Noah still here?"

"Hi." Noah stood from the couch and dusted some nonexistent crumbs off his jeans. "I was just leaving."

Noah had come into Serena's life a year ago. He worked at one of the local artisan coffee shops and wrote novels in his spare time. His wire-rimmed glasses, along with his dusty blonde hair, made him look smart but also adorable. The two of them had somehow found each other in a city full of millions. I'd never seen Serena happier, and I'd known her my entire life.

"Honestly, you don't need to leave on my account," I said to him. "If you're still hanging out, I can go up to the roof. The tenant on the top floor hasn't password-protected her wifi, so I can watch some Netflix and stuff my face with ice cream for a few hours."

"Uh oh, not the ice cream," Serena said with a groan. "What happened to our pact?"

Noah raised a questioning brow, so Serena explained. "Mia can't do anything in moderation but especially not ice cream. She eats a spoonful, and then the entire carton is gone within ten minutes. And then her stomach aches for days. A week ago, she vowed to go cold turkey." She eyed me warily. "So something must have happened."

"I found another job lead," I said tensely. "An audition to dance at a club. The owner turned me away because I don't look the part. That combined with the earlier rejection from the receptionist job has sucked the life out of my day."

"Wait," Serena said, folding her arms over her wrinkled t-shirt. "A club? Where?"

"All the way in Manhattan," I said with a sigh. "Hell's Kitchen."

"No wonder you were gone for so long." A moment passed before she spoke again. "A dancer at a club? Is that really the kind of job you want?"

"No. Yes. I don't know." I shrugged. "It doesn't matter either way. I didn't get it."

"The cafe is hiring," Noah interjected. "A girl quit last week, and business is booming. We need another barista as soon as possible. I could hook you up with an interview if you'd like."

I straightened, ice cream craving forgotten. Working in a cafe wasn't my first choice, but I didn't have the luxury of choosing. My business degree sat on a shelf, gathering dust, and my ballet shoes were tucked in the back corner of my closet. I didn't know much about coffee, but I could learn.

"You know what? That would be great. Thanks for offering to help."

He flashed me a smile as he gathered his things. "Anything for Serena's roommate. We'll get you back on your feet."

I read between the lines. He might be doing this to help me out, but there was a bonus for him. The sooner I got a job, the sooner I'd move out...but I didn't know how I'd afford rent on barista wages. At least not in Clinton Hill.

Still, I would take whatever I could get. I'd proved that tonight, auditioning for that stupid asshole and his stupid dimpled smile. Ugh. At least I would never have to see him again.

❦

A taxi horn blared louder than any alarm. I jolted up from the couch, heart hammering. Dawn light filtered in through the cracked blinds hanging over the single window. I glanced at the clock. It was only six. The symphony of the city began far too early.

After I climbed out of my makeshift bed, folded the blankets, and took a shower, I whipped up some breakfast and threw on the television. Noah had told me to be ready for my interview at ten, so I had a few hours to kill. When I was halfway into my stack of pancakes, Serena joined me on the floor with a bowl of cereal. There wasn't room in the apartment for a dining table.

"You're up early," she said as she rubbed the sleep out of her eyes.

"Couldn't sleep." I didn't mention the horns. Somehow, Serena always slept right through them. "Thought I might as well get up and get my day started."

"You'll be all right today?" she asked as she swirled her spoon through the milk. "I don't want to abandon you after last night."

Serena worked in Manhattan as one of the youngest lawyers ever hired by her firm. With that designation came long hours and little time spent at home.

"I've got that interview at the cafe. I'll be fine."

"Stay away from the ice cream," she warned.

I opened my mouth to throw back a retort, but a voice from the television cut through my thoughts. Serena seemed to notice it at the same time I did. We both twisted toward the screen.

"A new victim was found in Hell's Kitchen last night. Her throat was slashed, just like the others."

The reporter's lipsticked mouth was grim, solemn. "The police are investigating several leads, but..."

I sucked in a sharp breath and met Serena's wide gaze. "Another one? I thought those murders had stopped. Didn't they catch the guy?"

"They did. He's in jail...they must have been wrong...Mia, you were in Hell's Kitchen last night," Serena breathed as she leaned forward. "That could have been you."

My heart pulsed painfully in my chest. She was right.

After taking one final bite of my pancakes, I stood and brushed the crumbs from my jeans. "Well, it wasn't me. It was some other poor girl." I shivered just thinking about it. This was the fifth murder in the past few months. The police thought a serial killer was behind them all, and they'd caught a suspect a few weeks back. The murders had stopped...until now.

Either this was a copycat or they'd caught the wrong guy.

Serena frowned up at me. "Why aren't you more freaked out?"

"I *am* freaked out, but I don't want to drive myself crazy thinking in what ifs. Not anymore. I spent two years doing that." I strode over to the window, popped my head outside, and found Hendrix waiting for his morning treat. With a smile, I tossed him a leftover piece of my pancake. He caught it midair and swallowed it in one gulp. Spoiled pigeon.

Serena edged up behind me. "Just don't go

traipsing through the streets at night again, okay? Not even for a job."

"I won't," I replied, though I'd meant what I said. An asshole with a knife wouldn't make me cower in this apartment. I'd come to the city to finally move on with my life, so that was what I was going to do. As soon as I got a job. First up, I had to nail this interview. And hope they didn't decide to look me up online.

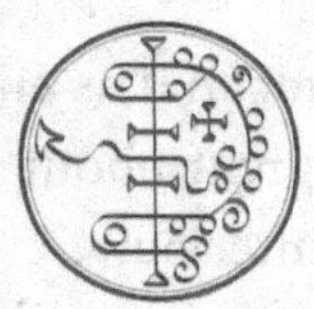

The little cafe sat on a tree-lined street in the nicest part of Clinton Hill and on the ground floor of a brownstone. Potted plants dotted the sidewalk, along with circular wrought-iron tables. Every one was packed with customers sitting in the sun and taking advantage of the warm summer day. I squared my shoulders and pushed open the door. A little bell jangled to announce my arrival.

Two harried baristas glanced up from behind the counter that curved along one wall. A line of customers trailed through the building, though most of the tables inside were vacant. Tiny, multi-colored mason jars lined the walls, and old pallets hung from the ceiling by mismatched chains and ropes. The scent of coffee wafted into my nose in a sudden blast of aromatic caffeine.

Noah popped his head out of a door in the far corner. He motioned me forward. I took a deep breath, wound my way through the crowd, and joined him in the back. He gave me a once-over, taking me in. Unlike last night's interview, I'd opted for a nice pair of black slacks, a sleeveless, button-up shirt that covered my belly button, and a basic pair of flats.

"You look nicer than usual," he said.

"Gee, thanks."

I knew he didn't mean it as an insult, but still. Way to make a girl feel great about herself two seconds before an important interview.

He led me down an empty hallway and stopped outside of a back office where an older man sat inside, rustling through a mound of paperwork. A pair of glasses perched on his thin nose, and the overhead fluorescent light gleamed off his bald head.

Noah knocked lightly on the open door. "Mia McNally is here for her interview. Mia, this is Abe, the owner of *Funky Froth*."

God, what a dumb name.

I pasted on a fake smile and edged into the room, perching on a small folding chair across from Abe's desk. He glanced up at me, put down his stack of papers, and gave me a blank stare before pushing his glasses up the bridge of his nose.

"Nice to meet you, Mia." He nodded at Noah, who left us to it, closing the door behind him. "Noah tells me you're interested in the barista opening."

"That's right. I've always wanted to work in a cafe." Lies, lies, lies. I had nothing against coffee, but it wasn't my top choice of beverage.

"I see." He shuffled through the papers, pulled out

a notepad, and clicked his pen. "Well, do you have any experience working in a cafe?"

I cleared my throat. "Not as such, but I'm a quick learner. And I was a server in a restaurant back home."

"Back home." He clicked his pen twice more. "How many years did you work in the restaurant?"

"Four years," I said. "All throughout college."

"I see. And what have you been doing the past two years? Have you had a job since graduation?"

My heart flipped in my chest. How did he know I'd graduated two years ago? I'd brought my resume with me, but he hadn't asked for it yet. Had Noah told him? Serena and I had been in the same class until she'd graduated early to go to law school, and he knew we'd grown up together, so he must have put two and two together. Still, why would he have mentioned that to Abe?

Unease slithered down my spine like a snake ready to strike. That old familiar feeling squeezed my heart. The realization that the person who sat across from me knew exactly who I was. When I'd moved to New York City, I'd thought I'd left that world behind, but it had followed me here. It dogged my steps on the sidewalks. It lurked in the shadows behind the lampposts. And it sat before me now with a pair of wiry glasses and a gleaming bald head.

Serena had asked me why I wasn't more freaked out by the serial killer roaming the nighttime streets, and this had a lot to do with it. I was far more scared of my past. It had a tendency of dragging me into the depths of hell.

"I took a little break after college," I finally said. "People in the UK like to call it a gap year."

"We're not in the UK." He tapped his pen against the notepad. "And you took two years instead of one."

Dammit. Gritting my teeth, I leaned back in the chair and fought the urge to tell this guy to shove his preconceptions about me right up his ass. "My family experienced a few personal issues during that time."

"Care to elaborate?"

"Not really."

"I see." He sighed and dropped the notepad onto his cluttered desk. "Mia, I agreed to this interview because Noah is one of our best baristas, and I understand you're old friends with his girlfriend. But I would be lying if I said I didn't have concerns about these personal issues of yours. With everything going on in the city right now, particularly in Hell's Kitchen, I'd be remiss to take you on. Noah mentioned you were there last night."

I bristled, hastily pushing up from the chair. "Wait. You mean the Hell's Kitchen murders, don't you? Are you suggesting I have something to do with those deaths? You think I'm *killing* those girls?"

He folded his arms. "I've read the articles. I know you only escaped a prison sentence because of a technicality."

I fisted my hands on his desk and leaned toward him. "The reason I didn't get convicted is because there was zero evidence against me."

"Then why did you refuse to testify?"

I flushed and pushed away from the desk, my

heart hammering my ribs. "I'm not going to stand here and get berated by you about something you know nothing about. I'll assume I didn't get the job. Fine with me. I wouldn't want to work in this shit-hole anyway. I hate coffee."

With that, I whirled on my feet and threw open the door. I stomped down the hallway past Noah and his shocked Pikachu face. I tried to rustle up a measure of guilt. He'd done me a favor, and things would no doubt be awkward next time he visited Serena.

"What the hell did you just do?" he asked, anger turning the edges of his words to steel. "You know I had to pull some strings to get you this damn interview."

"Well, you shouldn't have bothered if you were going to tell your boss about my past." I narrowed my eyes, and the guilt raced away as fast as Usain Bolt. He'd completely sabotaged any chance I had.

Noah folded his arms. "I didn't tell him. He looked you up, and then asked me about it. All I did was tell him the truth."

All the blood rushed from my face to pool around my feet. "The truth? So you think I did it."

"I think Serena loves you, and it's blinded her." He regarded me carefully. "Did you know she's put her life on hold because of you? She refuses to move in with me until you get your shit together, and she's taking a lot of flack from her bosses, too. They haven't put her on a few high-profile cases because they don't want some clever reporter to find the link between their firm and you. As long as you're living with her, you're holding her back."

"What?" I took a step back as the world tilted beneath my feet. "That can't be right. Serena would have told me."

He lifted his brow above his glasses. "You really think she'd tell you and hurt you like that? Serena is loyal to a fault."

I closed my eyes as the pain wrapped around my heart. He was right. There wasn't a chance in hell my best and oldest friend would ever tell me she suffered because of her association with me. She'd do anything to protect me. And I'd do the same for her. We'd always stood beside each other despite it all, and now she was paying for it.

"You better get out of here," Noah said, his voice cutting through my thoughts. "My boss is coming, and he looks pretty pissed."

"Yeah, whatever," I mumbled, turning away.

"Oh, and Mia?" he said just as I started toward the door. I paused but kept my gaze forward. I couldn't bear to look at him right now. "Think about what I said. If you care about Serena the way she cares about you, you'll find a way to move out of her apartment."

Blinking back the tears, I raced out of the cafe and onto the sidewalk. Cars rushed past. A group of teens stumbled by, laughing uproariously. The world continued on while my whole life was stuck in standstill. How would I ever get past that damn manslaughter charge? My only two friends in the entire world were my next door neighbor from elementary school, whose life I was ruining, and a pigeon who only liked me for my food.

My life had gone to hell in a hand-basket.

❧

I wandered around the neighborhood for a few hours before returning to Serena's apartment. She'd be at work, but I still couldn't face the tiny couch jammed into the tiny room. It felt like a cage, one I would never escape. The judge may have acquitted me, but I'd still ended up in another form of jail. And it felt like I was sentenced to life.

Back at Serena's, I changed into sweats, spooned out a massive bowl of ice cream, and settled onto the couch for some binge-watching. In the back of my mind, I knew I should power up my laptop and continue my hunt for a job, but it felt pointless right now.

As the episodes flashed before my eyes, I let my mind get lost in a world full of cakes, competitions, and British accents. A few drops of chocolate ice cream splashed onto my cream sweatshirt, and I found myself with my tongue halfway to the stain before I realized exactly what I was doing. God, I was a mess.

I paused the bakeoff show and drifted into the tiny cubicle of a bathroom to hunt for something to clean my shirt when Serena's door buzzer blared through the quiet apartment. I jumped, knocking my head against the medicine cabinet. Pain flickered through my forehead. Wincing, I pressed my hand against my head and found a massive bruise already forming.

I peered at myself in the mirror. Yep, there was a lump, and it was already turning blue.

Sighing, I padded out of the bathroom and pushed the intercom. "Who is it?"

A hissing crackle followed, and then his voice. The one I'd never forget. "It's Asmodeus. Is this Mia? I need to speak with you for a few moments."

I stumbled back and stared at the intercom like it would bite me if I got too close. Heart shaking, I crossed the floor and poked my head out the window. I spotted him through the slats in the fire escape. There he was, wearing low-slung jeans and a fitted black shirt. In the full light of day, he looked even more mouthwatering than he had in his shadowy club.

How the hell was that possible?

Suddenly, he dropped back his head and gazed up at me. "Hello, Mia. Are you going to let me in?"

"Fuck." I ducked back inside and crouched out of sight. I couldn't let him see me like this. I was wearing stained sweats and my forehead was turning blue. I looked like hell.

Why does that matter?!

This was the asshole who hadn't given me the job because I looked...well, like this, probably. *Ugh!* Why was he even here?

"Mia!" he called out. His voice sounded like it was right by my ear. I jumped and darted away from the window, trying to still my racing heart. Maybe he'd come here about the job. Not that I wanted it anymore. "Just give me five minutes of your time."

As much as I wanted to turn him away, my curiosity poked up its eager little head. Five minutes. And then he had to go. Before I could rethink my decision, I pushed the button and let him into the building.

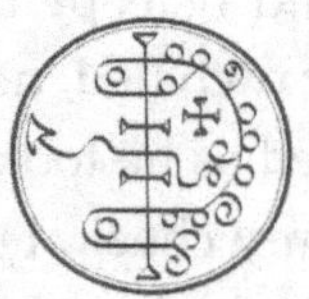

His brow lifted as soon as he saw me. Asmodeus, whatever-his-last-name-was, strode into Serena's apartment like he owned the place. His fitted tee highlighted his sculpted muscles, and the cut of his jaw was as sharp as a knife. Everything about him seemed effortless, like he'd just rolled out of bed looking like this.

Maybe he had.

I hated him.

"This is where you live?" he asked as he turned to take in the tiny studio. Clearly, he thought this place was beneath him and his fancy diamond-encrusted birdcages. His bathroom was probably bigger than this. "It doesn't look like you."

Um, okay.

"It's my friend's place. She's letting me stay here while I hunt for a job." I folded my arms and gave him a dark look. "Why are you here, Asmodeus?"

"You're sleeping on the couch?" He noted the

scrunched-up blanket, the empty ice cream bowl, and the pile of mismatched pillows. I flushed as his eyes drifted toward the brown stain on my shirt. If I'd hoped to impress him, I definitely wasn't going to now.

Luckily, I didn't want to impress him. He was an asshole.

"Where else would I sleep? It's not like I'm going to kick her out of her own bed, now am I?"

His brow furrowed as he took a step toward me. A finger lifted toward my cheek. Heat whispered across my skin like silken shadows. "What happened to your face?"

I flinched away. "I hit my head on the medicine cabinet. Now would you please just tell me what the hell you're doing here?"

An amused smile whispered across his lips. "I wanted to talk to you about the job you auditioned for last night."

"No need. You already turned me down."

"I may have been hasty in my decision."

I gave him a flat stare. "You've got to be kidding me."

He strode through the tiny apartment, tracing his fingers along the wall. When he reached the window, he glanced outside at the pots where Serena and I grew herbs, pretty unsuccessfully. "You have a pigeon out here, looking very expectant."

"His name is Hendrix. He wants his lunch."

Asmodeus chuckled. "You named a Brooklyn pigeon after one of the greatest singers of the past century?"

"At least you have *some* taste. It's a shame it doesn't extend further than that."

"How long have you been looking for a job?" He turned back toward me, and the intensity in his ice-flecked stare sent a bucket of fire down my spine.

I swallowed. "Too long."

"Do you think your lack of success might have something to do with your complete disregard for manners?"

I narrowed my eyes. "Look, *you* insulted *me* last night. And now you're here, wasting my time. Again. I have other things to do, you know."

He cut his eyes toward the paused Netflix show. "Oh yes. It looks that way."

"Whatever. Just get on with it already. Why are you here?" I threw up my hands and stormed toward him. "And don't tell me you came all the way out here to antagonize me. Because if that's the case, then you can leave. Now."

"I came here to offer you a job," he said easily, barely missing a beat.

I stopped in the center of the floor and stared. Was this some kind of joke? Had I fallen asleep and found myself in some bizarre dream? "You made it clear last night you wanted nothing to do with me."

"Now that's not true." He stepped forward, erasing the distance between us. "I was impressed by your talent. At the time, I thought you weren't right for the job, but I was too focused on your role as a dancer. There's something else I believe you'd be perfect for."

His dimpled smile made an appearance. Heat curled through my belly.

"A different job?" I couldn't help but ask.

"In a way. I'd still want you to dance, but that wouldn't be my primary reason for hiring you."

Um, well, *that* didn't sound weird *at all*.

"Explain."

"There are some important events for my business coming up in the next few weeks, and I need a date for each of them. Unfortunately, I don't have anyone appropriate I can take, and these potential investors have insisted I bring someone. So when the events arrive, you'll be my date." He folded his arms and smiled. "In the meantime, you can dance at the club to earn wages and tips. You'll be doing me a favor, so I'll do one for you in return."

I blinked at him. Surely I couldn't have heard him right. "Wait a minute. You're hiring me because you need...a date?" Okay, this guy really was trying to play a twisted joke on me. Did he think I couldn't see his face? And that body? He could have any girl in New York City. What would be the point of this elaborate plot?

Unless there was something wrong with him.

"You realize this is totally weird, right? What's the catch?" I asked, taking a step back.

"There is no catch. The final event is an important ball at the end of the month. After that, you're free to move on to another job, and I'll write you a glowing recommendation."

"So you want to pay me to date you."

"No," he countered, holding up a finger. "You'll be

paid to dance at the club. In return, you'll pretend to be my adoring date at a few events. One who doesn't hate me with the force of a thousand suns."

"You want me to be your fake girlfriend."

"Something like that."

"And why can't you just get a real girlfriend to go to all these things?"

"I don't want a real girlfriend," he said. "I have far too much on my plate for a relationship, and most of the girls who are interested in me aren't after an easy fling. They want my money and my hand in marriage. This way is better for everyone."

I scrunched my brow. "You do realize this is very strange."

He shrugged. "No stranger than most relationships. At least we both know what we want to get out of it. No feelings will be hurt, and no one will read intentions wrong. It will have a clear beginning and an end."

I shifted on my feet. Last night, Asmodeus had basically said I wasn't good enough to dance at his club. And now, he not only wanted to hire me but he wanted me to date him, too? Nothing about this made any sense at all. And yet...I couldn't help but be intrigued.

"Just so we're clear, this has nothing to do with sex, right?"

I didn't know why I was even considering this bizarre deal. A fake girlfriend? To an asshole who thought less of me for a reason he still hadn't explained? Obviously, I couldn't take him up on this.

Not to mention, there was a killer in Hell's Kitchen.

What if it….what if it was him? Surely not.

His eyes flashed with heat, and a strange thrill shot down my spine. "No sex, but a few carefully-timed kisses at public events would not be unwelcome. I wouldn't want my investors to think I hired a fake girlfriend, now would I?"

"No," I said flatly, rolling my eyes. "Because that would make you look like a lonely bastard."

"Careful," he said with a wicked smile, taking another step toward me. "If you take me up on this, I'll be your boss. And you wouldn't want to disrespect your boss, now would you?"

"*If*," I said with a smile I hoped looked just as wicked. "You're assuming I'm as desperate as you are."

He arched a brow and glanced around. "Aren't you?"

Ugh. He had me there. Damn him. When would I get another opportunity like this? Leaving Asmodeus out of it, the job was almost too good to be true. It was just a few dates, and I did love to dance. The only problem was…it would only last a month.

Would that give me enough money to save up for an apartment of my own? How long until I could get out of Serena's hair? Noah's words echoed in my mind. Serena had worked her ass off her entire life to become a lawyer. If she lost her job because of me…

"I just have one question," I said, shifting on my feet. "I need to get out of this apartment as soon as possible. Is there any way you can front me some wages?"

Holding my breath, I met his dark gaze. It was a bold request. In any other circumstance, I'd never ask something like this, least of all from a new boss. But nothing about this was normal. He'd asked me to work for him in exchange for pretending to be his girlfriend. If there was ever a time to be bold, it was now. The sooner I could get out of Serena's apartment, the better.

His lips curled, and a strange expression flickered across his face. "I can do one better than that. I have a guest room in my penthouse. You can stay there as long as you work for me, which will benefit our blooming relationship. It will be good for people to see us leaving the building together."

"Um. Say what now?" Surely I hadn't heard him right.

"It will be better if you're in Manhattan, too," he continued as if I hadn't said a word. "That way, you don't have to take the subway home late at night." His voice dropped to a lower octave. "The streets are dangerous right now."

Shivers stormed across the back of my neck.

"Yes, they *are* dangerous," I said, boldly striding up to him. "A psychopath is out there killing girls, and you just expect me to move in with you, *a stranger*? And pretend to be your *live-in* girlfriend?"

His face turned to stone. "I see. Well, Mia, if you think I'm a killer, then this ends here. My business is built on trust."

Shaking his head, he stepped around me and

made a move for the door. I turned to watch him leave, panic blooming in my gut. He was just going to let this go, as easily as that. I needed this job more than he needed me to do it, and he knew it. Plenty of girls would line up to be his fake date. He had options. I didn't.

Damn him.

Could he really be the killer? He was a massive dick and brimming with danger, but he'd had me alone last night. Nothing had happened. If he'd wanted to kill me, he'd had a chance.

"Wait," I said with a sigh when he reached the door.

He turned toward me, eyebrow raised.

"You understand why I'd be wary."

"Of course I do. But I am no killer, Mia, and just because my club is in Hell's Kitchen does not mean I'm involved."

"I mean, that *is* probably what the actual killer would say."

"I have an alibi," he said. "Which has already been given to the police. They came by the club last night after the poor girl was found—to ask if I'd seen anything. If you have any doubts, you're welcome to call them. But after that, I only want you to take this job if you can trust me. I mean it, Mia. Loyalty and trust are essential to me."

His eyes flashed as if to punctuate his words. Heat stormed through my veins, and an oddly familiar *zing* went down my spine. Where had I felt that before?

"All right," I said in a rush before I could stop myself. This was insane. Probably the most illogical thing I'd ever done in my life. But I couldn't bring myself to turn it down. I could move out of Serena's apartment immediately, and I'd have a month's wages behind me at the end of it. Hopefully, his recommendation letter would be enough to get me on the payroll somewhere else when our time together was up.

Of course, I would find a way to confirm his story, just for peace of mind. I was about to move in with a total stranger, after all…

His brows winged upward. "Are you saying you want the job?"

I nodded, gut twisting with excitement and unease. "When do I start?"

A slow smile spread across his face. "Tomorrow."

My heart flipped. That was soon. "And when do I move in?"

"I see no reason to hold off." His eyes drifted toward the TV. "I know you're very busy with your important plans. Think you could cancel them and move in tonight?"

I wet my lips as I stared into his chiseled face. Holy shit, this was happening fast. Could I really do this? Was I an idiot? Maybe yes. On both accounts. But it was the most exciting thing to have happened to me in months.

"I think I could manage to pack up my things by tonight."

"Good." He gave a nod and whispered over to the door. "I'll have a car pick you up at eight."

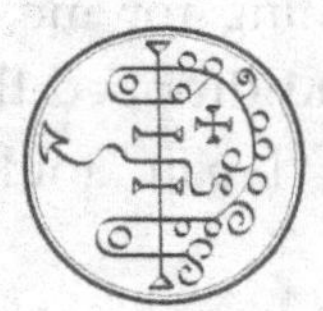

"Are you sure this is a good idea?" Serena asked as she perched on her twin-sized bed, watching me pack. It wouldn't take me long. When I'd run from my parents' home in Nashville, I hadn't brought much with me. A few changes of clothes, a Polaroid photo of me and my sister from when we were ten and eight, and a bucket-load of bad memories.

"No, I'm not sure, but I need this job, Serena. I can't keep living like this. Neither can you."

Serena hugged her polka-dotted pillow to her chest. "Of course I can. You're my best friend, Mia. I said it before, and I'll say it again. You can stay here for as long as you need."

"I don't want to be a burden," I said. "I've been in the city three months now. This apartment is barely big enough for one person, and I know you and Noah want your own place. Your life is on hold because of me."

"On hold?" Her voice dropped to a whisper as sadness flickered in her brown eyes. "I don't look at it that way."

"But it's the truth, isn't it? You and Noah want to move in together."

"Yes, but…"

"And you're waiting for me to move out before you do." I sighed and dropped the last shirt into my black duffel bag. "Noah told me what's been going on."

She stiffened, and then slowly stood from the bed, her arms still latched around the pillow. "He did *what*?"

"He told me you're waiting to move in with him until I'm out of your hair. And he told me what's been going on at your job." I zipped my bag shut and strode over to her, slowly prying the pillow out of her arms. "You could have told me."

She closed her eyes, and a tear slipped down her cheek. "I didn't tell you because the last thing I want to do is hurt you. And I knew it would. I can't believe Noah did that."

"He's only trying to look out for you."

Her eyes flipped open. "And *I'm* trying to look out for *you*. Mia, you can't move in with that guy and pretend to be his girlfriend. Not only is it bizarre as hell, he was an asshole to you, and you know next to nothing about him. For all we know, *he* could be the serial killer we saw on the news."

"He's not. I looked into him. He's been seen in public at the same time as some of the murders. It can't be him." I took her hands in mine and squeezed tight. "Serena, I love you, and you have no idea how much I appreciate everything you've done for me. You're the only person in the goddamn world who believes I didn't kill Audrey. You gave me a home when I had nowhere else to go. But I need to move on with my life now, and so do you."

"We can get a place together," she said fiercely. "A bigger place."

"And how would we afford it? I don't have a job."

"You'll find one eventually."

"What about Noah?"

"He's not really in my good books now," she muttered. "He never should have told you about any of it. It wasn't his place."

"Maybe not. But I'm sure he'll make it up to you. He just cares about you. Same as me."

The doorbell buzzed. I dropped her hands, stepped back, and grabbed my bag. It was eight on the dot, and Asmodeus's driver was here to collect me. I tried not to think about how weird it was that Asmodeus had his own *driver*. There were far too many other weird things to comprehend already.

"That means it's time for me to go." I slung the bag over my shoulder, smiled. "I'll text you as soon as I get there."

"You better." She rushed forward, sniffling, and threw her arms around my neck. The scent of her lemon body wash swirled into my nose. The same scent I'd smelled every morning for the past three months, every time she took a shower. I'd miss it. "Text me constantly. Let me know what's going on at all times. If at any point you want to back out of this, *call me*. You have a place to crash always."

With a sad smile, I clutched her back. If I had to abort this crazy mission, I didn't think I would have it in me to call her. If this was only about her future with Noah, I might have felt less firm in my decision. But I would not let her risk her dream career, the one she'd lost sleep, sweat, and blood over the past decade of her life. I'd never seen anyone work harder for what they wanted. I wouldn't be the thing to knock her down.

"I love you, Serena," I whispered into her hair. "I don't want you to worry about me. I'll be fine."

❦

*A*sleek black sedan with tinted windows stretched out along the curb outside of Serena's brownstone. I swallowed hard and inched forward as a desperate urge to flee rushed through my stomach. The driver's side window whirred down to reveal a suited man at the steering wheel. He motioned for me to get inside the car.

"Hello, Mia." His voice was deep, like the bass notes of a blues song. "I'm Asmodeus's driver. I'm here to take you home."

Home.

My gut clenched. Regardless of my new residential status, I would never consider my new boss's apartment home. A house was not a home, and it had been years since I'd felt like I truly belonged somewhere.

I cracked open the door and braced myself. But Asmodeus wasn't waiting for me inside. The smooth leather seats were empty. The chilly, air-conditioned air whispered across my bare arms. Before I could change my mind, I slid across the seat and slammed the door behind me.

The driver revved the car and took off through the streets.

He said little during the journey through the city. Every now and again, his dark eyes flicked up to his rearview window. I wondered how much he knew. Did this guy think I was Asmodeus's girlfriend? Or did he know I was an employee and nothing more? Either way, he didn't let on.

An hour later, the driver pulled up to the curb outside of a building located within the depths of Hell's Kitchen. I should have known Asmodeus would live close to his club. In fact, we were only three blocks south.

Situated on the corner, the sleek dark building rose high above the others around it. Large windows looked out onto the city streets, basking in the sunlight. A revolving door led into a spacious lobby with marble-tiled floors and sparkling chandeliers. I could see it all glisten even from inside the car.

What the hell had I gotten myself into?

Asmodeus pushed through the revolving doors and strode across the sidewalk, sporting a lazy smile that made my insides melt. He stood out from everyone else bustling past him. Probably because of the rich black suit that looked as though it had been made to fit his body. His dark hair matched the color of the fabric, making his bright blue eyes pop.

I swiped my sweaty palms against my jeans. At least I'd changed out of my ice cream sweatshirt.

The driver leapt out of the car and opened the door. I stepped onto the sidewalk, hoisting my bag behind me, but the driver quickly tugged it out of my arms. My whole face flushed.

"I'm glad to see you didn't back out." Asmodeus curled his lips into a wicked smile. "Welcome to my humble abode."

"There is nothing humble about this abode."

Asmodeus led me through the revolving doors and into the lobby while the driver trailed behind us with my bag. My boots clicked against the marble, and the door man glanced up from behind his podium. He gave a smile and a nod to Asmodeus before turning back to the screen before him. I gazed around as we continued toward a bank of elevators along the back wall of the lobby.

Everything glistened and sparkled as if every single surface was polished clean each day. The chandeliers flickered with luminous light, and expensive paintings adorned the cream walls. I couldn't guess how much one of these apartments cost, but I knew it had to be way more than the salary of a nightclub owner. Right?

After the elevator hurtled us up to the top floor, I followed Asmodeus into his penthouse apartment. I tried to swallow down my shock. Everything was sleek and black. The luxurious space ended with floor-to-ceiling windows that provided a view of the sparkling city lights. I trailed over to them and pressed my hand against the glass. My breath stuck in my throat as I gazed down at the very distant street.

Asmodeus stepped up beside me, following my gaze. "There's nothing else like New York City at night. Welcome home."

Darkness settled over my awe. Frowning, I stepped away from the window. Out of the corner of my eye, I spotted my bag beside the door. The driver had dropped it and left me alone with my new boss and his dimpled smile.

"This isn't home. I'm only here for a month." My tone was sharper than I intended, but this guy really set my nerves on edge.

"You're welcome, Mia." Sighing, he strolled over to the kitchen. With the open floor plan, most of the apartment was in one big space. The living room, dining room, and kitchen all fed into each other. There were three doors leading off from the main room. While Asmodeus rustled around in the kitchen, I let my curiosity lead me to the first of the doors. I cracked it open and peered inside. A luxurious bathroom looked back at me. A clawed tub sat in one corner where a rainfall shower-head hung low over the center of it. Plants dotted the entire room, basking in a strange humid heat that seemed to seep out of the floor.

I closed the door and moved on to the next room. Peering inside, I spotted a massive bed that hunkered beneath black silk sheets. The windows were covered completely with dark curtains.

"That's my bedroom. Not yours." His voice

sounded right in my ear, and something skittered down my spine. I jumped and twisted to the side, heart hammering. Had he crept up on me? But no... Asmodeus was still in the kitchen, pouring some gin into two tall glasses.

I blinked at him, my blood rushing through my veins. "How did you do that?"

He lifted his eyes from the drinks. "Do what?"

"You..." I pointed to the spot beside me, as if he'd been there only a second ago. "Your voice. It sounded like you were right beside me."

His brow arched, and he shook his head. "You must be tired. How about we have a quick bite to eat, and then you can get an early night? Tomorrow is your first day at your new job, after all."

"I thought I didn't start until eleven at night."

"You'll need to come in early, sign some paper-work, and go over some things with the other dancers." He lifted two plates from the counter and carried them over to the dining table. "And we'll need to take you shopping for a few outfits."

"Excuse me?" I asked as I joined him at the table. "Are you insinuating my clothes don't fit in at your fancy club?"

"That's exactly what I'm *insinuating*." He plopped the drink next to my plate and scowled. "You take everything as an insult, Mia, when you don't stop to think how your own words come across. You can't wear *that* to dance in my club. There are threads hanging off your shirt."

I glared at the plate before me. It held a steak with some butter-coated potatoes. My stomach growled, despite myself, and I pushed up from my chair. "You've insulted both my appearance and my clothes. How would you react to that?"

"Some jobs require a uniform. Being a dancer at a club is one." With a frustrated sigh, he took a long gulp of his drink. "I was hoping we could have a nice, enjoyable first dinner together to cheers to our new partnership, but I was an idiot to think you'd do anything other than pick a fight."

"You're right. I don't want to have dinner with you."

"Good." He gave me a bitter smile, and this time, no dimples dotted his cheeks. "I don't particularly want to have dinner with you, either. I was dreading it, actually."

With narrowed eyes, I whirled away from the table and grabbed my bag. I pointed at the only door I hadn't checked. "I'm assuming that's my room."

"That's the one." He picked up his knife and fork, and cut a piece of his steak, while my plate sat abandoned on the table. "You can show it to yourself. Sleep tight, Mia."

I squeezed the strap of my bag and stormed into the room. Once the door was firmly shut behind me, I let out an anxious breath. A large space stretched before me, cozier than the other. A thick rug spread across the marbled floor, and the draping curtains hung open to reveal the city beyond. I dropped my bag and kicked off my boots, curling up on the king-sized bed. The silk sheets brushed against my cheek as tears spilled out of my eyes.

What was I doing here? How had my life become

this? I was surrounded by glittering, sparkling things, and yet I'd never felt more unmoored. It was so quiet, eerily so. The blare of the taxi horns was distant and muted. I couldn't hear the rumble of trucks or the clatter of the subway. We were too far above it all.

A knock sounded on the door. I squeezed my eyes shut and tried to pretend I hadn't heard it, but it would do no good to ignore my new boss. If I kept this up, there was nothing to stop him from firing me. With a heavy sigh, I pushed off the bed and padded over to the door. When I pulled it open, Asmodeus was nowhere to be seen.

Frowning, I began to push the door shut again but stopped when something glimmered in the corner of my eye. I dropped my gaze to the floor, and my stomach twisted. He'd left the plate of food there for me.

I glanced around the dark, silent penthouse. There was no sign of him anywhere. He must have left to go to his club for the night. And he hadn't tossed out my plate. I knelt, grabbed the food, and then toed the door shut.

"This doesn't mean I like you," I muttered out loud to no one but myself. But then I had that same skittering feeling down my spine again, and I couldn't help but wonder if he'd heard me after all.

7

"Sign here." Asmodeus pushed the clipboard across the desk and leaned back in his office chair. My eyes flicked across the paper. It was the end of what looked like a twenty-page contract. I flipped through it all, eyes blurring. A spot for my signature sat just beneath his, next to that same *Infernal* symbol etched on the door.

"This seems a bit over the top," I finally said, setting the clipboard onto the desk. "And I should probably read through all of it."

"It's a standard employment contract," he replied, frowning. "Take your time, if you'd like. Unfortunately, that means you won't be able to start tonight. I'll have to put you on the roster for another day, one later in the week."

I sighed and picked up the pen. "It's fine."

As I scribbled my name across the line, a strange *zing* went through my body. Almost like someone had shot an electric charge into my arm. Wincing, I finished signing and tossed the pen onto the desk.

"What's wrong?" Asmodeus asked with a smile.

"Nothing, I think I just got a shock." I wrung my arm and pushed the clipboard toward him. "There. Happy now?"

"Delighted." He stood and motioned for me to follow him into the hallway outside his office. That afternoon, he had fulfilled his promise and had taken me shopping. In the end, we'd argued about every little thing until he'd angrily bought me three outfits I was to wear when I danced at his club. I hated each and every one of them. They were little straps of black fabric that highlighted my curves, but one wrong move, and I'd have a serious case of wardrobe malfunction on my hands.

He led me through the hallway and into a side room where a half a dozen guys were clustered around a folding table. They fell silent as soon as we walked in, and it was all I could do not to gape at them.

They were all tall and well-muscled, donning tight tanks that did little to hide their chiseled chests and biceps. In fact, I had a feeling that was the point.

"These are your dancers?" I asked, my voice rising to a higher pitch with every word. No wonder he'd said he needed a different kind of dancer. He'd meant men. Very muscled, very tall, very gorgeous men.

The guys all glanced at each other and laughed. Asmodeus chuckled from beside me, and that dimpled smile made a rare appearance.

"These aren't the dancers," Asmodeus said.

"They're the club's bouncers."

"Oh." My cheeks went hot. "That makes sense."

The guy nearest to the door had long dark hair that curled around his ears and an elaborate tattoo that swirled across his massive left bicep. He waggled his eyebrows at me. "I could put on a show for you if you'd like."

"Caim," Asmodeus warned in a dangerous voice. "No flirting with Mia. She's my *girlfriend*, remember? Starting now, we need to remember this, even when no one else is around. Otherwise, we might forget when it counts."

Ah, so these guys knew all about the fake girlfriend scheme. Good to know. So that meant they were inside his trust circle. Probably a good thing. I didn't know how well I could pretend on a day-to-day basis, on top of the events with his potential investors.

"Hi, Mia." Caim flashed me a brilliant smile. "Welcome to the crazy house. Buckle in. Your life is about to get turned upside down."

"Don't scare her, Caim," another one of the guys said. He had reddish hair with eyes I swore matched, even if that was impossible. People couldn't have orange eyes, right? *Must be contacts.* His voice was harsh and rough, a contrast to both Caim and Asmodeus. "If we want to pull this off, we need her to stick around, not run off into the night screaming bloody murder."

I raised my brow.

"This is Phenex," Caim said, jerking his thumb toward the ginger. "He's prone to exaggeration."

Phenex rolled his eyes and gave Caim a brotherly punch on the arm. Immediately, they both started bickering.

Not for the first time, I wondered exactly what I'd signed up for. These guys seemed friendly enough, but they were intense as hell.

I cleared my throat and tried on a smile. "Nice to meet you guys. So you know about the…" I glanced at Asmodeus.

"Girlfriend deal," Caim finished for me, nodding. "'Course we do. We came up with the plan together. In fact, it was Valac's idea."

I followed his gaze to the guy in the far corner, half-hidden in shadows. He had bleached white hair and pale skin that seemed to pull tight around his muscles. Something about him screamed danger, and every hair on the back of my neck stood on end. The whites of his eyes seemed to pierce my soul. Suddenly, the fangs of my memories threatened to scrape through my mind. I shuddered.

Caim sighed and rolled his eyes. "Stop it, Valac."

Confusion rippled through me, and my memories blinked away. "Stop what?"

"Nothing," Asmodeus said quickly, catching my elbow in his hand. "I need to take you to the other dancers now. They'll go through everything you need to know for the night. This lot will talk your ears off if we stay much longer." He shot them all a dark gaze. "Behave yourselves."

"Bye, Mia!" Caim called out as Asmodeus dragged me out of the room. I frowned up at him when our feet hit the hallway and yanked my elbow out of his grip. He motioned for me to follow him down the left side of the hallway, and we fell into step beside each other.

"You don't have to manhandle me."

"It's almost nine. The club will get busy soon, and we need you ready for your shift." He didn't even glance down at me, and he threw out his words as if they were barbed. Had I annoyed him somehow? *Again?*

"What have I done now?"

He cut his gaze my way. "You were eyeing up Caim like he was a steak dinner."

I snorted, nearly stumbling over my own feet at the shock of his words. "Wait a minute. You're mad because I noticed your bouncers aren't exactly ugly?"

"Stay away from them."

"Excuse me? You were the one who introduced me to them."

"Clearly that was a mistake."

I was starting to think the mistake was me agreeing to this bizarre deal in the first place. With a roll of my eyes, I considered the night ahead. At least I wouldn't have to work with him. I'd be up in a cage, dancing the night away. He'd be…doing whatever club owners did. Likely greeting his most prized guests and rubbing elbows with the latest winners of the Grammys.

At the end of the hallway, Asmodeus pushed open a door and ushered me into the dancers' dressing room and a flurry of vibrant energy. Girls sat along a slim table that hugged the wall, half-costumed and applying makeup before a bank of brightly-lit mirrors. Each and every one of them was breathtakingly beautiful, as if they'd walked straight out of the pages of a magazine.

My heart constricted as I scanned the room. Diamonds dotted earlobes. Their gowns were tiny yet classy, their hair shiny, their faces clear and bright. Asmodeus had not been wrong. I didn't fit in with these girls. They were fucking gorgeous.

"Everyone," Asmodeus spoke up from beside me with a booming voice. All the chattering girls fell silent and turned to gaze my way. "Meet Mia. She's our newest dancer."

A girl halfway down the table flicked her glossy brown eyes across me. "She's the one replacing Allison?"

"That's right."

The girls all gave each other uneasy glances. Hmm. I frowned. That was odd. Who was this Allison girl and why did they all look like they wanted to vomit from the very mention of her?

"Well, welcome to the crazy house," the girl said, repeating Caim's words. "I'm Priyanka. You'll be dancing in the cage by me. Come on in. Let's get you ready."

Asmodeus vanished from my side, and I was quickly surrounded by a gaggle of perfectly-coifed girls. They sat me down in a chair and applied a liberal amount of makeup to my usually clear face. There wasn't time for much discussion. They explained how the night went, what time to be ready for the cages, and how we needed to treat the patrons of the place.

By the time they'd taken me through a rundown of the job, it was time to climb into the cages and dance.

My palms were sweaty, and my heart beat a hectic drum in my chest. I couldn't help but feel like I was about to make a total fool of myself. But when I climbed into the cage and watched the floor shudder away, a strange sense of calm settled over me. And so I danced. For hours. I barely even noticed the minutes tick by, until suddenly, the night was done, and it was time for me to leave.

I'd even made three hundred bucks in tips.

I smiled as I counted out the wad and tucked it into my purse. Priyanka sidled up to me and gave me a high five, grinning. "You killed it tonight. The crowd loved you. No wonder Az has taken a shine to you."

My stomach tumbled, and the euphoria from the night took a sudden nose dive. "Taken a shine to me...so, you know?"

"About you and Az? Ha. As if he could get himself a girlfriend and keep it a secret. It's all anyone can talk about. He hasn't had a girlfriend in over a hund—" She cleared her throat. "In a very long time."

I flushed and felt a strange sense of pride surge through me, which was totally ridiculous. It wasn't like I was his real girlfriend. To be his girlfriend, I would have to like him. As it was, I could barely tolerate his presence.

"Aww, look at that." Priyanka grinned and tapped my cheek. "You're blushing. Better be careful, hun, or you're going to fall head over heels in love with that man."

"Don't worry. I don't think there's any threat of that happening." I grabbed my jacket off the back of the chair and tugged it over my dress. On my way off the dance floor, I'd spotted Asmodeus in deep conversation with a table of his patrons. I shouldn't interrupt, and his apartment was only three blocks away. I'd walk back while he wrapped up here. With my trusty can of pepper spray, of course. A girl can never be too careful.

"That's what we always say, eh?" Priyanka settled into the chair and pulled some makeup wipes out of a bag. "Well, it's been great to meet you. See you tomorrow night?"

I smiled back. "See you tomorrow."

I said goodbye to the other girls—Lexi, Ramona, Ellen, Piper, and Willow—and found the side door of the club. There were still several patrons wandering around the front, taking a smoke break outside. *Infernal* didn't close for another hour, and the night owls looked like they were only getting started.

With a slight smile, I turned the corner, aiming my boots south. Tonight hadn't been that bad after all. I might have even made some new friends. As much as I loved Serena, it wasn't fair to rely on her as much as I did. If I was going to make it in a new city, in a new life, I needed to meet other people.

The three hundred bucks in my pocket didn't hurt either.

Two large figures loomed out of an alley. They strode into the center of the sidewalk, turning to face me. My heart jerked in my chest as I came to a sudden stop, gazing at them with cotton balls in my mouth. They were both huge, muscled, and heavily tattooed. One had buzzed hair and was slightly taller than the other, but only by an inch.

The taller one stepped toward me. "Hello, Mia."

"Um." I took a step back and reached for my pepper spray.

"No need to be afraid." He smiled and held out a hand. "My name is Gabriel, and we just want to talk to you about your new association with *Infernal*."

"Gabriel," I repeated, ignoring his offered hand. Heart hammering, I glanced around me at the empty street. Should I turn around and run back to *Infernal*? Should I scream? Douse them in pepper spray? Probably all of the above.

"Yes, ah." He turned to the other guy, a golden-haired Adonis with a bicep bigger than my thigh. "This might be a little difficult for you to comprehend, so please don't freak out when we try to explain."

"We're angels," the golden-haired one said, folding his arms over his white, button-up shirt. "Now this might come as a shock, but...supernaturals exist, particularly in New York City. You're surrounded by them all the time."

Gabriel shot his friend a dark look. "Great going, Suriel. We were supposed to ease her into it. Humans freak out when they learn supernaturals are real." He turned back to me, and the brilliance of his encouraging smile was almost blinding. "It's all right, Mia. You don't need to be afraid."

I wet my lips and took another step back. Truth was, this wasn't news to me...but I couldn't tell them that. I'd known for a very long time that vampires and werewolves are real, but supernaturals live by strict laws. The most important one? Never let humans find out *anything*.

"Oh my god. You're crazy." I widened my eyes and pasted shock onto my face. "You must be on drugs or something."

Gabriel's smile dropped. "Oh. You already know about us."

"What? No. I—"

"You're a terrible actress," he said, sighing. "Who told you?"

"No one," I said through gritted teeth. "It's not particularly difficult to figure out. There's evidence all over the place if you know what to look out for."

That last part was true. The evidence *was* everywhere, but I hadn't magically deduced the existence of werewolves all by myself. Serena had told me. Because she was one herself.

I'd seen her shift with my own two eyes.

"Don't harass her, Gabe," the golden-haired one said, turning to me. "You don't need to tell us how you found out. That's not why we're here."

"Okay. Then what do you want?"

"We need to talk to you about the demons you're associating with. Asmodeus in particular."

At that, I blinked. Unease burned through my veins like acid, and my mouth went as dry as my bank account. "Wait a minute, did you say *demons*?"

I was aware of vampires, werewolves, fallen

angels, and fae. But surely *demons* didn't exist in the real world. If they did, I might have to start screaming. Blood-sucking vampires? That I could take. Human wolf-beasts with fangs and fur? All right. But horned monsters of the underworld? No, thank you. Serena hadn't mentioned anything about this.

Suriel's brows winged upward. "Perhaps she didn't know about supernaturals after all."

"At least not demons," Gabriel murmured, rubbing his jaw. "So you don't know what Asmodeus is? What *Infernal* is?"

My stomach dropped. "Are you trying to tell me that *Infernal* isn't a nightclub?"

"Oh, it's a nightclub." Suriel grinned and folded his massive arms. "For supernaturals only."

Wait a minute. My mind raced as it replayed everything that had happened in the past few days. The famous smiling faces on the wall inside the door. The strange way Asmodeus spoke of his club. His insistence that I stay away from the bouncers in the back room.

The demons.

I'm looking for a different type of dancer.

Everything suddenly made sense. It had nothing to do with my looks, or at least not completely. He'd turned me away because I was human. He needed a supernatural to dance at his club, which meant every other person I'd met tonight was either a werewolf, a vampire, a fae, or a…demon.

I needed to sit down.

8

"**A**re you quite all right in there?" Suriel frowned, leaned down, and peered into my eyes. Flecks of light shimmered in his dark irises like a multitude of stars against the night sky.

I steadied myself. "Yep, of course. Why wouldn't I be? I just found out my new boss is a demon from the actual underworld, and so are all my coworkers."

"They won't all be demons," Gabriel said. "Vampires and fae mostly."

"Right," I said in a small voice.

Even though I'd known Serena all my life, I'd never met another supernatural. That I knew of. She'd been such a constant presence in my life that I never even thought of her as a werewolf. She was just Serena. Sure, before she'd learned to control her shifts, I'd had to trap her in a cemetery mausoleum on full moon nights, but eventually, that had felt as normal as a Friday night football game.

I knew she'd made supernatural friends since moving to New York, but she'd never introduced me to them. Sometimes she even attended werewolf parties. Obviously, I never went. I wasn't supposed to know they exist, and she'd be in some deep shit if they found out she'd told a human about them.

"Listen," Gabe said, his smooth voice cutting through my shock. "We have some suspicions about Asmodeus and his club. We think he and his Legion are up to something dangerous in there, and it's impossible for us to get close enough to figure it out. Fallen angels are not allowed inside his club."

"You're human. You have no bond with him," Suriel added. "We need you to keep an eye on him for us and let us know the second he does anything that seems off to you."

I swallowed hard. "Did you say *legion*?"

"There's only six of them, including Asmodeus himself," Suriel said dismissively. "I don't know why he likes to call them his Legion."

"So what do you say?" Gabriel asked.

For a moment, all I could do was stare at the angels, my blood roaring in my ears. They both watched me with expectant expressions carved into their chiseled faces, and a strange hum of power rippled from their towering forms. A humid breeze rustled the hair around my shoulders, bringing with it the stench of a nearby dumpster. The street was silent and empty except for us. It all felt eerie and *wrong*.

"You're asking me to spy on a demon."

They shared a quick glance, and then Gabriel shrugged. "Pretty much."

"You realize how crazy that sounds, right?" I asked, taking a step away from them. "If he's as dangerous as you think he is, then I don't want to work for him anymore, let alone spy for you."

"I'm not sure you have much of a choice," Gabriel said. "Didn't you sign a contract to work at his place?"

"Yeah, but I mean—"

"You made a deal with a demon, Mia," Suriel said, his voice softening just a bit. "There's no way you can get out of it until you fulfill your end of the bargain. Not unless you're willing to lose your soul."

"Lose my..." Fear and anger ripped through me like a tornado. Sucking in a sharp breath, I fisted my hands, which started shaking by my sides. "Wait a minute. What are you saying?"

Gabe sighed and ran a hand along his buzzed hair. "When you make a deal with a demon, you lose your soul if you break the contract."

My heart lurched into my throat, and dizziness slammed into my skull. I reached out for something to hold on to but quickly realized there was nothing but the grime-infested building to my right and the towering angels before me. Shaking my head, I stumbled back.

"Let me get this straight. You're telling me that Asmodeus made a deal for my soul, and he didn't even tell me about it."

Suriel pressed his lips together. "Yes, Mia. We are. So you see why he needs to be stopped as soon as possible. Only an evil being would do something like that."

All the blood drained from my face as my mind spun through the implications. I'd made a deal with a demon. One who may or may not be totally, completely evil. And I had to live with him. If I tried to get out of it, my soul would…what exactly? Go to hell?

I really needed to sit down.

"We think the club is a cover for something else," Gabriel added, his boots thunking against the sidewalk as he stepped closer.

Suriel nodded. "Something nefarious. Perchance he is the one behind the recent murders."

I raised my brows as his words snapped me out of my shock. "*Perchance?* Exactly what century are you from?"

Suriel exchanged a glance with Gabriel. "Well, we are very old."

"And you didn't think to update your vocabulary during the past few centuries?"

Suriel cocked his head, and a lock of his golden hair tumbled into his eyes. "Why would I?"

"Nevermind." The fact that I was currently having a conversation in the middle of New York with two centuries-old fallen angels was not the craziest part of my night.

I was the fake girlfriend of a literal demon.

Oh my god. I shuddered as a new thought sprang into my mind like a ninja ready to chop into my brains. Asmodeus had mentioned kissing. I would have to *kiss a demon* if I wanted to keep my soul. Did he have normal lips? A normal tongue?

An unwelcome thought flashed through my mind.

Forget the tongue. Did he have a normal *dick*? Or did it have a weird spade-shaped end like a demon tail?

More importantly, did he have an *actual* tail, too? I wondered if Serena knew. I made a mental note to ask her later.

My cheeks burned as I realized I was thinking far too much about Asmodeus's dick. It wasn't like I was ever going to see it. He'd made it clear our deal had nothing to do with sex.

He'd better keep it that way.

"Here's our contact details." Gabriel slid a small business card into my hand. It displayed a telephone number in black letters against a white background. Nothing more. "Call us if you see or hear anything suspicious."

"You really expect me to carry on like nothing has happened," I whispered to them.

The two angels shrugged in unison.

"You don't really have another choice," Gabriel said with a gentle smile. "Just whatever you do, don't make him angry. Oh, and take this. You might need it. Just...never let him find out you have it, all right?"

He dropped a gleaming signet ring into my hand. A thin silver chain wound through it. When I took a closer look, I spotted that same emblem engraved into the center of it. The one on the flyer. The one on the door. *Infernal's* symbol.

"Great," I muttered as the angels vanished around the corner. For a moment, all I could do was stare after them, flipping the card over in my trembling fingers. If I were smart, I'd walk straight over to the subway entrance, climb on board the G train, and hightail it to Serena's apartment.

Strangely, it wasn't the demon part of the equation that had me spooked the most. Having grown up with Serena, I understood that supernaturals were a multifaceted group of people, just like humans were. They weren't all good; they weren't all bad. That might extend to demons…but Asmodeus had trapped me in a soul contract without telling me, and these angels thought he might be linked to a serial killer. Now I had to pretend like I didn't know about any of it.

How the hell would I pull this off?

Unease racing down my spine, I threw the chain around my neck, slung my hands into my jacket pockets, and started walking. I needed some time to think. Asmodeus was back at the club, unaware I'd been approached by two fallen angels who wanted to take him down. I still had a little time to make a plan. I wondered if I could convince him to tear up the contract. I knew next to nothing about demons, so I didn't know if that was even possible. How binding were these things? If *he* decided to renege on it, what happened to my soul then?

All I knew was, I didn't want to go through with this. I needed a job, but I wasn't *this* desperate.

Was I?

With a deep breath, I rounded the corner instead of continuing south to Asmodeus's apartment building. He wouldn't be there, but I wasn't ready to walk into that penthouse just yet. Not until I'd had a chance to clear my mind and make a plan.

The distant thud of footsteps sounded on the sidewalk somewhere behind me. Chills swept across my arms. Glancing around, I noticed this street was steeped in darkness. I was away from the bustling, twinkling nightlife now. Instead, the buildings were ghosts, full of shadows and darkened windows. I cast a quick glance behind me, but no one was there.

No one I could see.

Maybe it wasn't such a great idea to wander through Hell's Kitchen alone in the middle of the night, even with my trusty pepper spray. In fact, it was downright stupid. Why had I come out here alone? Idiot. Heart suddenly in my throat, I picked up the pace, only to hear the footsteps do the same.

Shit.

I started to run, tears pricking the corners of my eyes. A car squealed past and slid sideways as it jerked to a sudden stop beside the curb. The passenger door flew open. Asmodeus rushed out, eyes narrowed, jaw clenched tight. A burst of shadows exploded from his skin in the blink of an eye. And then they were gone.

"What the hell do you think you're doing?" he barked, thundering forward. The vein in his neck seemed to pop right out of his skin.

Swallowing hard, I stumbled back. Had he seen me talking to those two angels? Did he know what they'd asked me to do? Would he steal my soul now? Would he...would he *eat* it?

What the hell did demons do with souls anyway?

I didn't want to find out.

"I..." At a total loss for words, all I could do was

stand there. At least whoever had been following me would be long gone by now.

"I thought you'd seen the news," he demanded with flashing eyes. "There is a serial killer in Hell's Kitchen, and he is after girls exactly like you. It isn't safe for you to walk home alone at three o'clock in the fucking morning. Why didn't you tell me you were leaving? Why did you just vanish like that?"

He strode up to me and gently took my shoulder in his strong hand. His touch shot a flicker of warmth through my gut, even as everything within me screamed to run. Those dark eyes bored into me, and for a moment, all I could think about were his lips and his eyes, remembering my earlier conversation with the angels. If I didn't get out of this contract, one day I would have to kiss him. Heat curled across my goose-bumped skin.

I cleared my throat. "I just...well, you seemed busy. I didn't think it was a big deal. I'm your employee, not your prisoner...right?"

This guy was a demon. And he was touching me. Why hadn't I pulled away yet?

He sighed and let go. "Of course you're not my prisoner. And normally, it wouldn't be a big deal. I just assumed you'd wait for me to drive you home. It isn't safe. Not until the killer is caught."

One thing was for sure. If this guy was involved with the murders, like the angels thought, he probably wouldn't react like this. Unless he knew they'd cornered me in the street, and he was trying to throw them—and me—off the scent.

"Okay." I gave him a strained smile. "So...now what?"

"Now we go back home."

Home. My stomach clenched. That penthouse was not my home.

"Listen," I said, nervously tapping my finger against my thigh. "This whole Hell's Kitchen killer thing does have me a little on edge. I'm not sure this is the safest place to live right now. What would happen if I wanted to get out of our deal a little early?"

His expression darkened. "You signed a contract."

"Yes, but—"

"It's binding," he said with a growl, whirling away from me. He strode over to the car, yanked open the door, and motioned for me to climb inside. "It's just a month, Mia. And unless you go running off into the streets alone again, I'll make sure no one ever touches you."

"Erm, right." I shifted on my feet, eyeing the dark interior of the car. "It's just...you can't protect me twenty-four seven for an entire month. Can't you tear up the contract?"

His lips curled into a wicked smile. "I could. If I wanted to. But I don't. Now get inside."

"You know, some people might wonder why you're so insistent on getting me into that car."

"No, they wouldn't." His grip tightened on the door. "Because it makes perfect fucking sense. I know you don't like me very much, and I don't like you very much, either. But while you are in my employ, it is my responsibility to keep you safe. You're out this late because you were dancing in my club. I'm not going to let something happen to you when I should have been driving you home. Got it?"

I wet my lips, thinking back to the moments before Asmodeus had arrived. It pained me to admit he had a point. Someone had been following me. It might not have been anything at all. Just some weirdo. New York had a lot of them.

But I might very well have been in danger. A serial killer stalked these streets. He could have had his sights set on me tonight. Hell, he might still be watching me even now, waiting to see if Asmodeus would go away, leaving me out here alone again. As strange as it seemed, a demon was the better option.

Looked like I was going to become a spy after all.

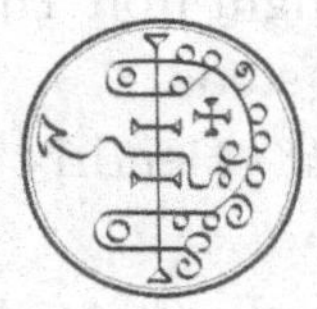

"Good morning." Asmodeus leaned back in one of the sleek black dining chairs. Dark, wet hair clumped on his forehead, and his soft heather grey t-shirt clung to his sculpted pecs. I slowed to a stop and rubbed the sleep out of my eyes.

My god.

Suddenly I was very conscious of my mussed hair and wrinkled sweatpants. Why did he always manage to catch sight of me when I looked my worst? Not that it mattered. I didn't care about impressing this guy.

He's a demon.

"Morning." I trailed over to the table and plopped down into a chair. "You look very alert and cheerful for someone who was up at the butt crack of dawn."

I'd heard him rustling around at six. I, on the other hand, had slept until noon.

"I have a couple of things for you." Winking, he

leaned forward and lifted a gleaming cloche off a massive stack of pancakes. My stomach grumbled at the sight of the fluffy circles. "You also have a visitor out on the balcony."

Frowning, I glanced over to the open sliding doors. A black-and-white pigeon perched on the back of one of the wrought-iron chairs. I sucked in a whistling breath and stood.

"Don't tell me that's Hendrix."

"The one and only."

My mouth dropped open as I plucked a chunk of pancake from the stack and padded over to the balcony. There was a single black spot above Hendrix's left eye. It was him all right. With a grin, I threw him a pancake. He caught it in midair and swallowed it whole.

"How?" I asked, turning back to Asmodeus who reclined in his chair with a smug smile. "Surely he couldn't find me."

"Pigeons are smarter than people give them credit for."

This had to be some sort of demon thing. He'd called Hendrix here. With his mind. Or something. Whatever he'd done, I didn't really care. It was an oddly touching gift. Grudgingly, I gave him a smile.

"Well, I don't know how you got him here, but it's good to see a familiar face."

"You're welcome." He motioned to the stack of pancakes. "Don't forget to eat. We have a big day ahead of us. Tonight, we'll attend a party together. It will be our first official outing as a couple."

My stomach dropped. Right. That explained the

pancakes and the pigeon. He was trying to soften me up before dropping the news about our impending date.

I eased back into the apartment, trying not to rush toward the pancakes like the greedy squirrel I was. "That's soon."

"It hasn't taken long for news to travel. People are already talking about you." He folded his arms. "It will be good to put in an appearance while we're fresh on their minds."

"So strategic." Throwing all caution to the wind, I dropped into the chair and pulled the plate close. To hell with it. I wanted these damn pancakes.

"I got to where I am today by being strategic," he said. "It's the only way I know to be."

"Doesn't that get lonely?" I asked as I jammed a forkful of pancake into my mouth. It practically melted against my tongue.

"I have plenty of people close to me."

"Who?" I asked.

"The bouncers you met last night, for one."

The Legion. That's what the angels had called them. Were they all demons? Caim and Phenex and the other three guys? It explained a few things if they were. They'd been just as intense and unnerving as Asmodeus was, and Valac had made me feel like knives were being dragged across my mind.

"And what about you?" he asked, leaning forward with an intent expression on his face. "Where are your friends?"

"You're looking at one." I pointed at Hendrix, who had flown into the penthouse to join us. Strangely,

Asmodeus didn't seem to mind a pigeon on his dining table.

"And the others?"

I swallowed down a lump of pancake. Suddenly, I was no longer hungry, even though my stomach still growled. "I don't really have any, other than Serena. I'm pretty much all I've got."

I braced myself for his next question. I knew what it would be. It was inevitable. Everyone always asked. *What about your family?* I didn't know how to answer him if he brought it up. Rarely could I discuss my parents, my sister, without tears forming in my eyes and blurring the world away. And I had zero desire to cry in front of a fucking demon who'd made a deal for my soul.

"Well," he said, leaning back into his chair again.

"Well," I repeated.

"Maybe it's time you changed that." His chair scraped against the floor as he pushed it away from the table. "You have one wild, precious, and very short life, Mia, made better by the people you surround yourself with. Make the best of it." With a sigh, he turned toward the door leading into his bedroom. "I have some business to take care of for most of the day, so I'll be out until tonight. Make yourself at home. We'll leave for our date at eight."

Asmodeus vanished into his bedroom, leaving me with a mouthful of pancake and a hell of a lot of questions. Stunned, I replayed his words in my mind. Had he really just said I had one wild and precious life? And not to waste it? That wasn't a very demony thing to say. Were the angels wrong?

No, I thought. Deep down in my gut, I had sensed something about him the moment we'd met. A strange energy seemed to pulse off his skin, and he could do things that weren't normal. At the time, I hadn't understood it, but I did now. He wasn't human.

And we had our first date tonight.

❦

The angels' business card burned a hole in my pocket as I paced from one end of the penthouse to the next. They'd asked me to spy on Asmodeus. Truth be told, I didn't really want to, but my curiosity made every hair on my arms stand at attention.

Asmodeus would be gone for hours. I was here in his penthouse alone. What if there was something here? Like…incriminating evidence that he was the bad sort of demon. And if there wasn't, maybe that would soothe my jangling nerves. I had to make it through the next month, or I'd lose my soul. Confirming that he wasn't hiding something big—bigger than being a demon—would go a long way.

On the other hand, if I *did* find something, I could call the angels and tell them everything. They'd arrest him, or whatever it was angels and demons did to keep the peace. Hopefully, they'd be able to get me out of my contract.

There. I nodded to myself. I'd convinced myself to peek into Asmodeus's things.

My stomach flipped as I scurried across the floor. I

was going to snoop through a demon's bedroom! Deep down, I knew I was far more excited about this than I had any right to be. But this was the perfect opportunity to find the answers to my burning questions. I might not get the chance again.

Did he have anything to do with those murders? Were there trophies hidden in his drawers? Would he have a list of everyone he'd targeted or an elaborate diagram plotting out his nefarious deeds? Did he wear a different type of boxer shorts? You know, for his tail. Not the other thing.

Adrenaline surging through my veins, I twisted the door handle and pushed. The door held firm against my attack. It wouldn't budge. Frowning, I released my grip and stepped back. He'd locked his door.

Now that was weird. And not a great sign. Why would he have locked his bedroom if he had nothing to hide? What did he have in there that he didn't want me to see?

There was only one explanation. No one else was here. He'd locked it to keep me out.

***

"You ready to go?" Asmodeus called through the door, and then gave it a light knock. I stood before the floor-length mirror, staring at myself with wide eyes. I hadn't seen Asmodeus all day, so I'd had a lot of time stuck alone with my thoughts.

I was going on a date with a demon who was hiding something.

To keep myself occupied, I'd dressed up for the occasion. Instead of my standard uniform of jeans and crop top, I'd chosen the only dress I'd packed. One I'd borrowed from Serena and hadn't returned yet.

She was a little smaller than me, so the dress hugged my curves. It was a little black number with a scooped neck edged in delicate lace. The bottom hem hit mid-thigh, the perfect length to pair with my boots. The outfit was a combination of class and edginess, and it gave me the boost of confidence I needed to get through this night.

I topped it all off with a pair of dangly earrings my sister had given me for my eighteenth birthday, a reminder of where I'd come from and why I was here. Her face flashed in my mind. Even after everything that had happened, I wouldn't go back and make a different decision. At least, not about sparing her.

"Yep, I'm ready," I called out as I turned from the mirror. Now was not the time to think about my sister. If I did, an avalanche of competing emotions would crash around me, burying me beneath the weight of it all.

I pulled open the door. Asmodeus sucked in a sharp breath and took a step back, his gaze sweeping across me. His eyes sparked as an appreciative smile lifted the corners of his lips. "You look incredible."

"Oh." I flushed, pressing my lips together. He didn't look so bad himself. A dark suit hugged his muscular frame in a way that should be criminal. The color matched his dark hair and the light stubble that stretched along his cutting jawline.

"No one will question why I'm dating you, that's a certainty," he said with a wicked smile.

My flush deepened. I cleared my throat. I'd never had anyone compliment me like this. Did he mean it? Or was it just for show, like everything else we were doing tonight?

"You don't have to start the fake dating just yet," I said with a strained laugh. "It can wait until we get to the party."

Tension bounced between us as his eyes darkened. "Right. I thought it would be a good idea to practice."

"No need. You've got it down, it seems. I'm guessing you probably date a lot." Rolling my eyes at myself, I stepped into the hallway and pulled the bedroom door shut. Why had I brought up his dating life? I didn't need to hear about that. He might think I was interested for other reasons, and I very much wasn't.

I did wonder though…how much *did* demons date?

"Well, there you'd be wrong," he said as he led me to the penthouse door. "I don't date. It's one of the reasons I made this deal with you. I have no desire for an entanglement."

An *entanglement*. His word choice reminded me of the angels who had asked me to spy on him. They were centuries old. Did that mean Asmodeus was, too? Obviously, he had to be. Even his name was evidence of that. So…how old were we talking about here?

I was desperate to ask him, and I hated that I couldn't. I'd have to admit I knew what he was. And then he'd want to know *how* I knew. I obviously couldn't tell him that, either. Not unless I wanted to face an angry demon.

And if he really was as dangerous as the angels thought he was, there was no telling what he was capable of.

"Listen." He paused at the door, bracing his hand on the wall behind my head. I swallowed hard as he leaned close and the scent of a bonfire wafted into my nose. I'd smelled that once before around him, and now I understood what it was. He was from Hell. I was smelling literal flames. "At the party, you should call me Az. Everyone close to me does. They'll find it odd if you refer to me as Asmodeus."

"Sure." I stared up into his sharp blue eyes, and my stomach churned. It was almost impossible for me to even remember my *own* name when I looked into them. "Az it is."

"Good." He lifted a finger to my neck and dragged it along my skin. Sparks stormed through my belly, and my chest went hot. I trembled as I leaned back against the wall, my body betraying me. His lips curled. "Also good. Keep that up. We want everyone to think you want me."

I didn't tell him that my reaction had not been fake. Because it sure as hell didn't mean that I wanted him. It was just my body being weird. He was an asshole. An asshole demon.

Why was I doing this again?

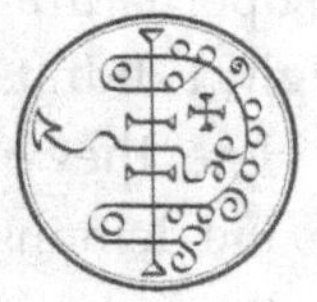

10

The party was being held on a rooftop bar smack dab in the middle of Hell's Kitchen. I'd hoped we'd get out of this little pocket of the city but no such luck. It seemed as though all of Asmodeus's business was wound up in these streets, as well as his friends.

As we waited in the gold-plated elevator, he dropped his voice to a low murmur. "I must warn you, some of the guests may be…wearing costumes. Don't be alarmed. Some of them are fond of gothic horror."

My heart flipped as I glanced down at my dress. "Costumes? Um, then shouldn't we be wearing some, too?"

He chuckled. "That won't be necessary."

I opened my mouth to ask him another question just as the elevator shuddered to a stop and the doors whirred open. Partygoers were crammed into the rooftop space. In the distance, the lights of New York glowed like a thousand stars. A fanged girl trotted into the elevator, her hand tucked into a guy's arm whose hands were covered in fur.

Realization slammed down on me as Az led me out onto the roof. He hadn't meant costumes at all. This was a party for supernaturals, and he hadn't told me. Because he thought I didn't know vampires and werewolves are real. Here, they let down their masks, if they chose to. Here, the demons came out to play.

Az gave me a gentle nudge. I glanced up at him, my heart pounding hard against my ribcage. Was I the only human here?

"Are you all right?" Az asked with concern in his voice. "You've gone pale."

"No, I'm just..." I pressed my sweaty palms against my dress and tried to clear my head.

This was fine. Totally fine. I could do this. Sure, I was probably the only human in a swarm of supernaturals, but there was no reason to panic. I just needed to calm the fuck down and act like it wasn't a big deal. Serena had told me about parties like this. She went sometimes. Supernaturals weren't inherently bad. They didn't just *attack* humans like the movies suggested they did. Vampires did drink blood, but only the worst of them killed for it. Werewolves rarely lost control of their beast. Fae liked to play games, but they were harmless unless they felt wronged.

This would *totally be fine.*

Maybe if I told myself that a hundred times, I would believe it.

"Mia." The way he spoke my name came out like a caress, his deep voice almost a purr. He took my hand in his and weaved his fingers through mine, and then he pushed me back against the wall. I sucked in a sharp breath when his body pressed tightly against mine. He angled in close and dropped his lips to my ear. "Relax. There is nothing to worry about. All you have to do is pretend you can't keep your hands off me."

Not an entirely difficult thing. He might be an asshole demon, but Asmodeus—*Az*—was maybe the sexiest guy I'd ever seen in my life. A part of me knew I should be afraid of him, but I wasn't. Not really. He set my nerves on edge, but it wasn't from fear. Deep dislike more like it. But...I didn't have to pretend I thought he was hot. I mean, it wasn't even a question. It was a literal fact. The man was a goddamn masterpiece.

Not that I would ever tell him that.

Loosing my pent-up breath, I tried to relax against the wall as I lifted my gaze to his. Flames flickered deep within the ice blue. I swore I could see the flash of them. That intense stare bored into me once more. That soul-stripping, piercing gaze. What kind of powers did he have? Could he see my soul?

He probably could.

Swallowing hard, I wound my hand around the back of his neck. He stiffened beneath my touch, but then shot me a wicked grin. "That's more like it. Ready to go into the party now?"

"Sure," I murmured back.

He pushed away from the wall, leaving a gulf

of cold air in his wake. I itched to draw him back to me, which was utterly ridiculous. I didn't want him to touch me. I mean...it was kind of fun. But probably only because we were pretending. It was like we had a secret from everyone else, and we were trying to get away with something scandalous.

That was why it felt so great.

The one and only reason.

Az and I drifted through the crowd. He introduced me to several businessmen before falling into some boring conversation about stock markets and real estate prices. I found my attention drifting away, even though the only reason I was here was to hang off his arm like some kind of human trophy.

The party was packed, and the crowd was more varied than I would have guessed. Suited men lounged on a sofa along with a crowd that had more holes in their jeans than stars in the sky. My gaze snagged on a familiar dark-haired beauty. Her eyes caught on me at the same time.

Serena jumped up from the sofa and rushed across the floor, her flowing crimson gown whipping around her feet. She grabbed my arm when she reached me, her fingernails digging into my skin. "Mia, what the hell are you doing here?"

"Not here," I mouthed to her.

She gave me a grim nod and dragged me away from Az, who barely seemed to register I'd vanished from his side. Serena led me off the rooftop and into the quieter space inside, down a long hallway, and into a restroom that was more like a lounge than anything. Everything was cast in shades of gold, including the toilet.

Serena threw the lock shut and then folded her arms over her slinky red gown. "Mia. Why are you at a party that's for supernaturals only?"

I winced. "Well, you aren't going to believe this, but my new boss brought me with him. Guess what he is. A demon."

"Wait a minute." Her eyes widened. "The guy you were standing next to out there. *He's* your fake boyfriend?"

"Boss." I flushed. "And yes, fake boyfriend, too. But mostly boss."

"I need to sit down." Serena leaned against the wall and clung to the hand dryer. "That's Asmodeus, a fucking Prince of Hell."

I blinked. "Say what now?"

"He's not just a demon, Mia," she whispered with wide eyes. "He's one of the Princes. He's like second or third in line to the throne. The one who will take over Hell if Lucifer is ever destroyed. Do you have any idea what you've gotten yourself into?"

"Sure. Yeah. I totally knew all that." I found my own wall to lean against and desperately tried to calm my heart before it exploded out of my chest. This couldn't be happening.

"So wait a minute," she said softly. "When you said you auditioned to dance for a club in Hell's Kitchen, you meant *Infernal*?"

"Of course I did. I told you all about it," I whispered. "You knew about *Infernal* this whole time? Why didn't you say anything?"

"You didn't tell me the name of the club," she hissed back. "And I never imagined that was where you went. They don't let humans in there to party. Let alone work for them!"

"To be honest, I think the only reason he gave me the job is because of this whole fake girlfriend thing. So…extenuating circumstances."

She closed her eyes. "This really isn't good. If he wants a human to be his fake girlfriend, there will be a reason for it. And it won't be a good one. He is a *Prince of Hell*, Mia. What were you thinking?"

"Well, I didn't know that until now! I didn't even know that Princes of Hell were a real thing!" I whisper-shouted the words, though a part of me was worried all those supernaturals out there could hear everything. Did they have enhanced senses? I knew Serena did, but only when she was in her beast form. What about the vampires? Or the fae?

Hell, what about the demons?

"Listen." Serena pushed off the wall and took my hands in hers. "You need to get out of this. Now. Before you get hurt. I know you're worried about being a burden to me, but you're not. Come back home. I don't care how long you have to stay. Just get away from Asmodeus."

"I can't," I said, squeezing her hands. "I signed a contract." Her mouth dropped open, and before she could tell me how stupid I was, I continued. "I had no idea he was a demon when I signed it. He didn't tell me. I only found out last night."

"For fuck's sake." She took a deep breath, nodded, and then paced across the marbled floor. "Listen, this is what you're going to do, all right? The contract is binding on your side, but not on his. He can end the deal by ripping up the thing you signed. Convince him this whole thing has been a terrible mistake. Get him to destroy it as soon as possible. And don't let him know you know. He'll never let you go. The last thing you want in your life is a demon."

The bathroom door flew open and in strode Az with his wicked smile and shadow-kissed skin. I sucked in a sharp breath as his eyes cut from Serena's face to mine. How much had he overheard?

"You can't just waltz into a bathroom when it's in use," Serena growled at him with narrowed eyes. "Get out."

"Neither one of you are using the facilities," he said smoothly as his gaze latched firmly on mine. A sizzling heat curled in my gut. "Mia, I need to speak with you alone for a moment."

"Nope." Serena folded her arms and shot Az a glare. "I'm not leaving you alone with her."

"Serena Mason," Az said, our eyes still locked. "Werewolf. Youngest attorney at Parkins, Weller, and Smith. Resident of Clinton Hill. Previously Nashville. You do know it is against our laws to inform a human of the existence of supernaturals."

"This isn't her fault," I said, gritting my teeth. If I dragged Serena into this mess, I'd never forgive myself. "I've known about supernaturals most of my life. That's what you get growing up next door to a werewolf. And no, she didn't tell me. I found out myself, accidentally."

We'd been five, playing in the woods behind our

houses. It had been summer, and a full moon had glowed in the sky, even before dark. Serena had begun to shift, and she'd had no idea what was happening to her. I'd held on to her the whole time. For hours. Until the sun rose. For years after that, I'd helped her through her shifts. Not once had she ever tried to bite me, even when she lost control.

Az's eyes widened a fraction of an inch, almost too little to notice. But I'd clocked the surprise. A smug smile lifted the corners of my lips.

"So this whole time you've known I'm a demon? And the others at the club? You knew about them, too?"

"Ah." I winced. "No. Idiot that I am, it never occurred to me."

He turned to Serena then. "So you did tell her what I am."

"Oh, don't be a dick," she countered. "I think it's fair game for her to know you're a Prince, especially since you had her sign a contract without telling her what it meant. That's not allowed, and you know it. You have to inform humans that they're signing a soul contract."

His expression darkened. "Just because you're an attorney at Parkins, Weller, and Smith doesn't mean you can lecture me about contracts."

I whipped my head back and forth, watching the exchange. What did he mean about Serena's job and demon contracts? Puzzle pieces began to click together in my mind. Serena had always been incredibly smart and driven, but she'd managed to snag a competitive job at a prestigious law firm in Manhattan at the age of twenty-three. Surely not…

"Serena," I said slowly. "Do you work for a super-natural law firm?"

She flushed, avoiding my gaze by staring at the soap dispenser by the sink. "I wouldn't really call it a supernatural law firm. It doesn't use magic or anything. It's just…most of our clients are vampires, demons, or fae. Werewolves, too, but mostly the others."

"And I am a client of the firm," Az added. "Which means you need to stay out of this. Otherwise, I will have to tell Parkins that you instructed Mia to tear up one of my contracts."

Serena growled and whipped her head to me. "This guy is a dick."

"Tell me about it," I replied.

"You're really not supposed to let a human sign a contract without telling them what it means," Serena said, not missing a beat. "It's against the rules. It won't hold up, regardless of who your lawyers are."

Asmodeus shot her a wicked smile. "For other demons, yes. But I am a Prince of Hell. Those rules do not apply to me."

My heart flipped, and for the first time, the reality of my situation sank into the very depths of my bones. A part of me hadn't believed it. The guy was an asshole, but he didn't look like the kind of person to feast on souls. Not that I had any idea what a soul-eater would actually look like. Maybe a red dude with horns. And a tail. Definitely a tail.

Did he have a tail?

"So it's true then," I said, my breath rattling in my lungs. "If I break our deal, you'll get my soul."

He leaned forward and tucked his finger beneath my chin. Those wicked eyes cut through me. "I will not only get it, but I will enjoy taking it straight to Hell."

11

"Now that we've settled that," Asmodeus said, pulling away. "All three of us are going to return to the party and act as though nothing has happened."

Serena snorted. "Not a chance in hell."

"Neither one of you has much of a choice," he said, his voice dropping into an irritated growl. "A deal has been made. One month, and then it's over. I'll give you two a minute to collect yourselves, but if either one of you does anything remotely against me, I will not hesitate to alert the law firm and take Mia's soul. Got it?"

I swallowed hard and nodded. Az had us exactly where he needed us, and he knew it. Too much was at stake. Serena's job, and…well, my entire life, apparently. If he took my soul, what would happen to me? Would I die? Or would my body continue to live on, like some kind of zombie?

Serena grunted but then relented. Asmodeus gave

us a wicked smile and then vanished through the door. A pocket of sound escaped into the bathroom: laughter, clinking glass, and booming music. It was a whole other world out there while we were stuck beside a golden toilet with our nightmares.

"Well." Serena blew out a long breath that rustled the ebony hair framing her face. "So I guess *that* happened."

"I don't think he is going to tear up the contract, shockingly enough," I said dryly. "I think it's more likely that hell will freeze over first."

She cut her eyes my way. "This is really bad. You know that, right?"

"Nah, I'm having a whale of a time. My soul is bound to a total dick of a demon. How could I have more fun than this?" I turned to Serena. "Speaking of dicks, I have a question. Do demons have weird ones? With a pointy thing at the end. You know, like demon tails? And also, does he have an actual tail, too?"

She gave me a blank stare. "Did you just ask about his dick?"

I shrugged. "Aren't you curious?"

"No. No, I am not." She shook her head. "I feel like you aren't taking this seriously."

Sighing, I pressed down the front of my dress, wondering exactly how my life had gotten to this point. Hiding from a demon at a party for supernaturals and hoping that I could hold on to my soul for a month. "I'm taking it seriously, but there's not much either one of us can do. Just gotta keep my head down and get through this next month. Shouldn't be that hard, right?"

Her lips flatlined. "My world is crazy, Mia. There's a reason I never invited you to come with me to things like this. Noah, too. I have to socialize because of my job. If I didn't have to, I wouldn't be here. These people can be dangerous, especially for humans."

My heart pounded. "None of them can be much worse than a demon, right?"

"You'd be surprised." She crossed the room and took my shoulders in her hands. Her dark eyes bored into mine. "As crazy as this sounds, I want you to stick close to Asmodeus. He needs you for something, which means he won't let anything happen to you. You're under his protection, which ironically, is probably the safest place you can be. For now. No one is going to fuck with one of the Princes of Hell."

"Sure," I said in a small voice. "No one is going to fuck with Lucifer's right-hand man, except maybe the angels?"

Her face clouded over. "The angels? What do you mean?"

A fist pounded the door, and a girl called out on the other side of it. "Hurry up! I have to pee, and you two are taking forever in there."

Serena grimaced and released her grip on my arms. "Our time's up. Remember what I said. Stick close to Asmodeus. And keep me updated. Some of the rules might not apply to him, but others do. If he does anything that seems off, let me know. I might be able to get you out of this."

She gave me a quick hug, and then we pushed back out into the party. The clamor of drunken supernaturals flooded my senses, and the crowd pushed in tight. At least fifty more people had shown up while we'd been hiding out in the bathroom, and the earlier partygoers were swaying and slurring their speech. And I couldn't help but wonder, how much alcohol did it take to get a vampire drunk?

Az loomed out of the crowd and latched his hand on my elbow. Without a word, he guided me down the hallway and into a dark room I hadn't yet seen. Inside, blue lights cast a haze across partygoers who were swaying to a live musician on a small stage. The singer gripped the microphone and whispered words in a language I didn't know. A guitarist sat just behind him, as well as a drummer. All their eyes were shut.

"Let's dance." He took my hand in his and pulled me close to his body. My lungs constricted; my heart nearly jolted into my throat. As we began to sway to the music, our chests pressed together and he leaned down to whisper into my ear. "I know all of this is a shock, but I need you to trust me."

I scoffed, tempted to pull away, but then I just continued on, my body betraying my mind. "You can't expect me to trust you after you tricked me into signing your demon contract."

"I didn't trick you," he murmured, his breath whispering against my ear. Shivers stormed down my neck. "You *wanted* the job. You came to my club, begging me to give you an audition."

"That's before I knew what kind of club it was," I replied through gritted teeth. "You should have told me."

"And would it have made a difference?"

I opened my mouth to retort that it absolutely would have, but then stopped. My heart pounded as his lips stayed close to my ear, teasing my skin with his wickedly hot breath. Would I have turned down the job if I'd known the club was meant for supernaturals? Probably not. I loosed a sigh.

"Fine, I still would have wanted the job, but I never would have signed the contract. It's my soul, Asmodeus. You say you're above all the rules, but fuck the rules. It's not right to make a deal with someone without them knowing what the consequences are. Not when their *soul* is on the line."

I could feel his smile against my ear. I had no idea how I could feel it, but I did. I couldn't see his face, not when he leaned so close to my neck. A strange familiar sensation rippled in my belly, one I'd felt a thousand times, but...I couldn't place where. Weird.

"You're talking about right and wrong with a demon."

"You say that, but I know you're not all bad." I turned to him then, catching the corner of his eye. "You made me pancakes. You brought me Hendrix. And you didn't want me to walk alone at night. If you were evil, you wouldn't have done any of those things."

"If someone kills you, you won't be able to fulfill your end of our deal," he said with a wicked smile. "And the other two things were nothing but bribes. You hate me, understandably so. I thought if I dulled your sharp edges then you would be easier to handle.

I don't have time to deal with your sarcastic pouting all the time."

A low growl rumbled in my throat as irritation stormed through my veins. "And you wonder why I hate you."

"I don't wonder at all. I'm an evil, vicious demon who likes to steal souls."

I rolled my eyes. "Being a demon is not your worst offence."

Slowly, Asmodeus pulled back. A strange expression flickered across his face, one I couldn't read. "You know, most human girls would go running and screaming in the other direction. You seem abnormally calm about this."

Shrugging, I tried to avoid looking too deeply into his ice blue eyes. I didn't like how they made me feel, like I was completely bare before him. "Like I said, I've known about supernaturals all my life."

"That doesn't explain it," he said with a slight shake of his head. "You didn't know I was a demon until tonight. Why aren't you scared?"

"I don't know," I said with a sigh. "I don't trust you or like you very much, but that's less about what you are and more because you're a total dick."

His lips twitched, and he pulled me close once more. My heart thundered against my ribs, and I hoped he couldn't feel the tremor of it. "I should be annoyed at you for that one."

"So be annoyed. I don't care."

"I know you don't." He chuckled. "You really aren't afraid of me, are you?"

Hmm. I wasn't sure that was *entirely* accurate.

There was still the small chance he was involved in a bunch of murders, but that didn't explain why he'd spared me when he'd had a dozen chances by now. Unless Serena was right. He needed something from me. Maybe after he got it, he'd kill me then.

My gut twisted, although fear didn't flood me with adrenaline. I just felt mildly uneasy. Not scared. Deep down, I didn't think Asmodeus was a killer, despite what the angels said. I also didn't think he *wanted* to steal my soul. The contract had been insurance and nothing more. To get me to do what he needed.

Not that it made it right.

"It's hard to feel scared when you're angry," I finally whispered to him.

He tensed against me, and then wound his hand around my back. His palm pressed against the dip just above my ass, and I suddenly forgot what we were talking about.

"We're being watched," he murmured, his cheek pressed against mine. "Now would be a fantastic time for you to use that anger as fuel for passion."

"Excuse me?" I squeaked.

"People saw you vanish into the restroom with Serena, and then me follow close behind. They know we were arguing about something. We need to convince them we've made up."

"Maybe I don't want to convince them we made up," I hissed back.

"Then I'll be forced to take your soul," he said in a deadpan voice that held little remorse or guilt. My fingers itched to curl into fists and slam into his gut.

But I couldn't. And he knew it. I was nothing more than a puppet to him, and I would never escape until he cut the strings.

"Fine," I growled back.

Rolling my eyes, I wound my arms around his neck and leaned in close to him. Heat curled off his body, caressing my skin. I swallowed hard at the feel of his light stubble against my cheek. His skin was soft and warm, and it drove away all thoughts of fighting him on this. To be honest, this wasn't too bad. He smelled good, like campfires and manly musk. His hand was warm against my back, and his shredded chest was like a steady rock, shifting against me each time we swayed.

If I forgot about the contract and the rude comments and the disdain in his voice when he spoke to me, I might even be able to enjoy this. Just a little.

Something buzzed by my ear. I jumped, heart raging like a bull. Az pulled his hand away from my shoulder and glanced at his smart watch. A frown pulled down his lips, and he turned away from me, his eyes shuttering.

"I'll be back in a minute," he said without even giving me a fleeting glance. "There's something I need to do."

"What?" I gaped at him as he pushed through the crowd, already halfway across the dance floor. "You're just going to leave me here?"

"Go find Serena and stay close to her," he threw over his shoulder, and then he was gone.

My mouth dropped open. What the hell was going on? Was he up to something? I should probably follow him and see if I could find out what it was. Maybe if I caught him with his hand in the metaphorical cookie jar, the angels could help me get out of the contract.

I glanced around. A few fanged dancers were eyeing me with eager interest. Yep, definitely time to follow Az. With a deep breath, I pushed through the crowd.

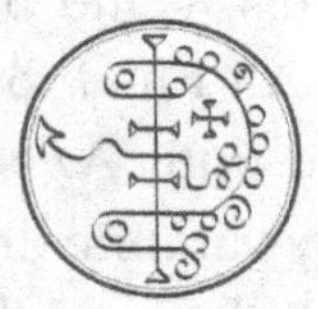

When I reached the hallway, Az was nowhere to be seen. I huffed and strode forward, my boots clicking against the floor. A few partygoers stumbled past me. Some wore horns. Others had fur sprouting on their cheeks. Every single time they caught a glance of my face, they stared.

Were they staring because they knew I was the girlfriend of a Prince of Hell? Or did it have something to do with my humanity? Serena had warned me about this world. Some of these supernaturals were dangerous, but which ones?

I didn't want to wait around and find out.

When I reached the end of the hall, I strode out onto the rooftop. All the tables and sofas were packed. Frowning, I scanned the crowd, searching for a familiar head of dark hair and piercing blue eyes. Where would Az have gone? He didn't mention leaving the party, but I couldn't spot him anywhere.

Surely he hadn't just left me here. Right?

It certainly seemed like he had.

My heart pounded. Asmodeus, the Prince of Hell, had left me at a supernatural party alone. And if I ran now, I'd lose my soul. *Fuck!*

I took in several deep breaths, hoping no one noticed my panic. This would be fine. It was totally okay. No. Big. Deal. All I had to do was find Serena. I'd stick by her side until Az showed up, and she wouldn't let a hungry vampire drain my blood.

A scream ripped through the party. My entire body tensed as the room fell into brutal silence. Another scream followed, and the distant pounding of rushing footsteps sounded like war drums in the night. My heart cantered, and then galloped right out of my chest. What the hell was happening now?

Several of the rooftop partiers jumped to their feet. They glanced around, as if searching for someone. One of the men, an older guy with salt and pepper hair, strode into the center of the patio and addressed the crowd.

"Everyone just needs to remain calm. I'm sure there's a reasonable explanation for—"

Serena rushed onto the rooftop like a tornado. Her gaze latched onto mine, and she visibly sighed. "Thank god. You're okay."

"What's going on?" I asked, keenly aware of the silence. Everyone was watching us.

"There's been another murder." Her voice shook with raw emotion. "A werewolf. A girl who dances at Az's club."

"What?" My blood rushed from my face and

formed a lump of coal in my gut. "Who? What was her name?"

"Willow."

Fevered whispers rippled through the crowd on the roof. Someone sobbed. My heart squeezed tight as I remembered the girl. We'd barely had a chance to speak last night, but she'd been kind and welcoming, vibrant and alive. Now she was dead.

My hands fisted. "Who is doing this?"

"I don't know, but it has to be the same guy as before," she whispered back, our voices now drowned out by the roaring buzz of conversation that filled the night air. "The, um, body was in the same position. And her throat was cut like the others." Suddenly, she seemed to notice I stood alone. "Where the hell is your demon?"

"I don't know," I replied. "He got an alert on his watch and vanished just before…"

Serena's eyes narrowed. "Just before the murder? Mia."

I pressed my lips together. "It looks really bad, but I don't think it was him."

"Why not? It makes sense."

"I don't know. It's just…a feeling I have. I can't explain it. Trust me, I've had my doubts and my questions. But every time I wonder if it's him, it just doesn't seem right. It's like a puzzle piece that doesn't fit the gap."

"That doesn't make any sense."

"I know it doesn't, but I don't know how else to explain it." I glanced around. Half of the roof had emptied now. No one wanted to stick around at a party where people got murdered.

The distant sound of sirens blared through the night air. They were drawing closer. My stomach dropped, and I latched onto Serena's arm. "The cops are coming."

She nodded. "Someone must have called them."

"Don't you have, like, supernatural cops or something?" My voice was rising as the panic clawed at my gut. I couldn't help myself. Rational thought rarely stuck around when my old fears rose up from the ash.

"Not really," she admitted. "We should. They're going to want to speak to everyone at this party, and there are things they aren't going to understand."

"I can't be here, Serena," I breathed. "If I talk to them, they'll look me up, and they'll find a way to blame this on me. A girl, our age, dead, at a party? The media will get ahold of it. It will be my senior year of college all over again."

"Okay, calm down." Serena glanced over her shoulder at the crowded hallway that led to the elevators. Everyone else heard the sirens and had similar thoughts. I tried not to think about what that meant. I wasn't the only one here running from the cops. "We'll get you out of here before they arrive. Dammit, Asmodeus, where the hell did you go?"

"I don't think we have time to find him," I whispered, my stomach twisting into knots. "I can't stay here, Serena. I won't go through all that again. *I can't.*"

"I know." Serena pressed her forehead against mine, and a sense of calm settled over me. A feeling only she'd ever been able to give me when I got like this. "The hallway is packed. You'll never even reach the elevator in time. We'll have to go another way."

Together, we pushed through the lingering crowd. Serena led me down the hallway in the opposite direction of the elevators. When we reached another door, she flung it open and strode inside. It was a small, cluttered office, likely for the manager of the bar. There was a single window overlooking a courtyard below. Sirens drifted through the cracked panes.

"You'll have to go down the fire escape," she said quietly. "Do you think you can manage it by yourself?"

My stomach dropped. "Aren't you coming?"

"I can't. I have clients here, and some of them might need me when the cops start to ask questions. If I leave now, my firm will not be pleased." She pressed her lips together. "But I don't like the idea of you running through the streets by yourself. As soon as you reach the bottom of the fire escape, head to the next block over. There are a few bars there, and they'll be open. If you can't find a taxi, call for one and wait inside one of the bars. Don't stand around in the street. And for the love of god, Mia. Don't walk home."

I rolled my eyes. "I'm not an idiot."

"I know you're not an idiot, but I also know how scared you are right now. Sometimes you don't think straight when it comes to the media and the cops."

"Gee. I wonder why." Dread filled my heart. "This is going to turn out just like Nashville."

"This is *not* Nashville all over again. You had

nothing to do with Willow's death, and the cops will quickly realize this matches up with the serial killer. There's no reason for them to think it's you. All right?"

"I had nothing to do with it then, either."

She sighed. "I know."

Shouts exploded down the hallway. Heart pounding, I threw my legs over the side of the window and jumped out onto a rusted fire escape. The metal groaned beneath me. I grasped the handrail that flaked against my skin. Gritting my teeth, I tiptoed down the first flight of stairs while Serena vanished back into the dying party.

I made my way down the fire escape as quickly as I could, scaling the final ladder until my boots hit the ground. Following Serena's advice, I turned the corner of the next block over. And came face to face with a line of police cars.

"Fuck," I swore beneath my breath and ducked back into the alley. Had I gone the wrong way? Steeling myself, I peeked around the red brick again. There were the bars Serena had mentioned. I glanced back in the direction I'd come, frowning.

Two lots of police cars? That couldn't be good.

Had the killer come here, too?

Chills swept down my bare arms. I glanced down, grateful for my boots. I might have to run, after all.

No, that was stupid. Serena was right. The killer was out here, somewhere. If he'd hit two places, there was no telling if he'd hit a third. A lone girl walking home in the middle of the night would become another likely target.

I pulled my head away from the corner and pressed my back against the rough wall. Time for a plan. One that made sense. If I wandered out from this alley, the cops would see me. Not a big deal if I didn't have anything to hide. Would they want to question me? Would they realize I'd fled the party?

That would look really, really bad.

Maybe I would just stay here, hiding in the alley, until the cops went away.

No, that wasn't any better. They'd search the streets for the guy, hoping they could catch him before he got away. I was a sitting duck. I couldn't stay.

I had only two options. Walk out of here and surrender myself to the cops. They'd question me. They might even suspect me. And my name would be plastered all over the internet again. The hounding reporters. The death threats. The chaos of it all.

Or I could sneak away through the alleys and risk stumbling into the path of a killer.

I'd told Serena that I wouldn't let fear control me, but it had controlled me for the past two years. Every decision I made. Every disappointment I encountered. Every pessimistic thought that swirled through my head. It all stemmed from my fear. I was scared that my past would never release its grip on me. It would shadow my steps for the rest of my days, no matter how far I ran.

It would always catch up to me. And it had found me yet again.

With a deep breath, I turned away from the flashing lights and the shouting cops. I wound my way through the dark, solemn alleys, fisting Az's apartment keys in my hand. I didn't think it would make much of a difference if someone attacked me, but it put a bounce in my step, a determination in my bones.

Az's building was only a few blocks away. The maze of alleyways would end, and I could curl up in the safety of a Prince of Hell's penthouse.

A gap in the buildings led to the sidewalk, one free of flashing red-and-blue lights. I picked up my pace. As I did, I heard the unmistakable clatter of footsteps behind me.

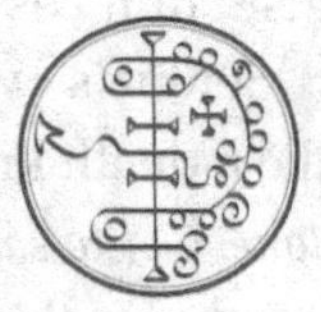

I didn't dare glance behind me. Terror shook my thighs, transforming them into jelly. All I could do was put one foot in front of each other and focus on the gap. Only a few more steps stood between me and freedom. Surely someone would be out on those sidewalks. A taxi would drive by or a couple would stumble home from a bar. There would be *someone*.

And whoever followed me would not strike.

As I drew closer to the sidewalk, the trailing footsteps suddenly thundered to life. My breath caught in my throat as I finally whirled to face whoever followed me. A large figure loomed out of the darkness, clad in black from head to toe. A mask covered his face, hiding every feature except for his slate grey eyes.

I sucked in a sharp breath and stumbled back just as he reached a meaty hand toward my arm. Blood roared in my ears. With a cry of alarm, I spun on my feet and raced toward the opening.

A strong hand landed on my shoulder, dragging me back into the darkness. I dropped my chin to scream, but his other hand clamped over my mouth. My cry came out as nothing but a muffled whimper.

I thrashed against him as adrenaline surged through my veins. Serena's whispered warnings echoed in my head like a death knell.

Don't walk home alone. Get to safety. Wait for me.

I'd done none of those things, ignoring every single thing she'd said. If I died here tonight, she would kill me.

"Stop fighting me," a deep voice growled into my ear, the sound of thunder cracking through the sky. "You won't get away from me, and you're only making this harder on yourself."

Tears sprang into my eyes as the taste of his skin melted against my mouth. Ash, oranges, and bitter herbs. What the hell?

"Let go of me," I said, my words muffled. "I will sic my demon on you if you don't."

He stilled. That had certainly caught his attention. Based on his presence at the party, I'd come to the conclusion that the friendly neighborhood serial killer was supernatural in origin. If he wasn't one himself, he certainly knew about them, which meant he wouldn't be shocked by the mention of a demon. Or, at the very least, he wouldn't think I was totally insane for talking about one.

"What did you say about a demon?" he asked in a dangerously calm voice.

I swallowed hard. "Take your hand away, and I'll tell you."

"No way in hell. You'll scream."

"Fine," I said, still muffled. "I have a demon boyfriend. If you don't let me go, I'm pretty sure he will tear all your limbs off your torso and then feast on your soul."

I didn't really know if that was a thing demons did, but might as well go with it. It wasn't a total lie. Asmodeus *wouldn't* be happy this guy had caught his little human pet. And I was pretty sure an unhappy demon wasn't high on anyone's list of favorite things. Except maybe Lucifer's.

Oh my god, what if this guy was Lucifer?

That was impossible, right? He lived in Hell. Of course I would have assumed the Princes of Hell lived in the underworld, too, so all bets were off.

"You're human," he said quietly. "Demons don't date humans. They only use them as playthings."

My mouth went dry. Well, that wasn't *at all* unnerving. Unfortunately, it probably wasn't that far off the mark.

"Plaything or girlfriend, it doesn't matter. I'm still protected by a demon, so you should probably run along home and give up on your big serial killer dreams. Because Az knows about you, and he will track you down. It's probably best for you to get out of the United States ASAP. Actually, make that this planet."

I was just talking out of my ass now. Asmodeus had shown no interest in finding the killer. He was far too wrapped up in his world of business ventures and rich, powerful friends. Sure, he didn't want me to walk alone at night, but it seemed like that was the extent of his concern. Why would a demon care about a killer in the streets?

The guy's black mask hid his mouth from view, but I could see a reflection of his wicked grin in his eyes. Anger flashed in his grey irises, a flash of steel, like a sword beneath the glint of moonlight.

I swallowed hard. I didn't think my fake bravado had done much to convince him to let me go. Time to come up with another plan.

My gaze drifted down the length of him and landed on his crotch. Hmm. Maybe if I was fast enough, I could slam my boot into his dick and run. *Yeah*, I thought to myself as I rolled back my shoulders. This guy deserved a good kick in the dick, and I was more than happy to be the one to administer it.

"I don't like that look on your face," he grunted as he pulled a large, serrated knife from his back waistband. "Time to stop messing around. Normally I wouldn't touch a human, but you chose your path. Now it's time for you to die."

My heart shot up into my throat and landed there like a clump of nausea I couldn't swallow down. Every hair on my arms stood to attention and begged for the world to open up beneath me and yank me into the darkness. I'd probably land in a nest of subway rats, but that would be a hell of a lot better than where I was now.

The hand that held the blade shot out toward my neck. I stumbled back, opened my mouth, and let out a scream that ripped through the night air. It was so loud my own ears rang. They could probably hear me all the way up in the Bronx.

Good. Hopefully someone would come running. I just needed to survive ten more minutes.

A low growl emanated from the attacker's throat. He stalked toward me with narrowed eyes and a white-knuckled fist that gripped his knife.

"You shouldn't have done that," he muttered. "I was going to try to make things painless for you. Nice and quick. But now I want nothing more than to see you suffer, you little bitch."

"I'll take that as a compliment," I said with a smile that betrayed none of the fear surging through my veins like acid.

He stalked forward, and I took a step away. My ass hit the grimy wall. Shit. He'd backed me into a corner, and the only way out was around his beefy frame. My heartbeat skittered like a mouse.

"You have a lot of nerve for a human, but you've run out of options now." He lifted the knife, angling the blade toward my throat.

I squeezed my hand into a fist and met his vicious gaze. My past flashed before my eyes, like a movie reel of unwanted memories. Dancing with my sister on the local playhouse stage. Running through the woods barefoot, laughing as we stumbled over fallen branches, scraping our knees. Dead eyes staring up at me. My sister's sobs. My parents' faces as they shouted at me to leave.

A tear slipped down my cheek. I didn't want to die like this.

Desperation rose up inside of me in a sudden

rush, like the waves against the shore. It filled me with an overwhelming heat. Invisible flames danced around my hand. The signet ring I'd tucked into my bra burned against my skin. The strange sensation built up inside of me until I could think of nothing else. It felt like it was going to explode within me, shattering me into a thousand pieces. Gritting my teeth, I let out a roar of pain.

The attacker's eyes widened as a sudden, invisible force slammed into his chest. His feet left the ground, and he hurtled through the air, landing in a heap right in front of the exit of the alley.

My grip relaxed; my eyes widened. What the hell had just happened?

Slowly, the attacker climbed to his feet. Fury ripped through his eyes. I swallowed hard and glanced at the exit. Why, oh why, couldn't I have thrown him somewhere else? He blocked the only way out.

"You have *really* just made things worse for you." As if in no rush at all, he brushed the dirt from his black jeans. "Your scream did nothing. No one is coming for you. And your little trick just then…whatever it was, it didn't work. All you've done is make me very angry. I will relish in this kill."

He strode across the alley. Heart in my throat, I fisted my hand again, trying to figure out what it was I did before. *If* I had even done it. I still didn't understand what had happened, but it felt like it had come from me. Or that ring. Of that much, I was certain.

So now I just needed to do it again. Simple, right?

Except I had no idea what I'd done. Heat had enveloped my entire body, and then…it had lurched out of me and slammed into the attacker's chest. Only he hadn't caught fire. He'd just been thrown back.

It didn't make much sense, but if I could do it again, I had another chance to escape. And I really needed it. As much as I hated to admit he was right, he was. If anyone had heard my scream, they weren't coming. They would have been here by now.

Suddenly, I sensed a pair of eyes on me. Darkness filled the alley like a storm, and a heavy sense of despair shuddered through my body. It was almost enough to knock me to my knees.

"Mia," a low voice spoke from somewhere nearby, but I couldn't see the man attached to it. "Don't move."

Listening to a disembodied voice didn't seem like it was in my best interests, but I also didn't want to be stabbed to death. Not exactly the two best choices, but it was all I had.

"Sure," I said, lounging against the wall like this situation was totally normal. "I'll just stay here while you do your thing."

Asmodeus slithered out of the shadows. Obviously, I'd had a hunch the voice belonged to him, but seeing him still made my breath catch. Pure and unadulterated danger rippled through his eyes, and the sword he held in his hands was...

Wait a minute. Was that a fucking sword?

He levelled it at the attacker. "If you touch her, I will fucking kill you."

"Um..." My jaw almost literally hit the floor.

"Stay back, Mia," he said, his voice so full of commanding anger that it shut my mouth. "Abaddon is feeling hungry for blood, and he struggles to understand the difference between friend and foe. I need you to stay back while I take care of this."

"Should I be worried you seem to think your sword is a living creature with a mind of its own?"

"As long as it makes you worried enough to stay the hell away from it, then yes. Very much so." He stalked further into the alley where the silent attacker was eyeing him like he was a platter of juicy meat.

Asmodeus growled, his entire body trembling with anger. "Get the hell away from her."

"You've finally come out to play," the attacker said with the hint of a smile in his voice. "Thought you were too cowardly to leave your little club to face me in the streets."

I whipped my head toward Az, who lifted his glittering sword before him. "I've had better things to do than engage with someone as spineless as you."

"Spineless?" The attacker barked out a laugh. "I'm the one out here taking care of things while you and your Legion are lost in your fancy drinks with your fancy friends."

"Who are you?" Az asked in a low, dangerous voice. "Why are you killing innocent girls?"

"Innocent?" He laughed again. "They are anything but."

"Mia has done nothing wrong." Az took another step toward the attacker just as police sirens blared through the air. I whipped toward the sound, surprised. There were more of them? Were they coming here?

My stomach flipped. Had they heard my screams?

Logically, I knew this was a good thing. The cops would save me from, you know, getting murdered. Az wouldn't have to go through with this weird sword fight, and the night would end without bloodshed.

There were two problems with this scenario, however. First, I'd definitely have to give a statement. This serial killer thing was huge news, and I would get wrapped up in the whole thing. It would turn into a circus, and my past would get dragged into it. I'd run from that party, too.

Second, I definitely didn't think it was legal for people to carry real-ass swords around Manhattan. As much as I hated the guy, Asmodeus had come to my rescue, and I didn't want to see him locked up because of it.

Could demons escape prison?

While I was distracted by the sirens, the attacker took the opportunity to bolt. One moment he was there, the next he was gone. It was almost like he'd literally vanished into thin air.

My demon let out a growl of rage.

That left me and Az alone in the alley with a sword and zero killers. This would definitely look way worse than it had before. Especially since there'd been two murders nearby already.

"We need to get out of here," I said at the same moment he did.

He stopped short, arching his brow. "Why do *you* want to run from the cops?"

I pressed my lips together. "It doesn't matter. You're holding a sword. Unless you want to get arrested for what I'm definitely sure is illegal carry *and* become a murder suspect, then we need to get out of here now."

He nodded and strode across the alley, stopping when he was nothing more than an inch away from me. Once again, my back pressed against the wall, but this time, the fear was replaced by something else. Something I didn't understand.

And it wasn't entirely welcome. This guy annoyed the shit out of me.

Still, I couldn't help but notice the flecks of ice in his eyes. The shadows that curled around his jaw. The power that rippled off of him, and the strength in the way he moved. The sword helped.

I swallowed hard. "Thank you for not letting me die in a grungy back alley in Hell's Kitchen."

His eyes flicked across my face. "Are you all right?"

I nodded.

"Good. I have to say, I'm impressed. It looks like there's been a scuffle. Did you fight him off for a bit?"

"Um." How could I explain what had happened? I was pretty sure it had something to do with the ring the angels had given me. If I told him about it, he'd know they'd been speaking to me. He might not be so willing to save my ass next time.

Next time. Fear tripped through my veins. The attacker had gotten away, and there was nothing stopping him from killing again. I'd pissed him off. He would bide his time and come for me again. I was certain of it.

Until this guy was caught, I needed Az on my side.

"He underestimated me," I said. "I don't think he's used to people fighting back."

"Hmm."

Thankfully, he didn't pry further than that. He took my hand and led me through the alleyways, away from the sirens. When we reached a single black door, he pushed it open to reveal the ground floor of his club. Somehow, we'd ended up here once again.

I glanced up at him with raised brows. His jaw was set firm, and his eyes had grown cold. "What are we doing here?"

"I need to tell the others what happened tonight. We lost someone." His shoes clicked against the slick floor as we strode down the dimly-lit hallway. Music bounced against the walls, and a distant shriek of laughter echoed toward us. The club had been untouched by this crazy night, but it sounded like it wouldn't be for long.

Az led the way into the small room where his bouncers sat playing cards around the folding table. There were only three of them tonight. Valac, Caim, and a third whose name I didn't know. His dark hair fell into silver eyes, and a scar ran down the length of his arm. The three of them spun on their chairs as we entered the room.

"Ah." Caim grinned. "Mia. You're back. I was afraid we'd scared you off. This place can be a little intense for humaaa....humanitarians. Not that you're necessarily a humanitarian. You just seem like a nice girl, so maybe you would be one. Shit."

"No need," Az said with a tense smile in my direction. "Mia knows about supernaturals. You can drop the act now."

Caim's eyebrows winged upward. "Well, this certainly took a turn. I didn't think you were going to tell her."

"I didn't tell her." He sighed and dropped into one

of the open chairs around the table. "She grew up next door to a werewolf."

"Ah." Valac nodded as if that made all the sense in the world.

"The killer tried to attack her tonight," Az said quietly as he palmed the table. "After murdering Willow at the party. I tried to save her. It was too late."

The third demon paled, and his hands clenched around the cards. "The dancer who started working here last week? That's two in a row. First, Allison. Now, Willow."

Oh. So that was why the other dancers had paled at the mention of Allison. The serial killer had targeted her, too. Shit.

Az's hands fisted. "He's killing people close to me. The closer we get to catching him, the bolder he gets. If I hadn't heard Mia scream, she would have died tonight."

Valac and Caim both turned to stare at me. I gave them a weak smile. "It's true. The guy backed me into an alley and—"

"Why exactly were you wandering around in alleys, Mia?" Az suddenly asked, whirling toward me, as if it had just occurred to him. "Why weren't you at the party? Why did you run off?"

"Um, it's complicated," I tried.

"Explain." His eyes flashed.

I glanced from his face to the others. They were all looking at me with expectant curiosity. It reminded me of the looks I'd seen from the neighbors, from my old classmates, from random people in Walmart. It made me want to crawl under the table and hide.

"Later," I said, clearing my throat. "When we don't have such a rapt audience."

Caim's brow arched.

Az folded his arms and leaned back in the chair. "Absolutely not. This is my Legion. Everything I know, they know."

"Yeah, about this whole Legion thing, I don't really know what that means."

Valac frowned. "How much *do* you know?"

"You're all demons. From the underworld, I guess." I drifted further into the room and shrugged. "I know you make deals for souls, but I don't know what you do with them. Or what your powers are. Or what a Legion is."

Caim let out a low whistle and glanced at Az. "Think we should fill her in?"

"Yes," I said, at the exact time Az said, "No."

We glared at each other.

"Look," I said. "You've dragged me into this whole thing without my knowledge, and now the serial killer wants me dead, too. He made it clear it has something to do with you, so I think it's time you explained to me *exactly* what it is you've gotten me into."

Caim grinned. "I like this one."

"Me too," Valac said with a strange, twisted smile. "Most humans go screaming in the other direction."

"Because you steal souls."

"No," the third demon said quietly, still staring down at the table. "We save them."

Az swore, and Valac dropped his head into his hands.

Caim sucked in a sharp breath and stood. "Honestly, Stolas. Think before you speak. The last thing we need is a human to tell someone what we're up to in here."

I blinked. "Wait a minute. You…*save* souls?"

Caim let out a heavy sigh and shot another glare at Stolas. "We're trying to help people instead of corrupt them. Lead them away from a path of destruction. Sometimes that means we end up saving their souls. Other times, just their lives."

"We shouldn't be telling her all this," Az said, voice hard, eyes cold. "If Lucifer finds out what we're up to, he'll drag us back to Hell. And I know none of us want that. We can't help humanity there."

Um, what?! This was a lot to take in. Numbly, I stumbled forward and sat hard on the only empty chair left. My gaze locked on the table. Not only were these actual, literal demons, but they were somehow working against the King of Hell himself. And I was all mixed up in it.

"Wait a minute," I said slowly, raising my eyes to Az's face. "If you're saving souls, then why did you trap me in a demon contract with you?"

"Because it was the only way," he said with a voice devoid of all emotion. "While we might be doing some good here, I am still very much a demon, Mia McNally. And I will do whatever necessary to get what I want."

Chills swept down my arms. My voice dropped to a whisper. "What is it that you want?"

"Entry into an exclusive party," he replied, his gaze locked on mine. Flames of darkness flickered in the depths of his eyes. "Invitations are only extended to supernaturals who have pretty, little human sacrifices on their arms."

All the blood rushed from my face. "Sacrifices?"

"He wasn't actually going to sacrifice you," Caim interjected. "It's just a trick to snag an invite."

I frowned. "But why do you want to get in?"

Fury rolled off Az's fisted hands. "I plan to stop the sacrifices."

"Oh." I leaned back in the chair. Everything was starting to make a lot more sense. I'd thought it was weird he'd fake a girlfriend just for a few dates. Why would business investors care if he had a plus one to some lame parties? Now I knew why. I was to be...bait.

I shifted on my feet.

"I need you to listen to me very carefully." Az's eyes bored into mine. I felt myself captivated by them, lured in, and held firm. His voice was as soft as a caress, even with the underlying danger in it. What would happen if I stretched out my hand and placed it on the table between us? With my breath locked in my throat, I palmed the metal.

Az leaned forward and gripped my fingers. Heat sizzled up my arm.

"These people need to be stopped," he said in a low growl. "They've held this party every year for over a decade, and at least twenty humans are sacrificed each time. That's over two hundred deaths. Two hundred souls lost to Hell. We can't let this continue, and the only way I can get inside is with a human companion. One meant to be a sacrifice."

My heart throttled forward into next gear.

"I never wanted you to know because I didn't want to scare you. We had a plan to keep you safe, none the wiser. You were my ticket in, and then the Legion planned to sneak you out safely before the bloodshed began." He sighed, and then his gaze went sharp. "But now that you fully understand who we are and what is happening here, I am going to give you a choice. Will you help us stop these deaths, or do you want me to break our deal?"

15

My blood crackled in my ears like static. Az dropped my hand and pushed up from his chair while my eyes followed his every move. This was…unexpected. He'd been dead set on forcing me to remain in the contract, and now he was offering up a way out as if it meant nothing at all.

Annoyingly, I didn't jump to my feet and accept. An hour ago, I would have. But an hour ago, I'd had no idea there was a group of supernaturals out there, sacrificing humans to…what exactly?

"What are the sacrifices for?" I whispered.

"Ah." Caim nodded. "Good question. And I don't think you're going to like the answer."

"They're for Lucifer." Valac lifted his gaze from the table. The silver in his eyes looked like glowing bullets, and there was an emptiness in him that made my soul shake.

"Lucifer," I repeated. "The same Lucifer you're hiding from."

"We're not *hiding* from Lucifer," Stolas corrected. "He knows exactly where we are. We just don't want him to find out that we're trying to help people instead of corrupt them. You see, he wants us to send more souls to Hell. It's getting too empty for his liking."

"Right, of course," I said as if that wasn't one of the craziest things I'd ever heard in my life. How had I gone from feeding pancakes to a pigeon to *this*?

"So now you understand our dilemma." Caim ran a hand through his midnight hair. "If you want to walk away from this, no hard feelings. But it'll suck for us. We'll need to find another human to replace you if we want to get Az inside that ball, and it'll look a little sus."

"Az never dates anyone," Stolas added. "To go from one girlfriend to the next in a span of a week…"

"Not to mention you're currently living with him," Valac said so softly that I almost couldn't hear him over my pounding heart.

I closed my eyes. "I need a minute to think."

The demons all fell silent. I wasn't seriously considering this, was I? Serena and I had *just* been talking about convincing Az to destroy my contract. And here was the perfect opportunity. I hadn't even needed to convince him. He'd offered. All I would have to do was say the word, and I'd be free.

Free from all this danger and supernatural insanity. I'd move back in with Serena and continue my life as a drifter. Drink mugs of wine in front of the TV every night. Better than the alternative. Death by demon.

But…these guys clearly needed my help. I was Az's ticket into this horrendous sacrificial party. If I walked away from this, he might not get an invitation, and the murders would continue another year. Could I really let twenty people die because I was too afraid?

Fuck. I couldn't. Sometimes I really hated being me.

When I flipped open my eyes, I found four demons staring at me. I jumped a little and glared when Caim cracked a grin.

"Honestly, you guys are creepy sometimes," I muttered.

"That's rich, coming from a human," Caim replied with a chuckle.

I glowered at him. "What's that supposed to mean?"

"Will you two stop flirting?" Az asked in a voice as hard as steel. Shadows rippled across his jaw.

"We're not flirting," I said quickly, although I didn't know why I felt the need to correct him. What did he care? He'd warned me away from Caim, but that was before I knew the truth about them. He'd clearly been worried I'd find out the truth. Now I knew everything. So what was the big deal?

Technically, I was very much single.

"Nevermind all that." Caim eagerly leaned forward. "What did you decide, Mia?"

"I'll stay." My voice sounded alien to my own ears. I'd decided not to run away from this, but it was hard to believe I'd said it out loud. This was totally idiotic, right? Serena was going to lose her damn mind.

Az sat up a little straighter, clearly surprised by my answer. "Let me get this straight. You *don't* want me to rip up our contract."

"No," I met his gaze and swallowed hard. There was a glint of appreciation in his eye, a softness I wasn't sure I really wanted to see. A good in him that betrayed my earlier impression. And as that good burrowed its way into my skin, I wanted to claw it out. It was easier to think of him as an asshole demon who wanted to steal my soul. Then I could ignore the way his touch made me feel.

Not that his touch made me feel any certain way, thank you very much.

He was just hot, okay?

A slow, delicious smile spread across his lips. It was the kind of smile that could melt most women's panties. Not mine, though. I was definitely one hundred percent immune. That little tickle down there just meant I had to pee.

"Mia," he murmured. "You have just made me a very happy man."

Flames engulfed my face. I cleared my throat and cast my gaze around to find anything that was not his wicked face. I turned to Caim, who wore a knowing smirk. Like he could see exactly what I was thinking. Or maybe I was just reading too much into things.

"I think this means I've earned a bonus," I finally said, turning back to Az. "You know, for the added danger aspect."

"Sure." Still smiling, he leaned back in his chair, his arms folded over his pristine black suit. "You can get a bonus. If you help us with something else."

"Something else?" My heart flipped. "I'm not sure I want to know."

His smile suddenly died, and shadows collected in his eyes. "We need to stop this killer, once and for all," he said with a nod to Caim. "Show her the thing."

Stolas let out a grunt, shaking his head.

"The thing?" I asked slowly, watching Caim jump up from his chair. He strode over to a wall where a thick black curtain hung over the windows. Only… when he pulled the curtain back, I saw it didn't block windows at all. It covered a massive map. Like, twice as tall as me both ways. Manhattan's famous grid stretched out across it, drowning in scribbles. String connected multicolored pins to each other. It kind of looked like something a serial killer would have in his dungeon.

"Meet the map," Caim said proudly as he gestured at it.

"That's deranged." Still, I popped up from the chair and trailed over to it. The pins obviously represented the murders. I didn't have to be a rocket scientist to figure that out. But not all of them made sense. I pointed at a few pins clustered together in the Lower East Side. "What are these for? I thought he only killed here in Hell's Kitchen."

"There have been some other murders downtown," Az said quietly. "Over in Queens, too. The cops haven't linked them, but we have. There are plenty of similarities. Every single victim has been a supernatural."

"This is…" I quickly counted the pins and whirled toward him, my heart hammering my ribs. "At least a hundred deaths. How long has this been going on?"

"Over a year," Valac said through gritted teeth as he joined us at the map. "We've tried dozens of times to catch this guy, but he's like butter through our fingers. He always vanishes into thin air."

"That's what he did tonight," I breathed. "As soon as he heard the sirens, he just…disappeared. Poof. He was gone. I thought maybe I was imagining things."

Az spoke up from the table. "You didn't imagine anything. He can hide himself somehow. We don't know if he's travelling through shadows, cloaking himself, or something else entirely. Either way, he's proven impossible to catch."

I jerked toward him. "He said you've never gone after him before."

"Usually we are much more discreet. We don't want him to know what we're doing in here. Tonight was the first time we came face-to-face."

Valac edged closer, his hollow, silver-white eyes staring at the map. "We cannot be as bold as we'd like, most of the time. Lucifer would not want us stopping this killer."

I nodded. There was still so much I didn't understand, but it felt like I'd been invited into a secret club. One that hunted killers. If this whole thing wasn't seriously dangerous, it might be a little exciting. Of course, it was also probably illegal. I had no doubt what these demons would do with the murderer once they caught him. Would they give him up to the human cops for a fair and honest trial? Not a chance in hell.

Could I really risk getting caught up in this? Would these demons throw me to the proverbial wolves after I'd helped them? What if we got caught?

I closed my eyes. "So this extra thing you need help with. It's catching a supernatural serial killer. Isn't it?"

"That's right." Stolas rested his hand on my shoulder and squeezed. "He'll try coming after you again. Why don't we let him?"

My stomach dropped to my toes. Slowly, I peeled open my eyes and whirled on all four of them. Caim jumped back with a laugh, holding up his hands in surrender while Valac continued to watch me with that really intense stare of his. Stolas kept one hand latched on my shoulder as if trying to anchor me in place. A calmness settled over me even as my heart yearned to break free of my ribcage. I shot him a glare. Was he using demon voodoo on me?

"You want me to be bait for you," I said to Az, who still remained seated, drumming his fingers on the table. "*Twice.*"

"Yes," three of them said in unison. Az remained silent, watching me.

"And you aren't at all worried the killer will succeed in his little quest? You said he's smoke. What if he just teleports in, stabs me, and then teleports out?"

"I don't think his power works that way," Valac said quietly. "Or he would have already used that technique to kill. He only shadows away to avoid being caught, which makes us believe that his abilities are limited in some way. Most powers are."

"Right. Uh huh. Of course." I glanced at each of them in turn before throwing up my hands. "You really want me to do this, don't you?"

"You're welcome to say no," Az murmured.

His voice slithered along my skin like a caress, and I fought the urge to shudder. Even with the others in the room, it felt like it was just me and him. The overhead lights seemed to dim. My breath stilled in my lungs. Heat pulsed between us as our gazes locked. We were on a date, I suddenly remembered. We'd danced. We'd had wine. And now here we were. A demon asking a girl to help him bait a supernatural serial killer.

"Fine," I breathed. "I'll be your stupid bait."

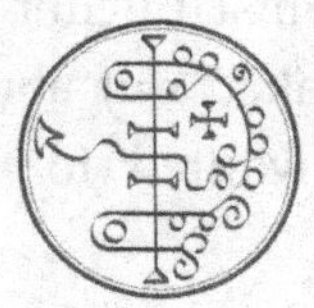

16

We took a car back to his building when the meeting was over. It was late, the club would soon shut, and there was little else we could do tonight. The Legion had been tasked with detailing a plan of attack. We'd go over it tomorrow before I had my second shift at the club.

When we stepped into his penthouse, tension punctuated the silence, so thick it was impossible not to notice. *I* felt it, anyway. I wasn't sure about Az. For the past several hours, after finding out the *real* truth about who he was and what he was doing in Manhattan, I couldn't help but see him in a new light.

A demon, trying to make his mark on the world. In a good way. It boggled the mind. It also made him a tiny bit less of an asshole than I'd originally thought. Not that I would *ever* in a million years admit that to him.

Yeah, I'd keep that thought to myself.

Despite all his attempted good, he'd still trapped

me in a demon deal without telling me what it was. For that, I would never forgive him.

"Today has been a long-ass day." I sighed as I trailed through the darkened penthouse. This was the first time we'd been truly alone since I'd discovered Az was a Prince of Hell—and some kind of vigilante demon revolting against Lucifer himself. Logically, I should be pretty freaked out about the whole thing. Instead, my bones wanted to crawl into bed and sleep.

"Yes, and we need to have a serious talk." He slid a key into his room's lock and twisted it to the side. Before he whispered inside, he cast me a quick glance. "Did you bring a swimsuit?"

I blinked at him. "Excuse me?"

"A swimsuit. I need to wind down after what happened tonight." A darkness churned in his eyes. "We lost someone, and the killer is still out there. I'm going to take a dip in the hot tub, and I need you to join me so we can discuss a few things. Did you bring a swimsuit?"

"The hot tu—" I flushed. "No. I didn't pack a swimsuit for my stay in a million-dollar penthouse as a demon's fake girlfriend."

He didn't even quirk a lip at that. Tonight really had gotten to him.

"Fine. Give me ten minutes. You can perch on the edge in your clothes if you want, but you're welcome to join me. A bra and panties is close enough to a swimsuit anyway." He vanished into his room and shut the door.

I swallowed hard as I stared after him. "No, it's not."

I mean, it really wasn't. There was something so much more…intimate about underwear. Still, a soak in a hot tub sounded like a hell of a good idea. Soothing, warm, relaxing. My pent-up nerves were about to pop right out of my skin, and if I went to bed now, I'd just stare wide-eyed out the window until the sun came up.

Before I could talk myself out of it, I slipped into my room, yanked my dress over my head, and pulled a fluffy white robe over my body. One Az kept in the closet for guests. I wondered if any other girls had worn this thing.

"What a stupid thought," I muttered to myself.

Suddenly, my phone rang. I pulled it out of my purse and checked the number. Serena. My heart squeezed. She was probably worried sick about me.

"Hey, Serena," I said as soon as the phone hit my ear. "Sorry I didn't call. I'm okay."

"Thank heavens," she whispered back. "I've been worried sick. I can't explain to Noah what's going on, and he thinks I've lost my damn mind. Where are you?"

My stomach twisted. She didn't know I'd faced the killer in the alley. And I couldn't bear to tell her. "Az's apartment."

"I can't believe I'm saying this, but good. Stay with him, okay? Just until the killer is caught."

"I will, Serena. You don't need to worry about me."

"Not happening. I'm going to worry about you

until this whole thing is over." She sighed. "I've got to get some sleep. I have work in the morning. Text me tomorrow?"

I squeezed the phone tight. "Always. Love you."

I found Az out on his balcony in the hot tub. Steaming water bubbled around him and droplets clung to his stubbled chin. He'd beaten me to it, which meant I wouldn't have a chance to see if he had a tail. On the other hand, I could *definitely* see his bare, sculpted chest. The guy looked as if he could bench press an entire car.

Maybe he could. How strong, exactly, were demons?

He arched a brow as I hovered nervously beside the hot tub. "You coming in?"

"Yeah, I just…" A flush crept up my cheeks. "Wow, it sure is hot."

"That's kind of the point."

"Yeah, I know, it's just, well, you know." Ugh. What was wrong with me? With an inward growl at myself, I turned my back to him, pulled off the robe, and quickly dipped into the tub before Az could get an eyeful. As the hot water engulfed me, I met his gaze. The intensity in his eyes shook me to my core.

"Lace," he said, arching a brow toward my bra. "Interesting choice."

"I didn't have many options," I replied with a roll of my eyes. "I rushed over here with my single suitcase, and I haven't done laundry yet."

"Is that one suitcase all you brought with you when you moved to the city?" he asked lightly, leaning back against the edge of the hot tub.

Instantly, I tensed. "Yes."

"I meant what I said." He closed his eyes and relaxed into the tub, the water glistening on his tanned skin. "You've been brought into the circle. Trust and loyalty are essential for this to work. They are the most important things to me."

Suddenly the hot tub seemed like a terrible idea. Here I was, in a small, enclosed space, with a total asshole. Forget all the good stuff he did. None of that erased the bad. "Says the guy who didn't tell me what would happen when I signed that contract."

His eyes flipped open. "I was never going to take your soul."

"Then why make a contract at all?" I fisted my hands, and the water slipped through my fingers.

"Lucifer is alerted every time one of us signs a contract. He doesn't know the details of the deal, but he receives a rolling tally. If we go too long without a deal, he grows suspicious. We have a quota we have to hit."

Narrowing my eyes, I folded my arms, hiding my lacy bra from view. "And so that's all I am? A quota."

"It was never supposed to mean anything more than that," he said quietly. "But you are impossibly complicated, Mia. And you've made things far more difficult than they needed to be."

"Gee, thanks," I replied dryly. "I guess you thought I'd be a good little pet human and fall in line just like everyone else."

"If it weren't for Serena, you never would have known. You would have walked away from this happy and content. Soul intact."

I fell silent at that. Obviously, he was wrong. The angels would have still approached me, telling me everything. But if I hadn't known Serena all my life, I probably would have run. I couldn't imagine how it would feel to be totally unaware of supernaturals, and then find out you'd signed a deal with a demon.

Az was right. Most humans would scream and run in the opposite direction.

"There is one thing I like about you," he finally said as he plucked a gin and tonic from the table beside the hot tub. He took a long, slow sip, meeting my eyes. Thankfully, the steaming water blanketed the flush in my cheeks.

"Oh, just the one thing?" I asked sarcastically.

He ignored me. "You don't try to obscure your emotions. You wear guilt, but it isn't a heavy anchor dragging you into the ground. Whatever you feel guilty about, it's a small thing. It's not for something as terrible as manslaughter."

I stiffened and slammed against the back of the hot tub. Water sloshed around me as my heart hammered my ribs. "What are you talking about?"

"Mia," he said as his piercing eyes latched onto mine. "You will never move forward as long as you pretend your past doesn't exist."

Blood rushed through my head, and my throat closed tight. "You looked me up."

I should have known it would happen eventually. His ignorance of my trial and the charges against me would only last so long. He might be a demon in a million-dollar penthouse, but he still lived in this world. The one with Google, social media, and clickbait headlines. The only thing I was surprised about was that it had taken so long.

And I bet he still wanted to use me as bait. Why not, right? I was just a trash human who had caused a poor girl's death. Hell, if I died, it would be no big loss in his eyes.

"I looked you up the night we met," he said as he took another sip of his drink. He set it back onto the table, edged forward, and took my shaking hand in his. "Mia, calm down. I don't think you did it."

"Wait?" I breathed, and instantly, my hand stilled. "What?"

He put his other hand on my shoulder. Tremors tiptoed down my spine. "I wouldn't have asked you to work for me if I thought you were capable of accidentally killing a girl and fleeing from the scene instead of calling for help. I can see it in you. You're not guilty of that."

All my breath whooshed out of me, leaving me lightheaded. And frankly, feeling a little weird. I must have been dreaming. No one had ever said that to me before. No one except for Serena.

"How could you possibly know that?" I asked in a whisper. I didn't think I trusted myself to speak any louder than that. Basically, I was a glass case of emotion on the verge of shattering into the steaming water. These were words I'd always longed to hear, just…maybe not coming from a Prince of Hell who had lied to me about a demon contract.

He leaned in close, and the hand on my shoulder drifted up to my cheek. I shuddered against his touch, my breath stilling in my throat. His gaze swept across me, piercing and dark and full of a strange intoxicating intensity. My eyes dropped to his lips just as his tongue swept across the bottom one. Shivers raced down my spine.

Suddenly I remembered exactly where I was, what I was doing, and who I was with. A demon, in a hot tub, on a balcony overlooking the sparkling city lights. His wet chest glistened, and my soaked lace clung to the curves of my breasts. Heat flickered between my thighs.

Oh shit.

Oh shit, oh shit, oh shit.

Was he going to kiss me? And was I going to let him? No, surely not. Nothing about this was real. We were in a fake relationship so we could stop a murderous group of supernaturals who wanted to sacrifice humans to Lucifer.

Wow, that sounded totally insane.

Still, I didn't budge an inch.

Slowly, his hand dropped away. "I'm a demon. I can read guilt. You have some, but it isn't for that. If I were to guess, it's because you're protecting someone else. The person responsible for Audrey's death never got caught because you wouldn't speak their name aloud. You wouldn't tell anyone who really did it. Loyalty, it is an admirable trait, even if the family deserves to know the truth."

I sucked in a breath and stood. Water streamed down my exposed stomach and thighs, but I forgot all my worries about letting him see my skin. "You don't know what you're talking about."

He gave me a sad smile. "You let the world attack

you because you were covering for someone else. And I have a good guess who it was."

Unshed tears burned my eyes, as hot as lava. "No, you're wrong. I don't know who did it. No one does. And if you think I want to talk to you about this, you're an even bigger asshole than I thought."

But I was lying. And he knew it. It really wasn't that hard to guess. That night, my little sister had visited me at college. We'd gone to a party and gotten into an argument, she'd gotten drunk, and then she'd raced off in my car. She'd hit Audrey, killing her instantly. And then she'd fled. I never told a single soul. Not even Serena. She'd done something so, so terrible, but it had been my fault. I shouldn't have yelled at her that night.

Disappointment flickered in Az's eyes. "Maybe I was wrong about you."

I climbed out of the hot tub, anger burning away whatever soothing warmth I thought I'd felt before. "Yeah. Maybe you were."

Gritting my teeth, I stalked back into the apartment and left a trail of dripping water in my wake. Normally, I would feel bad about messing up his pristine floor, but it served him right. He'd snooped into my past. Far more than a cursory search if he'd gleamed the truth. Asmodeus knew what had really happened.

Fuck.

What would he do with that information? Would he tell someone? Did he want to punish my sister for her terrible mistake? I pinched the bridge of my nose and tried to calm my racing heart. This couldn't be happening. I'd ripped up my entire life just to protect her. It couldn't all fall apart now. Because of a *demon*.

I stepped into my bedroom and immediately screamed. A note had been taped to the outside of the window, facing in. The words were written in red ink…that I had to admit had the dark, sickly color of dried blood.

My hand flew to my mouth.

You didn't escape me. You're next.

Az charged into the room, his eyes wild. He threw his body in front of mine and faced the window. Several unwelcome thoughts flashed through my mind all at once.

First, and most importantly, there was absolutely *zero* sign of a tail. He wore a skintight pair of black boxer briefs that would have made it very apparent if he had one. Instead, they hugged a round, perfectly buff ass that would put Henry Cavill's to shame.

Second, it became very clear that Asmodeus had the most magnificent body I had ever seen in my life. This fact was made even more apparent by the way rivulets of water trailed down his skin. It was difficult not to stare.

And finally, it was impossible not to notice the way he'd rushed in to save me within seconds of my scream. A growl shook through his body, and his fisted hands made him look like he was ready to rip apart the entire world.

"The bastard," he breathed as he stalked toward the window.

Oh right. The note. The serial killer who wanted me dead. I'd almost forgotten. My mouth went dry.

"Um, so," I said, clearing my throat nervously. He was practically naked in my bedroom, brimming with pure, unbridled demon energy. And it was trying to suck me in. "How easy would it be for him to get inside this apartment? Should I be worried about him, I don't know, teleporting in here while I'm asleep?"

He turned and regarded me for a moment. "Normally I would say no. These walls are warded against most magical attacks. But we've never understood this killer's powers. It might be best if you stay in my room tonight."

I swallowed and took a step back. "I'm sorry. Did you say…did you say *your* room?"

The room he'd locked me out of? The room where Az himself slept? Um…

"You're not staying in here." Az grabbed my suitcase and motioned for me to follow. "He knows where you are. If he wants to get to you, he'll have to go through me."

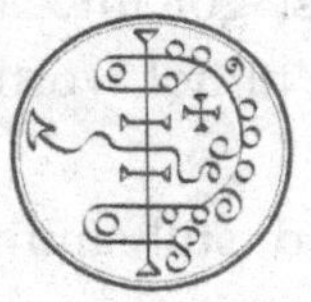

17

I stood just beyond the open door, shifting on my bare feet. On the way, I'd grabbed the fluffy robe, but other than that, I wore nothing but my soaked bra and panties. And now I was supposed to climb into bed with Az.

He'd carried my duffel bag inside and was tossing clothes into a hamper beside the open closet door. Inside, there were rows of dark, pristine suits, along with a dozen t-shirts in various shades of grey. The curtains were closed, just like the last time I'd seen them, blocking out the city.

Other than that, the room looked…normal. I couldn't help but wonder why he'd been trying to keep me out of it.

He slammed the lid on his hamper and turned to me. "What are you waiting for?"

"I mean…do you really think this is a good idea?"

Frowning, he grabbed a pillow from the floor and tossed it onto the bed. "Why wouldn't it be?"

I flushed. "You and me. Sharing a bed…"

A slight smile tipped up the corners of his lips, dimpling his cheeks. "You think you can't keep your hands to yourself?"

"I…" My flush deepened. "Don't flatter yourself. But we don't exactly get along, do we? Unless I'm hallucinating, we just got into a fight. Another one. What if you decide I'm not worth the trouble and eat my soul in my sleep?"

He shook his head, still smiling. "Just get into the bed, Mia. But do me a favor and change into some dry clothes first. The en suite is through there."

I followed the line of his finger to see an open door leading into a messy bathroom. "An en suite. Should have guessed."

After grabbing some sweats and a t-shirt, I quickly changed in his bathroom, resisting my itchy fingers' urge to poke around. When he wasn't here, it was one thing, but he was only one closed door away. And I was pretty sure he had enhanced hearing. He would for sure know if I started opening and closing his cabinets.

I made a mental note to search it when he wasn't here. If he ever let me out of his sight again.

When I pushed back into the bedroom, Az had already changed and climbed into bed. He wore a loose-fitting black shirt and his silken sheets were pillowed around his head. Even in the dark, his eyes pierced into me. Swallowing hard, I climbed into bed beside him.

Tension rattled my body.

I could smell him. The sheets were covered in the

aroma of bonfire and musk. Shadows curled across my skin, as timid as a light caress. I twisted my head to the side to catch him staring at me in the dark. Heat pulsed between my thighs.

"I'm never going to sleep if you keep staring at me."

His lips quirked. "And why is that?"

"Because it's creepy, that's why," I lied.

"Guilt is not the only emotion I can read, Mia."

Alarm throttled my heart. Oh god, please let him be lying. If he could read my emotions, he'd known every single time I'd felt even a hint of *anything*. I'd admired his body more than once. Not that it meant I wanted him. I just...noticed...that was all. And he knew it.

Oh my god, this was mortifying.

"If you can read my emotions, then you'll know I'm in no mood for games, and I just want to go to sleep," I snapped.

He chuckled.

I growled out my irritation and flopped sideways so that my back faced him. There. Now he couldn't lie there staring at my face all night, and maybe I could get some needed sleep. It was probably after five in the morning by this point. It had been a very long night.

Just thinking about what happened brought on an overwhelming wave of exhaustion. I was trying to think up another retort so I could snap back at Az some more, but sleep tugged me under as my thoughts grew heavy. Darkness curled around my mind, soothing my frayed nerves.

I awoke to a warm arm around my body. My heart jolted in my chest as my eyes flipped open. The room was still dark, even though it must have been hours into the day. And I was still in Az's bed with his arm around me.

Swallowing hard, I tried not to panic. It felt kind of nice, in an abstract kind of way. If he wasn't Az, the demon who had basically enslaved my soul. If I thought of him as just a guy trying to protect me from a serial killer, I didn't feel the sudden urge to leap out of bed and throw his arm off me.

"Good morning," he murmured into the back of my head. His breath whispered across my neck. I gritted my teeth at the sparks that lit up across my skin. Go away, sparks.

"I thought you were still asleep."

"I've been awake for a little while."

"Oh." Heat crept into my cheeks. "And so you just decided you wanted a cuddle?"

"You were shivering in your sleep. Your teeth were chattering."

"Right." I closed my eyes again and sighed. "That happens sometimes. Serena thinks it means I'm having a nightmare, but I never remember what they're about. It's all just hazy when I try."

"It's your past," he said quietly. "It haunts you."

I sucked in a sharp breath and slowly eased out from under his arm. "I don't want to talk about my past."

Something told me he wasn't going to let it rest.

Asmodeus did not seem like the kind of guy to let things go easily. I normally admired determination but not when it came to this. He needed to stay out of my life. In a month, we would no longer know each other. I wasn't going to let a stranger in on my darkest thoughts.

I pulled open the door and strode into the kitchen, leaving him in bed alone. The clock on the wall said it was well past two in the afternoon. We really had slept all day. For me, it had been sorely needed. Hendrix sat on top of the dining table, his head cocked expectantly. A smile crept across my face.

"Morning, Hendrix. If you go get Az out of bed, he might make you some pancakes."

He let out a little chirp and flew through the apartment, a tornado of feathers. *Huh*, I thought as I watched him vanish into the bedroom. It was almost as though he'd understood me.

❦

*B*ackstage was a whirlwind of activity. It was only my second shift at the club, which was crazy. With everything that had happened, it felt like I'd been there for weeks. Priyanka dropped down beside me as I painted on some eyeliner. There was a haunted look in her brown eyes.

"Are you okay?" she asked gently.

I glanced up from the mirror. "Yeah, I'm fine. More importantly, are you?"

She'd known Willow a little longer than I had. A sense of melancholy had settled over the dancers, but

Az had decided not to shut the place down for the night. He hoped the killer might be tempted to corner me here. And now that he'd met him face-to-face, albeit masked, Az was certain he would spot him in an instant.

Tears filled Priyanka's eyes, but she quickly blinked them away. "No, it's horrible. I didn't know Willow well, but she was a nice girl. Always said hello with a smile. Never complained. Even if she was the only werewolf here. The rest of us are fae."

I stiffened and lifted my brows.

"Az told me you know everything," she admitted. "To be honest, I'm glad. I hate secrets. I think it's about time humanity knows we exist. Here, let me help you with that."

She took the eyeliner from me and motioned for me to turn her way. I did as she asked and sat still while she flicked the edges of my lids.

"To be honest, I don't think a lot of humans would react the way I have. A lot would freak out," I said.

"You're probably right," she said, sticking her tongue out between her teeth as she did my makeup. "But that's not why we keep it secret."

I frowned. "Then why?"

"Ancient laws. Set forth by the Creator and Lucifer. We're supposed to control humans for whichever side we're on. If you know about us, it's harder for us to do that."

My stomach flipped. "Um, wait a minute. Control us?"

"Yep." She dabbed on the last flick. "We're

competing for souls. It's a game that's been going on for centuries."

Horror flooded through me. "You mean to tell me all of this is about a *game*?"

Priyanka leaned back and sighed, dropping the eyeliner onto the table. "I'm sorry. This is probably too much to unload on you."

"No." I shook my head. "I want to understand. Tell me about this game."

"It was a bargain struck between the Creator and Lucifer, centuries and centuries ago. Who could win fifty billion souls the fastest?"

"And what happens when one of them wins?" I whispered.

She pressed her lips together. "This world ends, and everyone goes to the winner's afterlife."

My hands fisted as I shakily pushed up from the chair. "So you're telling me everyone will go to Hell if Lucifer wins?"

"That's right."

"And you're okay with this?"

"Absolutely not." She patted my shoulder. "That's why I work for Az. The Legion does most of the dirty work, but I help out when I can. Fae can do things demons can't."

Priyanka's words stayed with me as I finished getting ready for my shift. Even though I'd discovered supernaturals as a child, I realized now I hadn't known the half of it. There was so much more to this, and likely loads more that I didn't yet know. This, the supernatural serial killer, and the sacrificial cult...I really, really needed a vacation. Preferably to a sunny beach where a hot guy would deliver me mimosas at regular intervals.

Unfortunately, I had to go dance in front of a bunch of supernaturals for the next four hours and hope a serial killer didn't teleport into my oversized birdcage.

"Mia." Az found me in the hallway just moments before I was due to step onto the club floor. He pulled me away from the other dancers and dropped his lips to my ear. "The vampire in charge of the invitations to the ball has come tonight."

I stared into his ice-flecked eyes, questions rolling through my head. There was so much I wanted to ask him. The game, the souls, the afterlife. More specifically, just how far along were the Creator and Lucifer on collecting their souls? How soon would the world end? It couldn't be far off.

Instead, I tried to focus on his words. "Is that a good thing or a bad thing?"

"Good," he said with a nod. "It means I've caught their attention. Now we just need to demonstrate our bond. I want you to step out onto the floor with me and pretend like you adore me."

"Right. That makes sense." I cleared my throat and ignored the heat tripping through my veins. This was exactly what we needed. A chance to pretend we had a thing in front of the very person who needed to believe it. Az needed that invite. If he got it, he had a chance at stopping the sacrifices.

"I have a question," I asked him as he pulled my hand into the crook of his elbow.

"What is it? We need to hurry before he leaves."

"The humans who get sacrificed at this ball... where do their souls go?"

"To Lucifer." He frowned. "They always go to Lucifer. Why?"

Of course they did. It was all starting to make more sense. Lucifer needed souls to win his game, and he would stop at nothing to get them. That meant he was ahead. If he won, the entire world would go to Hell.

"That's all I needed to know," I said with a nod. "Let's go convince a vampire we're in love."

18

It was only eleven, but the club was already thumping. The other dancers were up in their cages, swaying along to the hectic beat blaring from hidden speakers. Girls and guys spun around the floor. Groups clustered in the booths, the sparkling chandeliers casting eerie glows on their faces.

Every single person here was a supernatural, including the short, squat man lurking in the back booth with a gang of solemn-faced groupies. His flat nose reminded me of a spade, and half a dozen piercings dotted his ears. An elaborate tattoo swirled across his neck, at odds with his pristine suit and close-cropped hair. Frankly, he looked like a mobster.

"*That's* the guy?" I murmured to Az as he shifted me sideways so that our profiles were visible to the vampire and his gang.

Az leaned down and wound his arms around my waist. An electric *zing* went through me from his touch, bringing with it a strange sense of familiarity. "Yep. His name is Tony Soprano." When my eyebrows shot up to the top of my forehead, Az laughed. "I'm joking. His name is Lars. No last name. He likes his blood fresh."

A shiver went down my spine. Despite it, I pushed up onto my toes and laced my fingers around the back of his neck. "So he's a vampire who kills."

"That's the rumor. Of course, no one has ever been able to prove it."

"And so we're dangling me in front of him. Who's to say he won't try to drink my blood?"

"Because *I* have claimed you. And now it's time to make it look real."

Az dropped his forehead to mine. My whole body stiffened as he searched my eyes, almost as if he was waiting for my consent. I wet my lips and nodded, my heart raging like a bonfire. What the hell was I doing? Why didn't I stop this? This was crazy. A terrible, horrible mistake.

His lips brushed mine. Those pesky sparks stormed across my skin, burning away my intrusive thoughts. My hands tightened around his neck as the kiss slowly deepened. He groaned against my mouth and pulled me closer.

All logical thought fled from my mind as the hard planes of his perfect chest shifted against me.

I pressed up onto my toes, crashing against him. A shudder swept through me as his tongue speared my lips. Clinging on as tight as I could, my tongue melted against his, our mouths in sync and our bodies locked tight. Everything within me yearned for more of him. Heat coiled within me, clenching my core.

Slowly, Az pulled away. Darkness flickered in the depths of his ice blue eyes, and my chest thumped with the rhythm of my frantic heartbeat. I didn't know what the hell had just happened, but I knew I hadn't hated it. Had he felt that same spark? We weren't still pretending, right? Or had all that just been for show?

Even with the flicker in his eyes, I couldn't read his mind.

"Well," he said with a delicious smile that made my toes curl. "That will certainly do the trick."

"I mean, I would be convinced if I were him."

His eyes flashed as he spun me around and gave me a spank on the ass. I let out a little chirp of surprise. "I seem to have made you late to your shift. Better get to dancing, Mia. I'll see you after."

As he strode away, I reached my hands up to my cheeks. They were boiling hot. I took a deep breath and rolled my shoulders, trying to shake off what had just happened. I needed to get a grip. At the start of all this, he'd warned me that we might have to share a few fake kisses in front of people. That was all that was.

He was just a really, really good fake kisser. And I couldn't let myself think it was anything more than that.

❀

*A*fter my shift, Valac, Caim, Phenex, and Stolas were waiting for me in the hallway. There was a fifth demon among them, one I hadn't met yet, but whose name I'd learned was Bael. With dusty blonde hair and a winning smile, he looked like he'd strolled right out of a college football team. One of those wholesome, boy-next-door types. But luckily, I knew it was nothing more than a mask.

"I need a minute." I held up my hands when they tried to usher me into their little crime-solving dungeon. "It's hot as hell in there, and I need some fresh air."

Truth be told, I was still reeling from the kiss. But also, I'd spent four hours dancing. I needed to pee.

"All right, but we're coming with you," Phenex said with a nod. "We're not letting you out of our sight when there's someone out there intent on killing you."

I sighed and closed my eyes. I should have known I wouldn't get some privacy as easily as that. "I'm going into the ladies' room. You can't come in there with me."

Stolas frowned. "What if he climbs through the window and steals you that way?"

"Or does the whole teleporting thing," Caim added.

"Look, you guys. I appreciate your concern, but you can't go into the bathroom with me. If there's a problem, I'll just bang on the door. All right?"

They cast each other uneasy glances until Stolas

finally nodded. "All right, but only if you keep the door unlocked."

"Sure." With a shake of my head, I led the charge down the hallway, flanked by five massive demon guards. I would have laughed about the whole thing if my nerves weren't frayed down to their nubbins. The kiss had unmoored me, as much as I hated to admit it.

And I needed more than a breath of fresh air and a bathroom break.

The card from the angels still burned a hole in my pocket. The last thing I wanted was for Az to find it, and I needed to get these angels off his back. He and his Legion were trying to do a good thing here, but the angels could never know the full truth of it. If they didn't stop looking into things, they'd find out. And the news would reach Lucifer. The Legion would be forced back into Hell.

I couldn't let that happen to them.

After I ducked into the bathroom, I leaned against the wall and loosed a long, laborous breath that shook my whole body. The stench of the city streets wafted in through the cracked window, but with it came a soothing, cooling breeze. I really needed to get a grip. So what if the most gorgeous asshole demon I'd ever seen had kissed me tonight? It hadn't meant anything. We'd both only been pretending.

There was zero reason for me to feel so worked up by it all.

Shaking my head at myself, I pulled my cell from my purse and punched in a text to the angels.

This is Mia. I've done what you asked, and you're

wrong about them. You can stop looking into Infernal now. There's nothing to find. The Legion isn't up to anything bad at all.

There. I nodded to myself and headed into the bathroom stall. When I was done, I had a text message waiting for me.

That's impossible. You must not have looked hard enough. We need you to keep spying.

I rolled my eyes.

Absolutely not. And I don't want you to text me anymore. This whole thing is creepy. Please. Delete my number and never contact me again.

With that, I deleted the entire conversation, erased their number from my phone, and threw the business card into the trash. My heart hammered hard as I stared into the mirror. Had I just made a terrible mistake? Probably not. Az was definitely hiding something from me, but it wasn't dead bodies. I was in way over my head with this entire thing, and I didn't want a couple of pesky angels to complicate my life any more. Besides, I was now bait. I didn't want to be a spy on top of that.

A heavy fist banged against the door. "You all right in there, Mia?"

Shaking my head, I yanked open the door. Caim and Stolas both stumbled inside the bathroom, tripping over their feet. I grinned.

"Serves you right," I said. "For not giving me a little privacy."

"You were taking forever," Caim said, trailing after me as I left the bathroom. "What the hell do you girls do in there anyway?"

I shot him a conspiratorial smile. "You'll never know."

"Stop flirting," Az growled as he stepped up behind his Legion. He gave Caim a warning glare before whirling on his feet and striding down the hallway toward their meeting office or whatever it was.

We followed. Caim fell into step beside me and dropped his voice low enough that none of the other demons could hear. At least, I hoped they couldn't. "He gets very jealous when you talk to me."

"I'm pretty sure it's not jealousy," I muttered back.

Caim's brow winged upward. "What else would it be?"

I pressed my lips together. "I don't know, but it's definitely not that. He doesn't like me very much. Living under the same roof is getting a little dicey."

I didn't mention the fact we'd shared a bed last night. There was no telling what Caim would think.

"If he didn't like you very much, you wouldn't be here," Caim said with a brilliant smile. "Trust me, when Az doesn't like you, you *know*. He makes it clear."

I nodded. "Yeah, and he's made it more than clear."

"No, darling." He stopped and gave my shoulder a solid pat. "You're one of us now. He's brought you into the circle. If he didn't like you, you'd be out, and you would never, ever see us again."

My heart thumped. Surely Caim wasn't right. Az acted as though he could barely tolerate me most of the time. And *I* could barely tolerate *him*. I didn't want him to like me. It made things a hell of a lot harder. Could we...actually be friends?

No. Absolutely not. There was that whole demon contract thing! He'd hidden the truth from me when I'd signed it. Ugh.

We all gathered in the meeting room. As soon as the door shut, the place transformed into a supernatural detective agency. The curtain came off the wall. The map and its hundred little pins stared at us, reminding us exactly what was at stake.

"All the recent murders happened here." Phenex stabbed his finger at the corner of the city labeled Hell's Kitchen. "He knows Mia works and lives here now, too. I doubt he'll stray far."

"It's likely he's watching and waiting," Caim piped in as he strode from one end of the room to the other, his beefy arms folded over his chest. "I bet he's hiding in the shadows, making note of your routine and schedule, and planning for a time when he knows you'll be alone."

My mouth went dry. "Yeah, that's not at all terrifying."

Caim's lips quirked in the corners. Az narrowed his eyes and stepped in front of him, almost like he was blocking Caim from view. I rolled my eyes and leaned back into my chair. Okay, this was officially getting ridiculous. Caim was part of his Legion. He trusted him with his secrets and his life. So what the hell was his problem?

"We want you to walk home alone tonight," Valac said in an eerie voice, continuing as if nothing odd had happened. "You did it once before. So he might not find it strange."

"Wait." I leaned forward and palmed the table. "You want to do this whole bait thing tonight? As in…*now*?"

Stolas gave me a solemn nod. "The sooner we take care of this asshole, the better."

"Well, shit." I blew out a hot breath, my mind reeling. When I'd agreed to this crazy plan, I'd imagined some distant, faraway scenario that I didn't have to face for a while. Maybe in a few weeks. After I'd had time to get used to the idea. I'd never thought it would happen so soon.

"And we don't want him to get bored and target someone else," Phenex added. "Right now, he's focused on you. That's a good thing."

Yeah, sure. If you weren't me.

Az stepped in close. I swallowed hard and desperately tried not to stare at his lips. The lips that had been kissing me. Also, there had been tongue. "You'll be safe, Mia. I swear I would never let anything happen to you, not while you're under my protection. We'll be up on the rooftops the entire time. The second the killer appears, we'll be right by your side."

"Wait." My heart stopped. "You'll be on the rooftops? But it will take you ages to…oh." It was a demon thing. "Don't tell me you have wings."

A slow wicked smile crept across his lips. "Maybe one day I'll show you."

19

The Hell's Kitchen streets were full of shadows. Every thud of my boots brought on a fresh wave of unease. Frankly, it was stupid. The fear, not the trap. I had a Legion of demons watching my back. There was no reason to panic.

My breath shook in my lungs as I rounded the corner. Az's building sparkled one block down, a beacon in the dead of the New York night. Only a few more minutes, and I'd waltzed through that revolving door safe and sound. No one had jumped out of an alley to attack me.

Strange, really. Why hadn't the killer taken the bait?

Just as I started to relax, two massive forms stepped out of a doorframe and blocked my path. It was the beefy angels. Gabriel and Suriel. And they didn't look very pleased to see me.

Also, um, fuck? The demons were watching me from above. They wouldn't miss me chatting with two angels.

I took a step back and dropped my voice to a whisper. "I told you not to contact me anymore."

A deep frown pulled down Suriel's lips. "Your texts concerned us. How could we be sure they were coming from you? Maybe someone, like Asmodeus, stole your phone. We needed to see you were safe with our own eyes."

"Well, now you've seen me," I hissed back. "Go away."

Gabriel stiffened and glanced up. "They're watching us right now. Aren't they?"

"They are, and they're going to think it's pretty weird that I'm talking to you."

"So the texts *were* fake." Suriel nodded, his golden hair gleaming beneath the moonlight.

"No," I said through gritted teeth. "I meant every word. But I also don't want to get fired. And I will if they think I'm spying on them for some angels."

Suriel sighed and exchanged a glance with Gabe. "Mia, what you don't understand is that there's far more at stake than just—"

Caim dropped down onto the sidewalk, landing in a crouch between me and the angels. Massive wings stretched out behind him, the deep black feathers rippling in the breeze. They were like five times the size of his body. My mouth dropped open, and I stumbled back.

"Gabriel. Suriel," Caim growled out as a warning. "What the hell are you doing here?"

Suriel gave him a winning smile. "We were just introducing ourselves to your newest employee. Strange, isn't it? A human working at a supernatural club? One who knows everything about vampires, demons, and wolves?"

"Stay away from Mia," Caim said, his body trembling with anger. Slowly, he stood, and his wings flared wide. "You're not welcome at *Infernal*, and you're not welcome near any of us."

Gabriel arched a brow. "Us? Are you saying this little human is actually one of you?"

"Gabe." Az dropped down on my left side. I whipped my head toward him, swallowing hard at his wings. They were corded in pure muscle, clearly apparent even beneath all those feathers. Slick and black, pulsing with pure power. As much as I hate to admit it, I gaped.

"Hello, Asmodeus," Gabriel said, his voice going hard. "Seems you and your Legion have trapped yourselves another human soul."

"He hasn't trapped me," I shot back, but everyone ignored me as the rest of the demons landed on the streets. Their black wings beat behind them, shooting hot air across my face. And then the wings were gone, melting into nothing more than shadows.

I blinked as my mind tried to make sense of it.

"Well, this is bloody unexpected," Suriel said as he took in the six angry demons. "You're all here? Why?"

"None of your business," Az said, taking a step toward the angels. "Leave now, Gabe. These streets are mine. I don't want to fight you, but I will if I must."

Gabe rolled his eyes and let out a sigh. "Fine. But we'll be keeping an eye on things."

With that, the two angels pushed up from the ground, spread brilliant silver wings, and vanished into the cloud-filled sky. My heart thumped as I tipped my head back to gaze up at the dark.

"Mia," Az barked as he began to storm down the block toward his building. "Let's go. We need to get you home."

I pressed my lips together as I dragged my gaze away from the sky. He was already halfway down the block. The others followed behind him, bodies tense, gazes locked on the shadows they passed. Only Caim remained by my side, his hands slung into his jean pockets.

"Well, that was odd," he said, motioning me forward.

I fell into step beside him. "Tell me about it."

"I heard what they said," he murmured as the humid breeze brushed the inky hair away from his face.

My head jerked toward him as a snake squeezed my heart. "Caim."

"Don't." He held up a hand. "Like I said, I heard what they said. And I can put the pieces together to understand what happened. I don't need an explanation from you, but *he* does." He inclined his head toward Az who stormed ahead at the front of the Legion. "Loyalty. It is a very big deal to Az. I won't explain why. That's his story to tell. All you need to know is that he will never forgive you if you don't come clean to him."

I winced and glanced away. "You make it sound like I betrayed his trust or something."

"Didn't you?"

"No," I said, fisting my hands. "The angels approached me after my first night at the club. Things were different then. I didn't even know him."

"And you think you know him now?"

I flushed, my gaze locking on my scuffed leather boots. "As crazy as it sounds, yes. I mean, I've joined this dangerous mission, haven't I?"

He patted my shoulder and gave me a smile. "Then you know how important trust is to him. You need to tell him everything."

"Yeah, but..." My gut flipped over. More than once. It felt like it was doing somersaults. "Won't it make him angry?"

"Probably."

Sighing, I let out a frustrated growl. "This is so annoying. I didn't ask those angels to corner me in the street. They're really fucking creepy."

"Yes." He stopped suddenly, frowning. "They are."

He whistled and called the Legion back to his side. The others slowly fell into place, even Az, as unhappy as he looked about it. Caim clapped his hands and gave them a quick rundown of his newest idea, one I probably would have thought of myself if I hadn't been so distracted by Az's stupid lips and stupid scowl.

"The angels could be behind this," Caim said, glancing at each of the demons in turn. "Someone is killing supernaturals and targeting several people who were close to us. We've been thinking it's some psychotic supe who's lost control. But what if that's not it at all? What if *they're* killing anyone playing on Lucifer's side? They don't know what we're doing here. They think we're loyal to Lucifer. And so Gabe and Suriel show up and try to get Mia over to their side. She's human. They want her soul."

"Hmm." Az rubbed a hand against his stubbled jaw. "That doesn't explain why the killer cornered Mia in the alley the other night."

Stolas frowned. "Mia, did the killer try to talk to you at all? Convince you to leave *Infernal*?"

"Not really," I said. "He was pretty intent on the stabby thing."

"I saw the killer, too," Az said. "He was masked, but I saw enough to know he wasn't Gabe or Suriel. Might have been one of the others though. Raphael or Michael. They both like to keep to themselves. I might not have recognized either of them with that mask."

Phenex clapped his hands. "Oh, I hope it's the angels. That means we can have a little fun."

I gave Phenex a blank stare. "You do know this is my life we're talking about, right?"

But also, why would they have asked me to spy on the demons if they were behind the killings? They'd told me *Infernal* was a cover for something else, and they'd wanted me to find out what. A sudden dose of realization flooded my veins. Did they think the club was a venue for soul sacrificing? And they wanted me to find out if it was. So they could find a way to stop Az and get ahead in their little soul game.

Caim met my eyes. He clearly thought the same thing I did. But he wouldn't voice it aloud. He was leaving that up to me.

Meanwhile, Phenex had started laughing. "These guys have been fucking around with us for too long. You'd think they would have learned their lesson by now. Last month, they tried to send a spy into *Infernal*. Want to know where that asshole vamp ended up?" His voice morphed into a mobster's thick accent. "He swims with the fishes."

Chills swept through my body. I sucked in a sharp breath and stepped back. My eyes widened in horror as I stared at Phenex's cackling smile, turned to Caim's wince, and then finally landed on Az's ice-flecked eyes churning with unadulterated anger. Suddenly, I remembered exactly who these guys were. I'd started to think of them as harmless over-sized teddy bears, and I'd forgotten a very important fact. They were literal demons. From Hell. They might be trying to save souls, but that didn't mean they were fluffy bunnies.

They were nice to me now. What happened when they found out I'd been a spy, too? Caim gave me a grim smile. He hadn't said a word, but I had a feeling he hadn't been the one to throw the other spy into the Hudson River. It would have been Az.

"I'm really tired," I said in a small voice. "It's been a long night. Can we go now?"

Az nodded and motioned for the others to gather in close. They murmured a few words amongst themselves. I didn't even try to listen. It was too much. I just kept picturing a dead man's body floating in the Hudson River with fish nibbling his rotting toes.

After we said goodbye to the Legion, Az and I returned to his apartment. I couldn't stop the quick glances his way. Had he killed the spy? Would he do the same to me? I wanted to believe he'd never do anything to harm me. He'd said as much. But did it extend to this? If he believed I'd betrayed him, what then?

He frowned as he caught my one hundredth glance, just as he trailed over to his bar to pour a drink. "You seem on edge."

"Gee, I wonder why."

"Not because of that." Glasses clinked as he tipped the gin toward the crystal goblet. "You keep looking at me."

I nibbled on my bottom lip, tempted to tiptoe into my bedroom and lock the door behind me. But I took the offered gin and tonic instead. I doubted he'd let me sleep alone tonight. "The spy Phenex mentioned."

"Ah." He sighed as he took a sip of his drink. "That."

"Yes, that." I frowned. "What did you do to him?"

"It doesn't matter." Az toed off his shoes and trailed over to his black leather sofa that faced the floor-to-ceiling windows. He sank into the cushions, took another sip, and stared out at the twinkling city lights. "He was our enemy."

"But surely killing him is...a lot." I took a few timid steps closer to him, my heartbeat frantic. "Maybe he was just someone who didn't know what he was getting himself into, trapped between your heaven and hell games."

His eyes narrowed as he turned those piercing eyes my way. A shiver raced down my spine, even as heat curled through me. "He was a vampire. And he was spying on us. The angels have long guessed I'm hiding something. They're right, of course, and they can never find out. Do you know what would happen if they do?" He shook his head and leaned back into the sofa. "He needed to die."

I swallowed hard. So that was how he would see me if he found out the truth.

After a few moments of awkward silence, Az patted the open spot on the sofa next to him. The glow of the city curved across his jaw, highlighting the strong edges of it. He'd unbuttoned the top of his shirt, and his sculpted pecs gleamed like steel. He looked delicious basked in the shadows and the lights. "I don't know why you're so wound up about this. It has nothing to do with you. Come sit. Let's enjoy our drinks."

"No." I took a step back. "I think I just want to go to bed."

His frown deepened, but he didn't argue. "All right. But keep the door open just in case."

Before I could talk myself out of it, I placed my untouched drink on the dining table and vanished into his room. I climbed into his bed without bothering to undress. My eyes struggled to shut. Every muscle in my body stayed tense. Ominous thoughts flashed through my mind, taking me down paths of disastrous what ifs. I'd told myself never to play that game again, but I couldn't help it tonight.

What if I should have gotten out of the deal when I could? What if the Legion really was hiding something? And what if Az found out I'd been a momentary spy?

But the thing that kept me awake the most was that Az never came to bed.

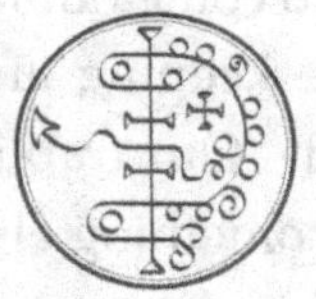

20

Time flew by, faster than an express subway train. Az and I fell into a daily rhythm even though things were tense and strained between us. Every night, I slept in his bed. Sometimes he joined me. In the morning, we had pancakes with Hendrix, and at night, I danced in his club.

I always walked home alone, continuing my role as bait. Thankfully, the angels hadn't tried to approach me again, but neither had the killer. Our entrapment plan wasn't working.

We all sat gathered around the folding table after another night at the club. My entire body ached, and my forehead glistened with a light sheen of sweat. I'd danced for five nights straight, something I hadn't done since high school. My muscles were making me pay for it, but the exhilaration in my tired body made up for it. Dancing drove the cobwebs out of my head. I might be mixed up in a dangerous, crazy situation, but I hadn't felt this good in a very long time.

Not since that night of my senior year in college when everything fell apart.

I could still see those flashing lights. The blood painting the asphalt. The terror in my sister's eyes.

"Right." Phenex leaned against the wall beside the massive map and folded his arms. "I don't think our little friend is going to come out to play."

"He knows we're keeping an eye on her," Stolas answered with a nod. "Our trap is too obvious. We're going to have to try something else."

"Like what?" I dared to ask. Walking home was one thing. Who knew what they'd come up with next?

Az rubbed his jaw. "We'll have to use the party somehow. That's the last time he showed his face."

"The party?" I frowned. "What party?"

He cut his eyes my way. "The second party we'll attend as a couple. It's part of your agreement."

"When is it?"

"Tomorrow night."

My heart flipped. That was soon.

"Would have been nice for you to mention it before now," I muttered.

"It's part of your deal," he replied evenly. "If you'd read your contract, you would have known about it."

I narrowed my eyes. Az met my gaze, clearly unaffected by the tension between us. He'd been like this ever since our argument. I'd offended him somehow, by asking about the vampire spy. Whatever friendship we'd formed had vanished like mist.

Fine with me. I didn't want to be friends with him

anyway. As soon as this whole thing was over, we'd never have to see each other again.

"Fine," I said. "We'll go to the party. But how exactly does that help us catch a supernatural serial killer?"

A strange smile slid across his lips. "We'll have a public argument. That shouldn't be particularly difficult, at least not for you. After, you'll storm off. Go outside to be alone. Hopefully, the killer will approach you then."

Heart thumping against my ribs, I nodded. "Sure, that could work, but won't that cause problems for the sacrifice ball? Have you gotten an invite for that yet?"

Az turned to Stolas, who shook his head. "Nothing. You haven't been invited to the Covenant Ball."

A shiver raced down my spine. "The *Covenant* Ball? Sounds like something straight out of a horror movie. Will I have to take some Holy Water?"

Caim chuckled. "You'll be safe. Two of us will go with you. We'll be waiting in the wings when you step outside."

In the wings.

"That was a terrible pun," I said.

"And by terrible, you mean so funny that you can barely contain your laughter, right?" Caim grinned.

Az puffed out an irritated sigh. "Back to the party. We'll need to be sure to argue about something stupid. Then it will be believable when we make up shortly after. I don't want our invitation to be rescinded. None of you seem to be taking this seriously, but there are dozens of human lives—and souls —on the line."

"Why don't you want Lucifer to win the game?" I suddenly asked.

Confusion rippled across Az's face. "What?"

"Why don't you want him to win? You're demons."

"Because," he said slowly, as if he were speaking to a child, "then this entire world will end. Everyone will end up in Hell."

"And that's definitely something you don't want?" I asked, my heart pounding. "In Hell, I'm guessing it doesn't matter if you kill people who get in your way."

Az drew himself up tall, so tall that a twinge of unease went through my heart. He strode toward me with his shoulders wide and chin strong. Shadows rippled across his skin. Flames flickered in his eyes.

Oh shit. I swallowed hard. He looked like he wanted to rip me to shreds.

"Maybe I should take you there and let you see for yourself."

I opened my mouth to say…well, I didn't know what yet. Probably something stupid. But he cut me short.

"I thought you were different, Mia. You didn't seem to fear us just because we're demons, but it turns out I was very, very wrong."

"It's not because you're a demon," I whispered back. "It's because you killed that vampire for spying on you."

"And you think an angel would have spared him,

do you?" he asked with an angry arch of his brow. "A fallen one, at that? They are far more heartless and coldblooded than we will ever be. But I suppose you'll never learn. You humans are all the same."

He left the room, leaving me in awkward silence with the Legion. Valac stared down at the table, half-hidden in shadows. Stolas paced nervously while Phenex fiddled with the map. Caim bounced on his feet.

"You know I don't have anything against you guys for being demons, right?" I finally said.

Phenex grinned. "We know, but Az doesn't. Bit of a sore spot for him."

"And you shouldn't hold anything against him," Valac said quietly. "He did what had to be done. If he hadn't, Lucifer would have found out what we're doing here." He lifted his gaze from the table and met my eyes. "Hell is not a very nice place to live."

Shivers stormed across my arms. "Even for you?"

"Especially for us," Bael said with a shudder. "The things we've seen, things we've been forced to do. We never want to go back there, and we sure as hell don't want the entire world in that place. All of this, it would be over."

"Not that Heaven is any better," Valac said with a hiss. "Angels can be just as ruthless as demons can."

My heart flipped as I looked from Valac to Caim. "But then what do you plan to do? If both sides suck?"

"We take it one day at a time," Caim said with a nod. "One fight at a time."

"One fight at a time," Phenex echoed.

"One fight at a time," Valac, Stolas, and Bael repeated in unison.

Hands fisted by my sides, I nodded. "One fight at a time."

❦

We entered the party with my hand tucked into Az's suit-clad arm. He'd chosen an all-black ensemble for the night, one that hugged his muscular frame with perfect precision. I wore a cute sapphire dress that hit my mid-thigh and earrings that matched. A gift from Az, though he'd just tossed the thing at me and told me to get changed.

He was still mad. Not that I could blame him. I understood exactly where he was coming from. He thought I'd made assumptions about him based on who he was. And he didn't seem to realize I hadn't. My unease was only based on what he'd done, and even I could admit that maybe I'd been wrong.

He made it really hard to tell him that, though. His smug disdain toward me got on my damn nerves.

This party was a little different than the other. Instead of a rooftop bar, the host had chosen her own penthouse apartment as the venue. As soon as we stepped inside, a strange chill swept across the back of my neck, like an ice cold hand had pressed against it. I shivered and glanced at Az.

He cocked his head at me, and something strange flickered in the depths of his eyes. "What was that?"

"I felt something weird," I replied in a low voice. "Like ice on the back of my neck."

"Hmm. Stay close to me." His words shot a new wave of unease down my spine. It was the first time he'd spoken to me without sounding angry. He almost sounded…concerned.

Great.

"What kind of party is this anyway?" I asked as we trailed across the empty floor toward a bar that had been set up along one wall. As far as I could tell, no one actually lived here. No sofas. No dining tables. No TVs or comfy rugs. It was just an empty space full of fancy supernaturals in their pristine dresses and suits, clinking drinks and chatting animatedly, probably about how they wanted to steal a bunch of human souls.

"It's a mixed party," Az said, shifting closer to murmur into my ear. "Like the Covenant Ball, you're not allowed in unless you have a human date. The host likes to call it a game. See how much we can get away with, all without humans finding out what we are."

I wrinkled my nose. "Great. It's one of *those* parties then."

"What kind is that?"

"The creepy kind." I glanced around and sighed. In the far corner, I spotted Serena's familiar head of midnight hair. She was speaking quietly with a group of older, suit-clad men, and Noah stood beside her like a steady, calming rock. My face transformed into what could only be described as cringing awkward turtle. I shifted closer to Az, hiding myself from view.

"Oh, are we already to that then?" he asked in a low purr, winding his arm around my back.

"Is there somewhere else we could go? A hallway or something?"

He arched a brow, and that dimpled smile made an appearance. "No one would be able to see us then, Mia."

The way he said my name shot a strange tremor through my gut.

"There are others in the hallway," I whispered back and pushed up onto my tiptoes. Peeking over Az's shoulders, I caught sight of Noah again. I really didn't want to face him right now. For one, our last encounter had been awkward as hell. And two, I didn't know how I could hold myself back if he gave me a smug smile and congratulated me on moving out of Serena's apartment. He'd gotten what he wanted, and I hated that with a passion. As happy as he made my best friend, he'd still been a dick to me.

Az twisted sideways to follow my line of sight, but Noah had vanished into the crowd. "Wait, isn't that your friend? Have you two had a falling out?"

"No, it's the guy with her." I grabbed his hand. As soon as my fingers touched his skin, his ice-flecked eyes zeroed in on my face. An electric charge passed between us. It ripped through my body, lighting my gut on fire. A sharp gasp popped from my throat, and the darkness in his eyes flared to life.

"What was that?" I whispered.

"I don't know," he murmured back. "I've never felt it before."

Okay, so that was good. Kind of. At least I wasn't

hallucinating these weird zipping sensations. On the other hand, it must have had something to do with magic and demons and souls and deals. Az, the Prince of Hell, didn't know what it was. And if *he* didn't know what it was, then it could mean anything.

"Hello, Asmodeus," a sickly-sweet feminine voice purred right beside my ear. I jumped two feet in the air, knocked out of my strange reverie with Az. Who was now…pulsing? Shadows leapt across his body in vibrant swirls of grey and black. His eyes turned pitch black. Tightening his grip on my hand, he pulled me behind him. A single feather poked up out of the back of his shirt. A piece of his hidden wings.

"Eisheth." Az's voice was pure steel, and it packed a powerful punch. If I'd been on the receiving end, I might have flinched. Who was this girl? Frowning, I leaned over to get a glimpse of her on the other side of him. Sleek raven hair hung down to her tiny waist, accentuated by a glistening silver gown. Diamonds dangled from each petite earlobe. Despite her small stature, she commanded attention. Power radiated off her body in waves.

She was also fucking gorgeous.

"It's been such a long time since I've seen you, sweetie," she said with a curving set of full lips that most girls could only dream of having. "I didn't think you liked to come to this kind of party."

"Maybe I've changed," he growled back.

She clucked her tongue and sighed. "No, I don't think so. You seem the same to me. Aren't you going to introduce me to your little friend?"

"No." He stepped closer to me, his back pressing into my chest. "I'm here to network and nothing more. Stay out of my way, Eisheth."

"It's *my* party," she said with a pout.

Az whirled on his feet, grabbed my hand, and practically dragged me into the hallway. I cast a glance over my shoulder at the woman staring after us in her perfect, sparkling gown. So many questions flew through my head. Who was she? Why had Az reacted the way he had? And how come she wasn't put off by his rudeness? It was almost like she'd expected it.

But all those questions fled from my mind the second my back hit the wall. While I'd been distracted, Az had pulled me into a quieter, darker corner of the hallway. We weren't alone. Several of the other party attendees were nearby, but it was as secluded as we would get without going into one of the bedrooms.

Not that I was thinking about going into one of the bedrooms.

Not at *all*.

Az leaned forward, bracing his hands on either side of my head. Swallowing hard, I tipped back my head to meet his eyes. "It's time to get to work."

"Yeah, all right," I whispered back as he trailed a finger along the edge of my jaw. Sparks soared behind his touch.

And then he kissed me.

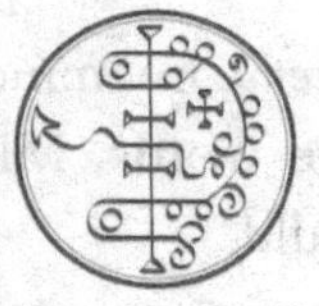

His lips were full of hunger. I pressed up onto my toes and wound my arms around his neck, pushing my body against the hard planes of his chest. All logical thought fled from my mind. A strange, unexpected need ripped through my gut.

Az's fingers tangled in my hair as his other hand dragged a soft caress across my chin. His touch made all the anger, the uncertainty, and the fear come undone within me. His mouth claimed mine, and the eagerness of his hands reflected a growing sense of need I couldn't ignore.

I kind of…liked this.

Soon, his hands found mine. He trapped them against the wall and pulled back. His dark gaze searched my eyes, those flashes of ice asking a question I didn't know how to answer. I realized then that my chest heaved. Hell, my entire body practically trembled.

With a slight smile, he dropped his lips to my neck. I gasped as a new wave of chills swept through me. Every time he trailed another kiss along my skin, my core built up an excruciating heat. Blood rushed through my ears. Everything around us dropped away until there was nothing left but me and him.

This is just for pretend, my mind screamed at me.

I blocked out the words. Might as well make it look as real as we could.

He released his grip on my left hand, and then palmed my hips. I sucked in a sharp gasp as his fingers teased the top of my thigh. My mind shouted something at me again, but I didn't hear it. I was too distracted by what Az was doing with his hand.

The hand slid further south until it hit the bottom hem of my dress. And then slowly, it crept a little higher, *beneath* the material. My entire body shook, and I swallowed down a moan. His mouth was still hot against my neck, driving me crazy, and his hand…oh my god, it was only an inch away from the apex of my thighs now.

"What are you doing?" I finally gasped, although a part of me wanted to slap myself for interrupting.

I could feel him smile against my neck. "I'm doing what we said we were going to do. Make everyone believe in our entanglement."

"Right," I breathed back. "With your hand up my dress?"

He pulled back and shot me a wicked smile. "Would you like me to stop?"

Swallowing hard, I shook my head. "No, you

should keep going. You know, for the fake rela-tionship."

"For the fake relationship," he repeated with a dark flicker in his eyes. He inched closer, his hand still on my thigh, and he gave me a gentle kiss that made my toes curl in my boots. I reached up and placed my palm against his cheek. His stubble tickled my skin, and the scent of him reminded me of tense nights spent in his bed.

His presence consumed me. The scent, the taste, the feel of him. What we were doing might be fake, but I had to admit something to myself or I might lose my mind. I *really* didn't hate him anymore.

That didn't mean he was a good guy who could be trusted, or any of that. But I definitely didn't hate him. *Dammit.*

His hand slid a little further up, and his thumb pressed against my panties.

Oh my god.

"Well, that's interesting," he said with a smirk. "You're wet."

"I…"

His thumb released its pressure, and I sagged against the wall. But then his finger slid beneath the thin, lacy material. My entire body shook as my heart leapt right up into my throat and stuck there. His eyes stayed locked on mine the entire time, and slowly, he slid the tip of his finger inside of me.

"I've been wondering what you would feel like," he murmured. "And you're just as I thought. Sweet, hot, tight. Most men would lose their minds to have someone like you."

My heart thumped painfully against my ribs. I literally had no idea how to respond to that, nor to the fact that *his finger was inside of me*. At a party. With a bunch of people nearby. Were they watching us?

Az slid his finger in further, and I moaned, shuddering against the wall. Without the slightest bit of control over my body, I felt myself tighten around him. A low growl rumbled from his throat, and then he pulled his hand out from beneath my dress, leaving me a mess beneath him.

"Fuck. Not like this," he said as the darkness in his eyes began to clear. "Not here. I'm sorry. I got carried away."

My chest expanded as I caught the conflicted expression on his face. Had that...had that been *real*? Surely not. We'd been playing around and nothing more, only to catch people's attention. But that didn't explain why he'd crossed the line he had. He hadn't really needed to touch me like that to make people think we were an item.

I wet my lips, trying my damnedest not to get carried away, but...

"What do you mean?" I couldn't help but ask.

"Nothing." His eyes shuttered over his emotions. "You're forgetting something, aren't you?"

"I think I am forgetting a lot of things right now."

He leaned forward and pressed his mouth against my ear. "We've made one type of scene, and now we need to make the other. *The argument*, Mia."

"Oh," I said numbly. "Right."

We've made one type of scene...

Now I was just getting whiplash. He'd said one

type of scene. So it *had* been fake. Or had it? Either he was a really good actor or he didn't want me to know he'd felt the same thing I had.

"Stop playing with my mind," I said in a booming voice as my hands found his chest. With narrowed eyes, I shoved him back.

He stumbled away from me with alarm plastered on his handsome face. "Mia, what are you doing?"

"You're hot and cold." My eyes narrowed. "One minute, you act like you want to rip my clothes off. The next, you look at me like I'm nothing more than a bug on the bottom of your boot. Make up your mind, Asmodeus. Do you want me or not?"

His eyebrows shot up. "I think I've made it clear what I want."

I fisted my hands and propped them on my hips. "Really? You sure about that? Because from where I'm standing, you don't even know what the hell is going on yourself. And I'm done with it."

With a frustrated growl, I whirled away from him and stormed down the hallway, jumping into the elevator as soon as it opened. Out of the corner of my eyes, I caught the shocked faces of the other party attendees. Thankfully, none of them were Serena or Noah. I really didn't want to have to explain what they'd just seen.

As the doors slid shut, I sagged against the wall and closed my eyes. Truth be told, I didn't even understand it myself. And I was starting to realize that I was in way over my head.

Like, *way* over my head.

The elevator shuddered to a stop, and the doors

whirred open. I made my way outside and pulled the cool night air into my lungs. My head began to clear, but only a little. The hardest part of the plan came next. If the killer took the bait, I had to trust that the demons would swoop in from above before he could sink his blade into my neck.

Throwing back my shoulders, I turned left, just like we'd planned. I would follow a prescribed route we'd gone over about five hundred times earlier in the day. Caim, Phenex, and Stolas were hiding on the rooftops above while Bael and Valac lurked in nearby alleys.

I was as safe as I could be. You know, in the "catch a serial killer with a bunch of demons" scheme of things.

As I wound through the late night streets of Hell's Kitchen, every now and then I caught the sound of distant footsteps. But nothing ever came of it. Before long, I reached the club, shut for the night. I used my key to get into the building and drifted down the dark hallway to the meeting room.

When I stepped inside, a sudden flash of *wrong* went through me. I hovered in the shadowy doorway with my fingers half an inch from the light-switch. Heart thumping, I took a step back. The Legion couldn't be more than a few steps behind me, but they weren't here yet. If the killer had somehow figured out our plan and had gotten ahead of us...he could be waiting in here for me.

Gritting my teeth, I fished the signet ring out of my purse and gripped it in my hand. Then, with all the bravado I didn't have, I flipped the switch. Light poured through the room, blinding me momentarily.

When my vision cleared, a gasp popped from my parted lips. The map, once an elaborate display of the killer's every move, had been ripped to shreds. All the pins were scattered across the floor like fallen soldiers. The yarn now hung from the overhead light. At the end of it was a folded note.

I swallowed hard and snatched the note from the string, heart thumping out a hectic beat. My eyes rushed across the words. A heavy stone crashed into my gut.

I know what you've been trying to do. Give up the hunt, Legion. This will be your last warning before I tell Lucifer everything about you. Need extra motivation? I have the werewolf friend. Her name is Serena. And I will kill her if you don't give me Mia. You have until tomorrow at midnight.

<h1 style="text-align:center">22</h1>

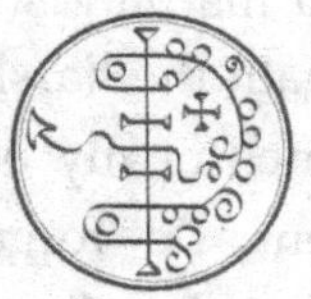

I dropped the note like it was made of poisonous snakes. It might as well have been. Its venom stung worse than the point of even the sharpest sword. My heart shook violently in my chest. It was pounding so hard I swore it would beat its way through my ribs.

This couldn't be happening. Serena had to be safe. She just *had* to be. I'd seen her at the party, not long before I'd left. She'd been fine at the time, surrounded by her fellow lawyers, her clients, and her boyfriend. How had the killer gotten to her? Why had she left the party?

Unease slithered through my gut. Horrified, I pressed my fingers to my lips. She must have seen me arguing with Az. And so she'd followed me out into the dark night when I'd left.

Fuck.

The Legion wouldn't have been watching out for her. They'd been too busy watching me.

I began to pace the length of the silent room, my steps growing more frantic by the minute. This couldn't be happening. This couldn't. Not to Serena.

Az stepped into the room. His presence pulsed along my skin, dark and dangerous. "Mia?"

With a shaky breath, I hurried over to him and shoved the note into his hands. As I did, the signet ring glimmered beneath the harsh light. My eyes flew wide. Every single inch of my body stiffened. In the terror of the moment, I'd forgotten all about that damn ring. I fisted my hand around it, desperately hoping he hadn't spotted it.

With a lethal glint in his eyes, Az ripped the note out of my hand and then slowly pried open my fingers. He gazed down at the ring. Obviously, he would know what it was, even if *I* didn't. And me having it was a very bad thing.

"Why do you have my ring?" His voice was edged in steel and full of danger. Shadows whorled through the room. Nervously, I couldn't help but wonder where Az had stashed his sword. Would Abaddon hear the anger in his demon's voice and fly out of the shadows to attack me?

I swallowed hard. "I want to tell you, but I don't want you to freak out."

Caim and Phenex chose that moment to step into the room. The former took one look at us and the ring, clasped his hand on Phenex's shoulder, and then practically yeeted the both of them out the door.

Traitors.

"Explain," Az demanded, barely missing a beat.

"Right, so." I took a deep breath and decided I

might as well go down in a blaze of glory. All I could do was tell him the truth, even if it meant he'd throw me into the murky, polluted Hudson River to swim with the radioactive fishes. "The first night I worked here, some angels cornered me in the street when I was walking back to your penthouse."

He sighed and closed his eyes, tension bouncing off his clenched jaw. "Gabe and Suriel. That's what they're up to. I should have known."

"They asked me to spy for them. And before you immediately toss me into the river, I need you to know that I never, ever told them a damn thing about you or the Legion. Nothing." I didn't even take a single breath. "All I did was take their card and this stupid ring, all right? I even texted them and told them to leave me alone. The only reason they came after me again was because they wanted to change my mind. I'm not a spy for them. I didn't tell them anything. I haven't betrayed you. Please don't kill me."

Slowly, Az opened his eyes. The torment in them shook me to my soul. "You really believe I would kill you?"

Tears pricked the corners of my eyes. "No. I mean, I don't know, okay? You killed the other spy because he threatened to destroy everything you and the Legion have worked so hard for. If I did the same, why wouldn't you kill me, too?"

He sighed and held the ring up before him. His expression was blank, unreadable. "You're under my protection. I swore an oath to you. I would rip a man's spine from his body if he tried to harm you.

And then I would grind up his bones and give them to the fae."

"Oh." I blinked, cheeks flushing. "Well, that was oddly specific."

"I mean it, Mia." He curled his fingers around the ring and then pocketed it. "I wish you'd told me sooner. I can't trust you if you can't trust me, and I've told you how important loyalty is to me. But this ring certainly explains a lot."

"Explains what?"

"The carving on the signet. That's my demon seal. It holds power. *My* power," he replied. "It explains why you were able to hold your own against the killer that night in the alley. You used it against him, didn't you?"

"I did. I think," I admitted. "I didn't really know what I was doing. All of a sudden, I just kind of threw him away from me with an invisible…fireball? But when I tried a second time, nothing happened."

He nodded. "It's because you don't know how to use it. You got lucky. Most humans wouldn't have been able to tap into the power without being taught how. If you hadn't been carrying this ring, he would have claimed another life."

My heart dropped. "Az, he *is* going to claim another life. Read the note."

Frowning, he unfolded the paper. A few moments passed before he said anything. It was only then that he seemed to notice the shredded map, the scattering of pins. He crumpled the note and hurled it against the wall.

"Dammit!" His voice boomed, echoing down the

silent hallway of the club. A moment later, the Legion appeared in the doorway. We quickly filled them in on what had happened. One by one, they shuffled into the room and dropped into a chair. The night had begun with eager excitement. Now every eye was hooded and dark. The killer had won. Again.

"What are we going to do?" I whispered, heart thumping.

"*We* aren't going to do anything," Az replied through gritted teeth. "I'm taking you back to my apartment, and you're staying there until we have a plan."

"But—" I started.

"But nothing," he insisted, turning to the others. "Serena is alive and well. He wouldn't have made a bargain with her life if she wasn't. We have time to find her and put a stop to this."

Caim pushed up from his chair and nodded solemnly. "Someone at the party must have seen something. We'll talk to everyone we can. Search everywhere he might have taken her."

Phenex and Stolas joined him by the shredded map. They began murmuring amongst themselves, plotting out a route to hunt down the killer. And Serena. Heart pounding, I turned my gaze to Az's shadowed face. "I want to help. I should search the streets with Caim and Phenex."

"The best way you can help is to stay safe," he said in a commanding voice that welcomed no argument. "Right now, he's keeping Serena alive because he wants you instead. If he somehow got his hands on you before tomorrow night…"

The rest of his sentence was left unsaid. I knew how it ended. Gut churning, I fisted my hands. It was all I could do not to break down in tears and rip the world apart trying to find Serena.

"I hate this," I hissed. "I don't want to run and hide."

He wound his arms around me and pulled me to his chest. "I know. But if we don't play this right, both of you will die."

❧

We returned to his apartment while the others took to the streets. The clouds had opened up, and rain poured down on our heads, sleeting sideways from a westerly wind. I shivered in my tiny dress and swiped my drenched hair out of my eyes. When we stepped inside the quiet penthouse, Az bustled into his room and returned with the fluffy robe he'd lent me for my stay with him.

"You're shivering. Change into this," he demanded.

Normally, I'd bite off his nose for ordering me around, but I didn't have the energy to do it tonight. Not with the exhaustion in my bones. Not with Serena missing. With a small smile, I took the robe, vanished into the bathroom, and quickly changed out of my wet clothes.

When I returned to the living room, he was waiting for me on the couch with a gin and tonic and a pigeon. I padded over to him and took the drink. He patted the cushion by his side as he tossed a dried kernel of corn into the air for Hendrix.

I sank into the soft sofa and downed the drink in one gulp. He shot me a raised eyebrow, but all I could do was shrug. "It's been a long night."

He nodded and handed me another. "I thought that might be the case. So I made you an extra drink."

"I'll probably need more than one extra." This time, I took a slower sip. Az curled his strong fingers around his own glass and watched me while I drank. The look in his eyes reminded me of that moment in the hallway. When we'd been pretending and nothing more.

I shivered.

"You're still cold," he said with a frown. "Do you want me to get the hot tub started? I can—"

"No." I shook my head. "It's okay. I'm not really cold. Anxious and worried more than anything."

"Serena means a lot to you," he said quietly.

I closed my eyes and leaned back into the couch, taking another sip of gin. "Serena is the best person in the entire world, and she's the only one I trust. I don't know where I would be if it wasn't for her. She's the only one who believed me about…well, you know."

"The only one?" he asked gently.

I nodded and opened my eyes to find him gazing at me with soft concern. What a strange expression to find on a demon's face. "The *only* one. You've read the articles. It looked bad, Az. Really bad. Why would anyone believe it wasn't me? My car. My street. On a night I was out at a party."

"But you testified that you didn't do it."

"Because I *didn't*," I said more harshly than I intended.

"Then who did?"

I sucked in a sharp breath and glanced away. "Despite all the evidence, Serena always believed me. She never once doubted my innocence even when the rest of the world did."

Az cocked his head, tossing another corn kernel to Hendrix. "You never told her who did it?"

My heart thumped. "Az, I can't."

I lifted my glass to my lips and drank the whole thing down. The gin burned my belly, warming me from the inside out and driving away the chill from the rain. Silently, Az took my glass and refilled his and mine both. Then he settled back onto the couch beside me to listen. No questions. No demands. Just patient silence. And for the first time in my life, I felt the knots around my fear unravel.

Tears burned my eyes as I took another drink. "You already know who."

"I have a pretty good idea," he said in a low murmur. "But I'm not the one who needs you to say it, Mia. You do. Ignoring it will never make it go away. You have to look the past in the eye and tell it to go fuck itself."

A tense laugh popped from my throat. That was not what I'd expected him to say. "There's a reason I've never told anyone."

"I know."

"I don't want anything bad to happen to her. Even though she's guilty as hell, even though she did a terrible thing...I don't want her life to be over."

"It won't, Mia." He shifted toward me and braced his arm on the back of the couch behind my head. His knee brushed mine. I tried not to stare at where his black pants melted against my skin. "You can trust me with this. I would never tell a single soul."

My eyes latched onto his, and that familiar electric charge went through me, starting from the spot where our bodies met. It sizzled in my gut like static. The world tunneled in around me, darkening at the edges, until Az was all I could see.

"It was my sister," I breathed.

He nodded, silent, as if knowing that was what I needed from him right now. A single tear slid down my cheek. It plopped onto my trembling hand that still clutched my drink. Shuddering, I tipped the drink into my open mouth and swallowed hard.

I had never said that out loud.

"My parents," I said after taking a deep breath. "They refused to believe me when I told them I didn't do it. They kicked me out of the house. I spent two years sleeping in my car, buying food from some savings I built up during college. I got a full-ride scholarship, so all the hours serving tables at Applebee's went right into my bank account. Of course, that money eventually ran out."

"And that's how you ended up on Serena's couch," he murmured, eyes sparking.

I nodded. "I used the last of my money to buy gas so I could drive up here. I thought I could start a new life in New York. Find a job. Thrive in a place where no one knew my name. But everyone looks me up. No one wants to hire someone with such a rocky past.

Some think I did it. Others might not, but it doesn't matter. My name would be attached to their company. No one wants that."

Except for you.

"Now I understand why it's so hard for you to trust people." He sighed, stood from the sofa, and refilled our drinks. When he sat back down, I couldn't help but notice his chiseled face was a little hazy around the edges. My body had begun to relax despite our conversation and my worries about Serena. Distantly, I wondered if I'd had too much to drink.

"I think we're more alike than I first thought," he said.

My attention zeroed in on his words. "What do you mean?"

He reached out and wound a strand of my deep red hair around his finger. My heart stopped as he lightly caressed my thick strands. "You may have realized by now that the Legion is a very close-knit group. We rarely allow anyone into the circle, not unless we trust them. Unfortunately, I trusted the wrong person once. Someone who did not realize I was a demon until our lives were tangled up together. When she found out the truth about me, she did not take it well, even though she *knew* me. She assumed the worst. And she took it out on my Legion."

I shifted on the sofa, my mouth suddenly dry despite the multitude of drinks I'd consumed. "She?"

His lips pressed tightly together. "You've met her. Eisheth."

Right. Of course. The gorgeous vampire who had

hosted the party. I should have guessed. They'd been incredibly weird toward each other, and it was because of this. Clearly they'd once been involved. Not fake involved. *Real* involved.

"Oh." That was all I could manage.

"She attacked me, stole all of my funds, and stabbed Morax in the gut with my own sword." He closed his eyes. "Morax fought back. He nearly killed her. But when we found him, she was already gone. A vampire had found her and decided to take her under his wing."

"You mean he turned her."

He nodded. "That was over a hundred years ago."

"What happened to Morax?" I asked in a whisper.

His jaw rippled as he tipped the rest of his drink into his mouth. "He didn't make it. She destroyed him completely."

My stomach clenched, and my hand found his knee. "I'm so sorry, Az. I had no idea about any of this."

"I should have known what would happen," he said in a pained voice. "Everyone assumes the worst of demons, and frankly, I don't blame them. But I can never let someone get that close to me again. The Legion are my *family*. And I would do anything to protect them."

The emotion in his voice shook my heart. Suddenly, everything was shockingly clear. Why Az was the way he was. Why he'd killed that spy. Why he'd kept me at arms length even as we danced around our strange connection. He'd been burned.

Horribly so. Trusting Eisheth had cost him almost everything.

"I don't think the worst of you," I finally whispered as the soft edges of the robe slipped down my shoulders.

Az lifted his eyes to meet mine. "Yes, you do."

"I don't," I argued. "You annoy me sometimes, but that doesn't mean I think you're evil."

He slid his fingers to the ends of my hair and paused when they were mere inches from my exposed skin. "What about the situation with the vampire spy? You seemed to think the worst then."

"I told you," I insisted, shifting closer to him. "That had nothing to do with you being a demon. The whole thing just freaked me out, that's all. I'm not used to your world. I've known about supernaturals all my life, but I've never been among them like this. It's...different."

"The alcohol is lowering your inhibitions. It's making your emotions roll off of you in waves. I can read them perfectly," he murmured as the scent of bonfire wafted toward me. "There is fear, intense worry, and beautiful earnestness, Mia. But there is also something else."

"What?" I whispered.

"Desire."

My heart thudded in my chest. For a moment, I swore I couldn't breathe. Az's ice-flecked eyes roared with eternal flames, and the temperature inside his penthouse suddenly went up a few degrees. He'd read my emotions which meant he knew exactly how I felt. He knew the secrets of my soul.

Deep down, I knew I should be embarrassed, but I wasn't. Not after all that liquid courage.

"Maybe you're just being hopeful," I finally managed.

Shadows swirled across his skin. "It's the same emotion from the party."

"Yes, well." I swallowed hard as memories replayed in my mind. His thumb brushing my thigh. His finger *inside of me*. "I *am* only human. That is a perfectly normal reaction to being touched like that."

His lips quirked as his dark gaze dropped to my bare shoulders. A hint of cleavage peaked out from the fluffy robe. In my hurry to get out of my clothes, I hadn't bothered to put a dry bra or panties on. Whoops.

"You didn't tell me to stop," he practically purred with lethal attention. Like I was his prey.

"We were putting on a show. We had an audience."

"We don't have an audience now."

My heart flipped, and his hand dropped to my shoulder. He massaged the skin just below my neck where knots had formed from all my pent-up anxiety and fear. Sparks rushed across my skin.

"You're very tense," he murmured as he took my empty glass from my fingers and placed it on the coffee table next to his.

"Yes," I said around a trembling breath. "Trying to trap a serial killer will do that to a girl."

"I know a way to make you relax." His knuckles dug deeper into my shoulders, and I bit back an explosive moan. God, his touch felt good. *More* than good. It was euphoric. And that was just from a massage.

"I'm sure you do."

Smiling, he pushed me back against the couch and tugged at the tie around the robe. I swallowed hard as I watched him work his deft fingers. Soon, it came undone. My heart did another flip. "Az..."

He slowly opened the robe, pushing the soft material onto either side of my naked body. I trembled as he gazed down at me with his ice-flecked eyes. They swirled with flames, sparking up the dark apartment.

As he sank to his knees before me, everything within me clenched tight.

I could barely find the words to ask him what exactly he thought he was doing. "Did you forget what you just said? We don't have an audience."

"Mia," he said in a deep growl. "Let me take care of you."

When I thought about someone taking care of me, I imagined a bowl of chicken soup and some fluffy pajamas. Maybe a cooling wet towel on my forehead to lower my temperature. You know, the kind of things you got when you were sick. I sure as hell had never imagined something like this.

Az dropped a kiss on my knee. I shuddered, and my eyes practically rolled back into my head. My god, how did every single thing he did feel so incredibly amazing? His fingers tiptoed along the outside of my thighs, stilling when they reached my hips.

My heart thundered as I gazed down at him. Leaning forward, he kissed my belly. Shivers stormed through me. His kiss went lower. Another storm of shivers rocked my body.

Core aching, I reached down and wound my fingers through his soft hair. I could barely stand it anymore. I wanted—no, I *needed*—his mouth on me.

His lips came agonizingly close. My lungs stilled. Everything within me tensed. Even my hands gripped his hair like I would fall if I let go.

He dragged his tongue across my core.

My breath exploded from my throat as I arched toward him, tremors of pleasure shaking through me. All the last remnants of my inhibitions vanished as I tugged him closer. With a low, delicious growl rolling through his body, he licked my folds with a feverish intensity.

I shook against him. His fingers gripped my thighs. Losing all control, I rocked against his mouth, barely holding on as I slid further and further toward the edge of an endless cliff.

His tongue slid inside of me, and that was all it took. I came undone, my need shattering like ancient stars. My body pulsed around his tongue as he kept his grip tight on my thighs. When my quaking finally slowed, I relaxed against the couch, my heart beating a million times a minute.

Az leaned back with a smug smile on his face. "I told you I would make you relax. Don't you feel better now?"

"You're right," I breathed.

"Did I just hear you say I'm right about something?" Slowly, he pushed up from the floor to tower over me, blocking out the city lights. "Hmm. You really did enjoy that."

Conscious of how exposed I was before him, I reached for the edges of the robe, but the tone in his voice stopped me short.

"Mia."

I sat up a little straighter, suddenly alert all over again.

"Are you sure you're *fully* relaxed?"

My eyes dropped to the thick bulge in his pants. Heart pounding in my ears, I understood at once what he meant. He'd driven me wild with need, but he wasn't immune to the spark between us. Need clenched my thighs.

Slowly, I stood from the couch and let the robe slip all the way off my body. It pooled around my bare feet. I reached up and fingered the buttons of his shirt. As I fumbled with the top one, he shook his head, grabbed the fabric, and ripped the shirt right off his body.

"I can't wait that long," he said in a growl that made goosebumps pop up on every inch of my skin. The heat in his eyes burned me up from the inside out, and all I could do was stare as he tore his pants clean in half. He tossed them across the room, locking his eyes on mine.

I shuddered as I stared at his glistening, muscular body. Every single inch of him was chiseled to perfection, including a deep V that led down to his well-endowed cock. A cock that, as far as I could see, had no weird demon tail spade attached to it.

Thank god.

He lifted me into his arms and carried me across the apartment, his mouth claiming mine. Hunger roiled off his body as he dropped me back onto the dining table and braced his arms on either side of my head. Heart pounding, I spread my thighs for him.

He groaned as he pushed inside of me. His hard length stretched me wide, almost filling me completely. With his fingers gripping my thighs, he thrust deep. I dropped my head back onto the table as a desperate pleasure built up inside my core.

"You looked so good with my finger inside of

you," he growled as he thrust inside of me again. "But you look even better like this."

His carved chest rippled beneath the lights of the city that poured across him. Tightening his grip on my thighs, he thrust even harder. I watched him over me as a delicious heat spread through my body. This powerful demon who locked out the entire world. Except for me. And he was now claiming me as if he were mine.

There was no audience anymore. We weren't putting on a show for anyone else. It was just him and me and this passion charging between us. And I didn't want it to end.

As his eyes locked on mine, another explosion of pleasure shook through my body, taking me over the edge. He thrust into me once more and came only seconds behind. A deep growl echoed through the silent penthouse as he shuddered against me. Sweat dripped down his chest, our bodies melting as we became one.

He sighed against me. Slowly, he pulled me off the table and carried me back over to the sofa. We collapsed into the cushions together, our limbs all tangled. He'd been right, of course. I *was* very relaxed now, even as my mind spun with new questions.

What the hell had just happened? Was it a tipsy one-night stand and nothing more?

I didn't manage to hold on to those questions for long. Exhaustion tugged on my tired bones, begging me for sleep. Sighing, I curled up on his chest and gave in to the call. Soon, a dreamless sleep enveloped me.

❧

A banging jolted me from sleep. My head pounded as I climbed off Az's body, rubbed my eyes, and blearily glanced around. The pounding was coming from the door.

My stomach flipped.

Grunting, Az climbed to his feet and wrapped his torn shirt around his waist. He padded over to the door and cracked it open. Caim rushed inside, followed closely by Phenex.

I let out a little cry of alarm and tugged the robe over my chest.

Phenex stumbled to a stop and glanced around. "Oh."

Caim grinned. "*Oh.*"

"Stop gawking and get the hell on with it," Az growled, stepping between me and the guys so they could no longer get an eyeful of my very obvious nakedness. "You're banging on my door in the middle of the night. What did you find?"

"Nothing. I'm sorry, Mia," Caim said as the grin slid from his face. "We looked all over the city. There's no sign of Serena anywhere."

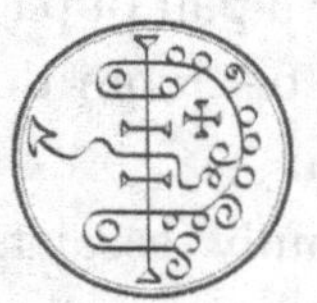

24

Az paced as I tiptoed into the bedroom to find some clothes. I was not about to have a naked chat about my best friend's life with a bunch of demons. Serena was out there, in danger. And I was rolling around on a dining table with a Prince of Hell. *Idiot!*

I shook my head and grimaced as another wave of nausea pounded through me. What had I been thinking? *Not much*, I grimly thought as I found a comfy t-shirt in my bag. The five or six gin and tonics had gone straight to my head. And my vagina, too, apparently.

How stupid could I possibly be? It clearly hadn't meant anything, and now we had to survive the next week, save Serena, stop a human sacrifice, and who knew what else. All while knowing that we had seen each other naked. Who was I kidding? We'd done far more than just *look*.

Of course, I couldn't help but wonder...had it

really been a mistake? He'd opened up to me, and I'd done the same to him. Az understood me in a way I'd never expected. Hell, he was one of the only people in the world to give me a chance. We'd been tiptoeing closer to each other ever since I'd moved in. Maybe… maybe there was something there.

After I tugged on a pair of pajama bottoms, I eased toward the cracked bedroom door. Voices drifted in from the living room.

"Well, *that* certainly escalated quickly," Phenex said as he elbowed Az in the ribs.

Az's jaw rippled as he clenched his teeth. "She's upset about her friend, and we had a few drinks. One thing led to another, that's all."

I paused, heart thumping. Really, I shouldn't stand here eavesdropping on their conversation, but I couldn't help myself. They were talking about me and what we'd clearly just done. It didn't take a rocket scientist to tell we'd had sex.

"So, it was just a drunken hook-up?" Caim asked with arched brows. "Come on, Az. We've all seen the way you look at her."

"Of course that was all it was." Az collected the empty glasses from the table and carried them into the kitchen. "She's a human. I'm a demon. Our worlds can never intertwine. I was having a little fun, and there is nothing more to it than that. Now can we please move on?"

"Yeah, alright, boss," Phenex said, shrugging. "If that's what you want."

"We have a couple of ideas on how to tackle this

ransom note situation," Caim said, nodding as Az handed him a drink.

With a deep breath, I slithered back into Az's dark bedroom. My heart pounded, and an unwelcome burning sensation filled my eyes. It was just as I'd thought. A fling. A random hook-up. Something to pass the time. A little fun. Nothing more.

And that was *fine*.

It wasn't like I wanted anything more than that from him.

Most of the time, Az annoyed me. I didn't like him. Hell, I barely tolerated him. And, you know, *he's a demon*.

Nodding to myself, I squared my shoulders and pushed out into the living room. The three demons fell silent as soon as I stepped in front of them. "Hi."

Phenex cleared his throat. "Hi, Mia. I see you, ah… cute pajamas."

"They have pigeons on them," Caim said with an amused grin.

"I like pigeons." I strode across the room and eyeballed them both. "What are you going to do about finding Serena?"

Phenex ran his fingers through his blazing hair. "We have an idea, but I don't think you're going to like it very much."

"Wonderful. What is it?"

"We've talked it over. Valac, Stolas, and Bael agreed. They've gone back to the club to clean up the mess and see how much of the map we can salvage, but…we're never going to find the killer like that. If he's smart, he would have gone somewhere we'd never think to look."

I folded my arms. "I don't like any of the words coming out of your mouth."

Caim clasped Az's shoulders. "We think we should go through with the trade."

My stomach bottomed out. Shaking my head, I sucked in a sharp breath and stepped back. I couldn't have heard him right. No way in hell one of the Legion—Caim especially—would want to toss me to the mercy of a supernatural serial killer who clearly wanted me dead. There had to be another option, one that would end in no one's death. Not Serena's. Not mine.

Az would never agree to this. Heart squeezing, I turned to him. His words echoed in my mind. I was under his protection, but…what was more important? Saving one human life or saving his Legion from having to go back to Hell and face Lucifer's wrath?

He'd known me for all of three weeks. He'd known them for centuries.

Fuck.

Maybe it was time to run.

"That's not an option," Az said firmly. Inwardly, I sighed. "I'm not handing Mia over to a killer."

"That's not what we said," Caim replied. "We want to set up the trade. If we do it right, we leave with Serena *and* Mia. And the killer leaves empty-handed."

"And by empty-handed, we mean he'll join Vlad where he's swimming with the fishes." Phenex waggled his eyebrows at me and grinned.

"You really like talking like a mob boss, don't you?" I rolled my eyes, but inexplicably, I felt my heart soften. Just a bit. These demons were violent and rash, but they were also trying to save me and Serena. And, you know, all of humanity.

Kind of hard to think of them as evil when I looked at it like that.

Phenex pounded his chest. "I'll make you an offer you can't refuse."

"You're too late." Caim elbowed him, snickering. "Az already did that."

My entire face flamed. Awkwardly, I coughed and tried to find something to look at that wasn't Az's sculpted chest. He still hadn't put his shirt back on, probably because it and his pants were in ribbons now. The shredded material of his shirt draped over his waist and barely hid his cock. I wasn't sure why no one but me seemed to notice.

"How can we be sure this will work?" Az asked, changing the subject back to the new plot to stop the murderer. "We already tried to trap him. He'll likely expect us to try again."

"We'll come up with a good plan," Caim said firmly.

Az folded his arms. "And that is...?"

Caim and Phenex exchanged a glance. "Well, we don't know yet, but we have some time. By tomorrow night, we'll have something."

"There's another thing you need to know, boss," Phenex added.

"What now?" Az growled.

"You and Mia had a public argument tonight.

She stormed off. As far as the supernatural community knows, you've broken things off." Phenex grinned again, but then forced his lips into a frown when Az shot him a glare. "We're running out of time to get an invite from Lars. If you don't do something soon, we'll lose our chance to get into that ball."

"We don't have time to worry about this," I said, throwing up my hands. "We need to focus on finding Serena."

"We're going to have to worry about both, darling," Caim drawled. "You and Az need to have a public date where we know Lars will see you. As soon as possible. Like…tomorrow. While you're out getting your invite to the ball, we'll huddle and form a plan for the killer."

Phenex nodded. "After your date, you can come back to the club, and we'll fill you in on the plan. We can do both. Easy peasy."

"This sounds like the opposite of easy peasy," I said flatly.

"As much as I hate to admit it," Az finally said. "They're right. If we don't get an invite to the Covenant Ball by the end of this week, we aren't getting one. All of those human lives will end."

"Fine," I relented. "On one condition."

Az frowned. "I'm not sure I want to know."

"Before we go rushing headfirst into this plan, whatever it ends up being, can we try something else first? Serena's boyfriend was at the party with her tonight. He was by her side the whole time. If someone took her, maybe he saw who it was."

Az cocked his head. "You mentioned him before, but I didn't see him."

"He was there," I insisted. "Trust me. He might have stepped away for a moment, but I doubt she would have left the party without telling him. He *must* have seen something. Maybe he could at least give us the identity of the killer. That would help, right?"

"Maybe," Caim said, nodding at Phenex. "If the killer is part of the supernatural community, there'll be an address for him somewhere. If we could find out his name, we might be able to track him down."

I loosed a breath. "So we could find him that way, instead of trying to set a trap for him again. Like Az said, he isn't stupid. He'll expect us to try something during the trade."

"Okay." Az nodded. "It's a deal then. Shall I draw up the contract?"

My heart dropped. "You can't be serious."

A little, dimpled smile tickled the corners of his lips. "No, I just wanted to see your reaction."

"I wonder what your reaction would be if I slammed my fist into your face," I replied sweetly.

Caim cleared his throat and jerked his head at Phenex. They locked eyes and made a few strange noises before they simultaneously drifted toward the door.

"It's late. We'll be going now." Caim's hand hovered over the handle before he turned to find me hugging my t-shirt to my chest. "Don't worry, Mia. We'll do everything in our power to save your friend."

I nodded. All I could do was put my trust in them. We were up against a supernatural killer who wanted me dead. My only hope was a Prince of Hell and his five loyal friends. Logically, I knew it was a long-shot that we would win, but my gut told me we'd be able to save Serena and those sacrificial human souls.

As long as Lucifer never found out.

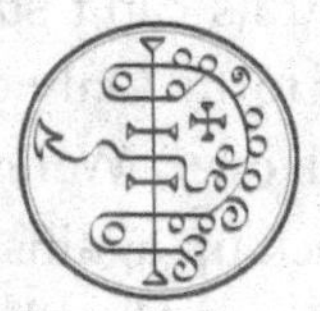

25

An unsetting awkwardness formed a lump in my belly. With Caim and Phenex gone, there was nothing to distract me from the fact I'd just had sex with Asmodeus, the most powerful Prince of Hell. Tipsy. While my best friend was missing. Thankfully, Az didn't seem like he wanted to discuss it any more than I did.

"Would you like another drink," he asked as he moved over to the bar. Glasses clinked as the muscles in his back rippled beneath the city lights splashing through the windows.

"I think I've had enough."

His shoulders tensed. When he turned toward me, it was all I could do not to stare at his chest. Why hadn't he put on a shirt yet? "Right, of course. You're exhausted. We should probably get you to bed."

I hugged my arms around me, sighing. "To be honest, Az, I don't think I can sleep right now. Not while Serena is out there. She's probably scared. Or hurt."

"She might be scared, but she's likely not hurt," he said with a frown. "It's a shame it's not a full moon or she might have a chance of fighting her way out of wherever she's trapped. Werewolves are as strong as hell. Most supernaturals can't stack up against them when they're in wolf form. Only demons and angels."

My heart flipped over. Werewolves were strong, but how did they stack up against literal angels? I had to ask, even though I was already sure I wouldn't like the answer. "How strong *are* angels? Can they even die?"

He shook his head. "Not permanently. They're immortal, just like demons. The only way to stop us is to rip our hearts out, but then you have to keep the heart away from the body or we'll heal ourselves."

I blinked at him. "Are you telling me that you literally have to hold onto a demon's heart if you want him dead?"

"The heart will never stop beating, and if you try to destroy it, it will regrow itself. Same as the body. Morax is the only one we've ever lost, and that's only because Eisheth buried his heart and then had another demon erase her memories of where she hid it. So that no one could ever find it again." He took a step closer, his eyes darkening. "There are plenty of hunters who have tried to kill us over the centuries. It is impossible. The heart always finds a way of returning to its body if it's close enough. We're talking within a thousand miles."

Shivers stormed across my skin. *A thousand miles?*

"So you're all immortal. How are we ever going to stop this killer?"

"I plan to take his heart. And then I will drop it into the deepest ocean, as far away from here as I can manage." Az reached out and fingered a strand of my hair. My heart lurched into my throat, despite everything. "But don't you worry about that. You need to get some sleep. We have a big day tomorrow."

I opened my mouth to argue. Hadn't he heard me tell him I was too worried about Serena to sleep? Damn demons and their selective hearing. But just before the words popped out of my mouth, a strange sensation whooshed through my veins. My limbs suddenly grew too heavy for me to move. Lightness filled my head. As the world went black, Az wrapped his arms around me and kept me from toppling to the floor. The last thing I knew before sleep dragged me under was being lifted off my feet and carried into the bedroom. The scent of fire soothed my soul.

❦

I awoke with a start. A gasp shook my lungs as I popped up straight, sweaty hair tangled against my forehead. Darkness still hung heavy in the bedroom, but pinpricks of light shone around the edges of the curtains. Az was already up. I could hear him moving around in the kitchen, clinking dishes.

With a frown, I padded into the main section of the penthouse. A glass of orange juice sat waiting for me on the counter, but I still shot the back of his head a glare. Mister Nice Demon wasn't going to cut it this morning.

"What did you do to me last night?" I asked in a low voice.

He turned, nodded at the juice, and went back to the stove. The scent of freshly-grilled bacon wafted into my nose. "Drink."

I folded my arms. "Not until you tell me what you did to me."

"You needed some rest. All I did was help you along."

"You knocked me out." Narrowing my eyes, I grabbed the juice and took a sip. Damn, it was good, especially after all the booze I'd consumed last night. The annoying thing about Az was that everything he did was frankly amazing.

"Not exactly," he said smoothly as he slid his spatula beneath the bacon and deposited it onto a plate. "All I did was make you relax with a small bit of my power. It released some of your anxiety. The exhaustion did everything else."

Grudgingly, I took the plate. Bacon, toast, and poached eggs, along with a little spinach. The greens stared up at me. I didn't know what the hell that was there for.

"Something wrong?" he asked as he followed me over to the table with his own plate of food.

"I'm not a big fan of spinach." I lowered myself into a chair. "But everything else looks delicious. I'm still mad at you for knocking me out, by the way… but thanks for making me breakfast. To be honest, I'm surprised you didn't go with pancakes again.

We've had it…what? Every morning for three weeks?"

"I've forgotten to think of you as a human," he said as he joined me at the table. "We need to look after your health. Protein, carbs, and greens. It's important for you to get them all. Pancakes don't have a lot of nutrients."

I arched my brows. "You can't be serious."

"Of course I'm serious." Confusion rippled across his face. "You're mortal. You can subsist on nothing but pancakes every day if you're a demon, but not if you're human."

I decided not to argue. My stomach grumbled, and the bacon smelled like heaven. Who was I to complain about a home-cooked breakfast made from the finest ingredients in all of New York? Not this girl. I gobbled up the entire plate in record time. Even the spinach.

Az didn't mention anything else about the night before. Neither did I.

After I'd eaten, we both got showered, dressed, and then headed for Brooklyn. My thoughts grew darker as the car rumbled across the bridge. Would Noah be able to tell us anything important? Or would I have to make up some crazy story to explain Serena's absence? He didn't know about supernaturals. After our run-in at the coffee shop, would he think I had something to do with her disappearance?

"You seem uneasy," Az said from where he lounged beside me on the black leather seat.

"Noah isn't very fond of me," I said with a frown. "He believes the…you know, stuff."

I glanced up at the driver, who kept his gaze forward. This really wasn't the kind of thing I wanted to talk about in front of someone else, even if he probably already knew all about it. If Az had looked me up, maybe his driver had, too. Hell, maybe the entire Legion had. A rock tumbled through my belly. It was one thing for Az to believe in me and quite another for five whole other beings to believe in me, too. Did they know? If they did, surely they wouldn't want me around much longer.

Not that I *would* be around much longer anyway. As soon as the deal was done, I was gone.

Az's gaze went hard. "I see."

I shook my head. "Maybe this was a mistake. I was so eager to talk to him about last night, to find out if he'd seen anything, that I didn't fully think things through. How will I explain all of this to him? Will he think I'm involved?"

"You let me do the talking," Az insisted.

"But..."

"Your friend's boyfriend isn't the first asshole I've had to deal with," he said with a slight smile that looked kind of evil, if I were being honest. "I'll make him understand you had nothing to do with it."

"Please tell me you don't plan on ripping out his heart if he says the wrong thing," I said dryly. "Or his spine."

The evil glint spread to his eyes. "What an excellent idea, Mia."

I rolled my eyes, trying not to focus on the way he'd said my name. Deep, melodic. Almost like a purr. Memories flashed through my mind of the night before. Az's body on top of mine. The hunger and need in his eyes.

None of it had been real. We'd been faking things so much we'd gotten confused, that was all. Combined with the alcohol, the fear and worry from the night, it only made sense we'd ended up like that. It was a classic case of "one thing led to another" and nothing more. It would never happen again.

Still, I couldn't help but flush at the memory of his lips between my thighs.

The driver saved me from my thoughts when he stopped the car outside of Serena's apartment. Az and I took the stairs together while the driver waited by the curb. My heartbeat pounded in my ears as I knocked. Moments passed in excruciating silence. Noah didn't answer.

"He's probably at work," I muttered, trying to ignore the heavy sense of doom. I didn't know Noah's schedule, but it seemed weird he'd head into the cafe while Serena was missing. Or maybe he was out in the streets, searching for her. That made more sense.

Az placed a comforting hand on my shoulder. "Try your key."

Nodding, I unlocked the door. It creaked as it swung wide. Total carnage swept through the silent apartment, and a strangled gasp of shock popped from my throat. I stumbled inside, gazing around at the destroyed apartment. Remnants of the sofa were scattered across the floor—the cotton tufts fallen like soldiers on a battlefield. Broken dishes from the kitchen joined them, and lemon-scented body wash bottles rolled out from the open bathroom door.

I stepped back and into Az's firm, unyielding chest. His heartbeat pounded against me. "Az…"

"It's all right," he murmured, squeezing my shoulder with his warm hand. "Serena wasn't here when this happened."

No. Because she'd already been taken.

"But what does this mean?" Tears filled my eyes. The reality of the danger we faced flooded in hot and fast like a river of molten lava. Az and his Legion were Princes of Hell, but they hadn't been able to stop this from happening.

"It was the killer, wasn't it?" I asked in a small voice. "Whoever took Serena came and destroyed her apartment."

"Most likely, yes." His voice was hard and edged in steel.

"But why?" I whirled to face him, searching his eyes for answers he didn't have. "What's the point of this?"

He shook his head and gazed around at the ransacked apartment. "Honestly, I have no idea. He was clearly looking for something. Maybe he thought you'd left something here?"

My heart skipped a beat. "Like what?"

"Something that smells like you," he murmured. "If he knows your scent, he can find you more easily."

Ice slid down my spine. "That's horrifying."

"Don't worry. I won't let him get you," he said. "But I think we might need to pay Serena's boyfriend a visit at his cafe. See if he went into work today. See if he's…alive."

All the blood drained from my face. "You think he might have been here when the killer broke in."

He glanced around again. "Perhaps."

And if that was the case, then Noah might be dead.

We left Serena's apartment as it was. There was little we could do there now, and if the cops got involved, we didn't want to leave any evidence behind that we were there. Next stop: *Funky Froth.* The place was as lively as ever. A line of coffee addicts stretched down the entire block. We cut past them— much to their shouted dismay—and flagged down one of the harried baristas, neither of whom were Noah.

"Is Noah in today?" Az asked in an easy voice that betrayed none of the tension I knew we both felt.

The girl cocked her head, scowling. "No, the bastard. He was scheduled to work this morning, but he never showed up. Probably with his girlfriend, like he always is. And we're fucking swamped."

"Thanks," Az said with a nod. We stepped back out onto the sidewalk before we got too many questions—and before the owner spotted me inside his cafe again.

I sucked in a breath of the smoggy city air. Deep down, I'd known we wouldn't find Noah at work. He'd been with Serena last night. If he'd seen something, he never would have escaped.

"Noah's dead, isn't he?" I asked softly, my words almost drowned out by the constant blare of taxi horns.

"It's possible."

The killer needed Serena to get to me, but Noah was nothing but collateral damage. I didn't like how the guy had turned on me, but he didn't deserve a fate like this.

"What are we going to do?" I asked, glancing up at him. "How are we going to stop the killer from claiming another life?"

His face hardened as he gazed across the Brooklyn streets. "We're going to rip out his fucking heart."

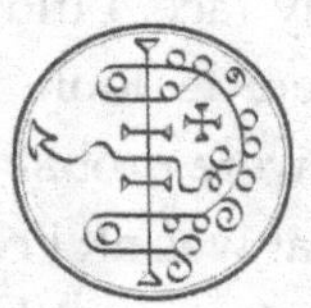

26

The day felt like it stretched out for years. I waited in the Legion's meeting room while the demons hunted down the killer. After stopping by the cafe, Az and I had returned to Serena's apartment to grab one of her shirts. The killer's actions had given him an idea. If we had her scent, we might be able to find her before the trade tonight.

No such luck.

Phenex returned first with an apologetic smile. He tried to keep me distracted with a game of poker, but my heart wasn't in it. I didn't care if my hand won or not, so I kept throwing low number cards on the table. Valac drifted in second. He didn't say a word. Just perched on a chair and frowned.

Slowly, the rest of the Legion arrived. Bael and Stolas were next, followed by Caim. Az was the last to walk through the door.

"I'm sorry, Mia." His hands hung heavily by his sides. "We haven't been able to find her."

A twinge went through my heart as I stood on shaky legs. "Then we'll get her back with the trade. We have to."

His lips lifted in the corners. "You really are brave."

The compliment caught me off guard, and a sudden heat filled my face. I didn't really know what to say or do or where to look. Definitely not at the other demons. They were probably smirking at me.

Clearing my throat was all I could manage.

"The trade it is," Caim said, striding over to the ripped map they'd managed to tape back together. Slivers of it were still missing, but the pattern was clear. The killer had claimed far too many victims, and we couldn't let him add to his collection. There was also that little issue of him running to Lucifer. If he spilled the beans about what the Legion was really up to here, the people of New York weren't the only ones at risk. The future of this world was at stake. And this all depended on whether or not I could keep my shit together during the fake trade.

No pressure, right?

"But first, you two lovebirds need to go on your date," Phenex piped in as he poked a finger at the West Village section of the map. "Rumor has it, our friendly neighborhood vampire mob boss will be dining at the Waverley Inn tonight. We've already booked you a table for eight."

I swallowed hard, avoiding Az's gaze. "Can't this wait until tomorrow? *After* we get Serena back?"

"Afraid not, love," Bael drawled in his charming

British accent. "Word is that Lars is finalizing his list of invites first thing tomorrow. That info could be wrong, of course, but we'd rather not risk it."

A date. With Az. While Serena was missing. And after what had happened between us last night. Still, I couldn't ignore the repercussions. There were human souls on the line. Actual mortal lives. And it was too late for Az to find another human date that would be convincing enough. Besides, the idea of him taking someone else made me feel a little funny.

Not jealous, *obviously*. Just…funny.

Az glanced at his thousand dollar watch and nodded. "If we want to get there on time, we need to head back to my apartment now. You'll need to get changed."

Frowning, I glanced down at my outfit. Faded, ripped jeans, a rumpled black tank, and my signature knee-high boots. Maybe he had a point. Not that I had any other options.

"Ah, about that. I have something." Phenex winked and vanished out the door. Narrowing my eyes, I gave the others suspicious glares. I didn't really like the sound of that.

"Where's he going?" I asked.

"You'll see, love," Bael said with a wink.

"You guys bought me a dress. Didn't you?"

"We love you, Mia," Caim said. "But you can't go out to a fancy dinner where you're meant to convince a rich vampire to invite you to his exclusive ball wearing…that."

"I am very comfortable."

His grin widened. "Yeah, you look it."

Az let out a low, menacing growl. "Maybe you two should go on the date. Your flirting would convince anyone."

Phenex returned just in time to break the tension. He held up a silver slip with diamonds sewn into the neckline. The rest of the material shimmered like a waterfall as it moved. My mouth dropped open. That thing must have cost...who the hell even knew? I certainly didn't. Definitely more than anything I'd ever owned, including my car.

My poor car. I'd sold it the second I'd arrived in New York.

"You want *me* to wear *that*?"

Az shot me a wolfish smile.

❦

*M*y boots paired with the dress nicely, and if anyone tried to tell me otherwise, I'd punch them in the face. Okay, I'd probably just threaten to sic my harmless pigeon on them, but I refused to wear heels. The slinky gown that cost as much as a Tesla? Fine. Heels? No fucking way. There was a supernatural murderer out there who wanted me dead. If I needed to run tonight, I had no intention of doing it teetering around on little sticks attached to the bottom of my shoes.

No thank you.

Az waited for me in the lobby of his building. He'd wanted to make a few phone calls, apparently out of my earshot. Once again, I got the sneaking suspicion he hadn't told me everything yet. Maybe he never would. Az was a puzzle. A very dangerous, annoying puzzle. And as a human, I doubted I would ever have all the pieces to solve him.

When the elevator whirred open before me, I caught sight of his suited back. The silky material stretched tight over his muscles, accentuating that raw power he carried with him everywhere. His damp dark hair curled across his neck. One strong hand clenched into a fist while the other held a phone to his ear.

Slowly, he turned to face me. The scowl on his face melted as his eyes sparked with light. He murmured a few words into the phone and then slid it out of view. I swallowed hard. Everything about him was eye-wateringly hot. The light stubble on his sharp jaw. The sleek cheekbones. The flaming crystal eyes. His hands. His body. My god, *everything*.

And he was looking at me like he wanted to eat me up. After last night, I very much wanted to let him.

No, my mind screamed at me. That had been a drunken mistake. It didn't mean anything. It would certainly never happen again. We had a determined path ahead. Save Serena. Rescue the human souls from sacrifice. Prevent Lucifer from finding out about any of it. And then I would go on my merry way.

But for tonight…I was Az's fake date.

"Hello, lovely," he said with a wicked smile curving his lips. My stomach squeezed. *Lovely*. It squeezed a second time when I spotted his dimples had made a rare appearance.

With a deep breath, I took his offered hand. Warmth flooded my belly, and a *zing* shot up my arm and into my heart. He pulled me toward him and brushed a strand of my curled hair behind my ear. I rarely did much other than let it hang loose and messy around my shoulders, but I'd made a bit of effort tonight.

To be convincing for the vampire mob boss, of course.

"You look captivating," he murmured.

"Thank you. You aren't ugly."

Smiling, he tugged me toward the door. "Our table is booked for eight. We only have fifteen minutes to get there."

I hurried after him. As soon as we climbed into the car, he stretched an arm behind my head. I could almost feel the heat of him burning against my neck. The car rumbled into drive, and soon, streetlights flared through the windows as we spun downtown.

"Relax." He massaged the back of my neck. The sudden contact made my thighs clench.

"I'm not going to relax until Serena's safe."

"Fair enough," he said. "But try not to show it, if you can. We don't want Lars to have any suspicions about us. If you're on edge all through our dinner, he'll know something is up."

"Maybe he'll think I just have date nerves."

"You're supposed to be my live-in girlfriend, Mia," he said in a delicious purr that made chills sweep across my skin. "By now, you shouldn't be so nervous."

I turned to face him, my heart throbbing. "It's not you I'm nervous about. It's Serena. It's this vampire mob boss. It's me being bait tonight. You are the last thing that would cause me nerves right now."

My lungs froze as I held my breath, waiting. He still hadn't mentioned what had happened last night. How long could he dance around it? Was he worried I would think it meant more than it had? Or was he waiting for me to bring it up? *Ha!* Hardly. Az wasn't the kind of guy to wait for anything.

"Well, then just focus on me for a couple of hours, lovely." His wicked smile burned right through me.

The car slowed to a stop outside of the Waverley Inn. The driver opened the door for the both of us, and we headed into the restaurant. Inside, the lights were dim, and the clinking of glasses mixed with a soothing folksy music filtering in from hidden speakers. The elaborately-painted walls were lined with quiet maroon booths and small pockets of tables were dotted throughout a larger room beside a bar. It screamed old money.

A brunette smiled at us from behind a podium. "Last name, please?"

"Asmodeus," my date replied with a smile.

"Ah." The girl flushed bright red and grabbed two menus from the rack behind her. Her eyes darted to his chest. "Of course. So sorry. Right this way, sir."

My eyebrows shot up my forehead as we followed her to a small corner booth. As soon as she bustled away, I couldn't help but ask. "What the hell was that?"

"This is a popular locale with the supernatural community. Most of the waitresses here are fae. She'll know who I am."

She looks like she creamed herself.

I didn't say that out loud. Frankly, I didn't blame her. As long as she kept her hands to herself.

When I opened the menu, I couldn't help but sneak a few glances around the place. It didn't take me long to find him. Lars sat in the far left corner in a booth slightly larger than ours. A few other men sat with him. Also vampires, I was assuming. They all wore their brown suits, their tattoos, and their piercings. One of them gazed across the restaurant with red-lit eyes.

Shivering, I ducked behind my menu and wondered—not for the first time—what the hell I'd gotten myself into.

"Why does he have red eyes?" I hissed at Az through the menu.

He pushed the paper down, and it took all my self-control not to grimace. We'd come here to be seen, but the idea of those vampires watching me made my skin itch.

"He's hungry," Az said in a frank tone of voice that I didn't feel properly conveyed the severity of that statement.

"Hungry," I repeated.

He turned back to his menu. "Sometimes this restaurant caters to those with varied tastebuds. Have you decided what you'd like to order?"

I swallowed down the urge to jump to my feet and get out of this restaurant as quickly as possible. They served human blood here. No way I wanted to put anything they cooked into my mouth.

"Pancakes," I said tensely. "With ice cream."

Az cracked a grin. "I'm afraid they don't do pancakes here. Mia…"

"Yes?"

"Relax." He pushed up from the table and joined me on my side of the booth. As he slung an arm around my shoulders, my heartbeat kicked up into the next gear. A moment later, his hand disappeared into the inside of his jacket, and then he fished out a small black box.

It looked like a damn *wedding ring box*.

"Whoa," I hissed. "Wait a minute. We didn't agree to take things this far."

With a chuckle, he snapped open the lid. The signet ring twinkled at me from within folds of black silk. His seal practically glowed with firelight.

"I want you to have this," he said as he took the ring from the box and pressed it into my hand. "It will help keep you safe tonight."

My heart thumped. "I thought there was nothing to worry about."

"There isn't," he said. "But just in case something goes wrong, I'd rather you hold on to that ring than me."

I squeezed my fingers around the treasure. "Okay. I'll admit. Having this does make me feel better."

"Good." His hand gripped the back of my neck, and suddenly, his lips were on mine. Chills burned across my skin as desire coiled in my gut. I fisted my free hand around his suit jacket, breathing in the scent of his flames. Hunger tore through me, matched by the intensity of his kiss.

When he pulled back, he gave me a wink. "If that doesn't convince him, I don't know what will."

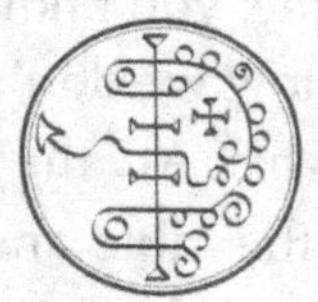

"Asmodeus." The stocky vampire mob boss strode up to our table and held out a hand toward my fake demon boyfriend. As they shook hands, I turned my eyes onto my plate. I'd ordered the halibut, and the meal had been pretty tasty until now.

After our little kiss, I'd been lulled into a false sense of security. We'd had drinks. Our food had arrived. Everything was going well. We were going to get through our dinner without a confrontation. But the vampires had decided to take notice.

"It's been a while since I've seen you around here," Lars said. "Thought you might have forgotten about those of us who don't live and breathe all things Hell's Kitchen."

"My friend here has said the same thing," Az said easily, lounging against the booth's maroon seat. "She says we don't get out of Hell's Kitchen often enough."

Lars flicked his greedy eyes my way and gave me a knowing smile. "More than *friend*, don't you think?"

"You caught me." Az flashed Lars a smile full of teeth. "Mia is my paramour. She moved in with me a couple of weeks ago."

"So I heard. So I heard," Lars murmured, turning back to Az. "What's the, you know, taste like?"

Az tsked. "You know we don't drink blood, Lars."

"I don't know why. All the other demons do." He leaned closer to the table and dropped his voice to a whisper. "Some of the fallen angels, too. Why do you Princes have to pretend you're so above it all?"

"Because we are." Az gave him a smile that masked the rage I could clearly see flickering in his eyes. Did the vampire notice it, too? "We don't need to subsist on blood like you do."

"Yes, yes," Lars muttered, flicking his eyes to Az's porterhouse steak. He wrinkled his nose. "You and your animal meat. I don't know how you can stand it. The human kind is much more enticing."

Right. So…this guy was more than a little creepy. He and his desire for human flesh was downright terrifying. And I had to sit here and pretend that I didn't care what he said.

He jerked his thumb toward me. "Why'd you end up telling this one about us? I thought it was against your rules."

Az folded his arms and gave me an appraising glance, like I was some kind of puppet on display. "She accidentally found out the other night at a party."

"Ah." Lars nodded. "I heard about your little fight."

"We've made up." Az flashed me a wicked grin. "She's all mine now."

"Oh, I bet," Lars said, licking his lips. "You've made a deal, right?"

"Absolutely."

"She just looks so delicious."

My hands drifted down to the edge of the seat. I wrapped my fingers around the leather and clung on tight. If this fucking vampire said one more creepy thing about me, I didn't think I'd have the willpower to hold back.

I'll show you delicious, asshole. When my knuckles connect with your teeth. I hope you like the taste of your bones.

"Mia," Az murmured.

I snapped my attention back onto his eyes. The ice shards had grown darker. Flames flickered deep within, calming me down. Only a little.

"Just because I'm okay with you being a demon doesn't mean I want to hear you talk about me like I'm a little trophy you won."

Az's eyes darkened even more in a warning.

But Lars just laughed. "You've got a feisty one here, old friend. Good luck."

The vampire gave me one last look and then drifted back to his table. Az waited until he was out of earshot before leaning forward with a growl.

"You couldn't wait until he walked away before you snapped at me?"

I folded my arms. "No."

Rolling his eyes, he turned back to his meal. "It's a good thing he didn't take offense. I think we may have bagged ourselves an invite. So just play nice for the rest of our dinner."

"Great," I replied as I stabbed my halibut with my fork. "I'm really looking forward to the ball."

"Mia."

"What? You want me to play nice? I just said something positive."

"With sarcasm."

I gave him a sweet smile and dug into my food. The sooner I ate this halibut, the sooner we could get back to *Infernal*.

The sooner we could save Serena.

❦

"Here's the plan," Bael said as he paced from one end of the map to the other. He held a little pointer stick and kept stabbing it at the shredded page to accentuate his words. "The Legion, minus Az, are going to head to the warehouse now. We'll find some good places to stay out of sight."

"And wait for the fun to start." Phenex grinned.

Valac folded his arms and leaned back in his chair, his bleached white hair falling into his eyes. "We'll check for cameras before we go in. The killer could be monitoring the place. If he knows we're there, he'll never show up with Serena."

I grimaced. "The only thing I ask is that you don't do *anything* to tip him off. If he knows we plan to trap him…"

"We'll be careful," Valac said, meeting my gaze. A shiver went down my spine at the pure darkness within his eyes. Valac had seen some shit in his life. I couldn't help but wonder what, even though I knew it would probably scar me for life.

What could scare a demon?

"You'll start your shift," Caim added. "Get ready with the girls. Be prepared to go out and let the patrons see you. But just before you're set to go into your birdcage, leave through the back door and go straight to the warehouse. We think he'll be in the crowd watching for you."

"If you hear anyone following you, don't freak out, love," Bael added. "It might be him, but that's okay. He'll be checking to see if any of us are with you."

"And, as much as I hate it, we won't be," Az said as a muscle in his jaw ticked. "But I'll be keeping an eye on you from the sky. It's a cloudy night. He won't know I'm there."

"Okay," I breathed, glancing around at the six of them. "Anything else?"

"You don't have to worry, Mia." Phenex clapped a hand on my back. "We've got you. You're one of us now."

"And we protect our own like we protect our own lives," Stolas murmured as he stepped up beside Phenex. Caim edged in, along with Bael. Valac even joined. The five demons formed a protective circle around me, and a low chant spilled from their lips.

"One fight at a time," they shouted in unison.

My heart thumped as a strange sense of belonging

washed over me. It had been a very long time since I'd felt this way, like I was part of something else. Part of a *family* almost.

A family of demons, sure, but that didn't matter. All that mattered was that it truly felt as if they were on my side.

In another week, this would all be over. No more demon contracts or vampire mob bosses or weird supernatural parties where people got killed. But no more Caim or Stolas. No more Phenex and Valac. No more Bael.

And no more Az.

Before they could see my unshed tears, I blinked them away. How embarrassing would that be, right?

As the Legion shuffled away, Az stepped in close. He captured my eyes with his. "You ready?"

"Not really," I admitted. "I feel like a million things could go wrong."

"That's life, Mia," he said. "But as long as you trust us, you don't have to live in fear."

"I know," I said, meaning it. "I could see it in their eyes. They won't let anything happen to me."

"No, they won't." He wound his arms around me and pulled me against his chest. "But more importantly, *I* won't. I will not let anyone in this world harm a hair on your head. Do you understand me?"

Swallowing hard, I nodded. "Actually, I think I do."

✤

he dressing room buzzed with activity. The dancers swirled through the space, along with the scent of sweet perfume, pizza, and chocolate cake. They were filling up their stomachs before they took to the cages, and I joined in with great abandon. I hadn't been able to stomach much at the restaurant.

"You look confused and concerned," Priyanka said as she twisted my hair into an elaborate braid. "Everything alright with Az?"

"Not really," I admitted, careful with my words. I wasn't sure how much she knew about our relationship or our plans to save Serena from a supernatural serial killer tonight. "It all kind of started off as a…joke."

"A meaningless fling," she said with a knowing smile. "And let me guess. You've developed feelings."

I flushed. "I don't know if I'd say that."

"And you don't know if he feels the same." She tightened the braid, spinning the strands together. "Az is difficult to read, so I understand how you might be confused."

"It's more complicated than that." I sighed.

"Because you're in a fake relationship?" She arched a brow when I shot her an anxious glance. Chuckling, she shook her head. "You forget. The most important thing to Az is loyalty. Every single person who works for him is in his circle of trust. He tells us everything, including what's been going on with you."

I should have known. Of course he wouldn't have kept any of it to himself. These dancers were part of his family, same as his Legion. But if they knew about our fake relationship, then surely they knew about…

About me.

I pressed my lips together. "He's really told you everything?"

"Most of it, I'm guessing."

I closed my eyes. As understanding as he'd been about my past, I hated the idea he'd discussed it with anyone other than me. Those were my skeletons. Not his. My shadows. My nightmares.

"I wish he hadn't done that," I whispered.

Priyanka's hands slowed. "Why is that?"

"Because some of that…it wasn't his to share."

"You mean your past." Her fingers got to work once again. She was almost finished with the braid now. Just in time to end this awkward conversation. "He didn't tell us about that. We got an anonymous letter the other day, slid beneath the door while the club was shut. One of the girls found it, took it to the Legion. Az was so mad it looked like he would burn the whole place down."

"Wait, what?" All the blood rushed from my face, pooling in my gut like a stubborn rock.

"He wouldn't hear a word against you. Said that if anyone had a problem with you and your past, they could get the hell out."

My eyes flipped open, and our gazes caught in the mirror. "Az said that?"

She gave me a solemn nod. "He certainly did. And so we all stayed. If you say you didn't do it, that's enough for us."

I was literally speechless. Not just because of Az's

reaction to that letter but because of *theirs*. These people barely knew me. I shouldn't fit in, even if it sometimes felt like I did. They were demons, fae, werewolves, and vamps. I was a scrawny little human with bad memories, an empty bank account, and a pigeon I'd named Hendrix.

Tears filled my eyes. I couldn't stop them this time. My own damn family hadn't believed me, but these supernaturals did. For the past two years, all I'd wanted was an escape from accusing stares and hastily-made assumptions. And somehow, I had found it. In the most unexpected place imaginable.

In a week, I would have to leave it all behind. It wasn't like I could actually stay in this life…could I? Would Az even want me if I decided I'd like to stay? We'd made a deal. Soon, that deal would be done.

I would have to say goodbye to this place and these people.

Unless…unless I was wrong about how Az felt about me. He'd defended me, viciously so. Maybe I was wrong to think last night hadn't been real.

After all was said and done, maybe I actually could find happiness here.

But first, I had to save Serena.

28

Just before we were set to go on stage, I ducked into a doorframe and watched the other girls go. Priyanka gave me a nod and a thumbs up before disappearing into the club. The thumping bass pounded against my feet. This was it. The moment I'd been waiting for all day. My heart thundered so hard in my chest, I could feel the aftershocks in my neck.

With a deep breath, I pushed out the back door and turned my feet west. The warehouse was only two avenues over, near the piers. My footsteps echoed through the quiet streets, and the closer I grew to the river, the fewer pedestrians I passed.

Az was in the sky, watching me. The rest of the demons were waiting inside the warehouse. They were with me every step of the way, even if I couldn't see them. As long as I remembered I wasn't alone, I could do this.

For Serena.

I stopped on the street corner and gazed across the avenue at the nondescript warehouse that squatted on the next block. Banks of windows were blacked out, and rust splashed across the metal rolling doors. Tipping back my head, I took note of the roof, just in case. It was four stories high and flat on the top. A good place for Az to land.

A crack beneath the doors spilled dim light onto the pavement. With a deep breath, I pulled it up, wincing as the metal screeched into the night. I stepped inside just as the door crashed down behind me. Flickering fluorescent bulbs barely illuminated the expansive space. The entire place was empty, except for a few plastic sheets that hung from the ceiling, blocking my view of the far left corner.

My heartbeat picked up speed. There was nothing in here. No place for the Legion to hide.

Where the hell are they?

Sweat beaded on my brow. If they couldn't find somewhere to wait for me, they would have come back to the club to warn me, right? They wouldn't have just let me wander into a killer's warehouse all alone with no backup.

But what if something had happened? What if they hadn't been able to get to me in time?

I took a step back toward the door.

"Mia," a familiar voice drawled from behind the plastic sheets. Frowning, I whipped toward it and narrowed my eyes, trying to make out the vague form through the sheer material. Was that one of the Legion? I recognized his voice, but...no. It definitely wasn't Caim or Phenex. Maybe Valac? I hadn't spoken to him much.

The sheet rippled as the man pushed it aside. Noah stepped into the warehouse wearing black sweats and zero glasses. His green eyes gleamed beneath the overhead bulbs. Confusion pounded against my skull as I stared at him. Wait. Why was he here? Had he gotten a note from the killer, too?

Shit. He probably had no idea what he'd just walked into.

"Noah," I said, rushing across the floor. "You need to get out of here. Now."

A smile flashed across his face. "I'm surprised you were actually brave enough to show. You've run from everything else in your life. I thought you'd run from this, too. A pity, almost, that you chose guts this one time. You'd be better off if you'd fled."

My lungs rattled as I gaped at him. Thoughts flicked through my mind almost too fast for me to comprehend them. Noah wasn't here because the killer had lured him into his trap. He was here because…

"You can't be," I breathed as I took a step back. "Not you. You're just…you're *human*."

He was a nerdy coffee-addict hipster who had swept my best friend off her feet.

Chuckling, he reached behind his back and pulled out a very, very sharp knife. The fluorescent light gleamed against the serrated edge. Specks of blood clung to the metal. I swallowed down a hard lump in my throat.

"I was shocked when Serena's useless roommate walked right through Infernal's doors without any trouble at all. At first, it annoyed me, Mia. But then I saw it for the opportunity it was." He flipped the knife in his hands. "You would finally give me what I have wanted for decades. A way to find out *exactly* what Asmodeus and his Legion are up to in his fucking club."

My heart thumped. "Seems a little over the top, don't you think? You could probably just ask him."

Sneering, he edged a little closer. "Asmodeus would never tell me a goddamn thing. Don't you know who the hell I am?"

"Um. Actually? No." I shrugged, trying my best to appear nonchalant. I needed to keep him talking long enough for the Legion to get here. And then we'd grab Serena and go. Was he keeping her behind that plastic sheet?

"My name is Raphael," he growled.

I blinked at him. "Like the ninja turtle?"

"No." He fisted his hands, and anger poured off his body in waves. "Like the *fallen angel*. How could you have never heard of me? Don't they teach you humans about us in church?"

"I've only been a few times, and I never really paid attention." I folded my arms and lifted an eyebrow. Somehow, my body remained far more calm than my mind did. Inside, I was screaming to run. "So tell me. What's your plan here? You're going to give me Serena, and in exchange, I give myself up to you. And then what? How does that tell you what's going on inside the club?"

A wolfish smile flashed across his face. "You'll see.

Az will arrive any minute now. He won't be able to help himself. I sent the Legion off on a wild goose chase, and he'll soon realize you're facing the killer alone."

Realization pounded through my veins. "You want him to show up."

"Now you're beginning to understand."

"But why? I don't understand." I shook my head. "If he's the one you wanted all this time, why do all this? You had a chance to face him in the alley. Why'd you run?"

He scowled. "That was Michael. Not me."

"Michael?" I started to ask, but then stopped. "Oh. There's two of you."

"Four," he corrected. "Though we don't claim Gabriel or Suriel as ours. They want different things than we do."

I arched a brow. "Care to explain?"

"Gabriel and Suriel both want to save humanity from Hell." His eyes glittered as he took another step closer. "Michael and I, on the other hand, have seen the light. Lucifer needs to win this game, and I'll do anything it takes to ensure it. That means killing Asmodeus, his Legion, and anyone who sides with him. Just like all those other supernaturals out there who are trying to save souls. Lucifer doesn't know what the Legion have been doing, but I do. And I intend to prove it tonight. When Asmodeus comes to rescue you."

All the blood rushed from my face. Of course this wasn't about me. It never had been. It was about something far greater. The future of humanity, of this world. Az had been careful, but he'd still caught the notice of his enemies. Noah and Michael had been killing any supernatural that sided with him. And if Az showed up tonight and was unable to stop Noah…erm, Rafael…the fallen angels would take this information straight to Lucifer.

That couldn't happen.

So how exactly was I going to save Serena, save my own damn self, *and* stop this crazy angel guy from running to the King of Evil?

I'll tell you how. I had no fucking clue.

The door thundered open and Az ducked inside. The moment he saw me, he crossed the floor and threw himself in front of me. His entire body trembled as he glared at the fallen angel who stood before us, ripples of shadows flooding off his skin.

"Mia, get out of here," he said in a low growl that sent skitters of fear—and maybe a little bit of desire— down my back. He sounded like he wanted to rip Noah's head off. That probably wasn't far off the mark. The only way out of this was for him to take his heart.

"Not so fast," Noah-Rafael said, fisting his hands. "You and Mia have signed a contract, have you not?"

Az tensed. "What the hell does that have to do with anything, Rafael?"

Rafael smiled. "Mia, tell Asmodeus you're breaking your end of the contract. You will no longer fulfill your duties."

"What? No," I shot back.

"Don't do it," Az warned, edging further in front of me.

"Mia," Rafael said. "If you don't do what I say, I will kill Serena. Michael has her behind that sheet. Do as I say, or she will die."

I swallowed hard, horror pounding like a drum against the back of my head. My eyes swam as I stared at the angel's glittering smile. So much anger. So much hate. No wonder he'd been kicked out of the afterlife. And now, he wanted me to break my deal.

I wasn't an idiot. I knew what that meant. If I broke the deal, I'd lose my soul.

With a heavy sigh, I closed my eyes. Serena needed me to do this. She'd die if I didn't. I had no idea what would happen to me next, but it didn't matter. Not when her life was on the line.

"Mia, don't," Az said, his voice rising to a shout.

"I break my end of the deal," I whispered.

My entire body tensed as I waited for something to happen. The horrible excruciating moments stretched by. When at least five minutes had passed, I cracked open one eye. Az stood before me, his hands hanging heavily by his sides.

"Is that it?" I asked with a frown. "I thought something would happen."

Rafael's vicious chuckle echoed off the warehouse walls. "Something *should* have happened, Mia McNally. If you'd actually made a deal with a demon."

"We did make a deal," Az muttered. "I ripped it up."

Rafael stepped closer, narrowing his eyes. "To save her soul. You decided you didn't want to risk losing her to Lucifer, and so you destroyed your contract.

Because you aren't who you once were, are you, Asmodeus? You've become something else. Something far too mortal."

A growl erupted from Az's lips. My heartbeat flickered in my neck as I glanced back and forth between them. I wasn't entirely sure how to take this news, but that didn't matter right now. I needed to get to Serena before Rafael ordered his angel friend to kill her.

Az launched toward Rafael just as the heavy warehouse doors flung wide. The Legion rushed across the floor, shouting in anger as they raised their swords high. I took one second to gape at five sword-wielding demons before throwing myself toward the plastic sheet at the back of the warehouse.

Rafael was so busy focusing on Az that he didn't notice me.

My feet thundered against the concrete floor. When I reached the sheet, I threw it to the side and fell to my knees beside a bound Serena. The other angel was nowhere to be seen, but I didn't dare stick around and wait for him to return. With a grunt, I wound my arms around her trembling body and dragged her back into the warehouse.

She peered up at me with bleary eyes. Her face was beet red, and her hair hung in messy clumps around her shoulders. But she was alive, and she wasn't bleeding. Thank god.

"Serena." I knelt beside her and got to work on the knots around her wrists, ignoring the total chaos raging on behind us. "Are you okay?"

She yelled against the sock in her mouth. Heart

hurtling into my throat, I whirled just in time to see Rafael rush toward us with anger flashing in his eyes. I braced myself, wishing I had a damn sword myself.

Az slammed into Rafael's back with a roar, knocking him down onto the concrete. Rafael rolled onto his back and launched a kick into Az's chest, but Az leapt to the side just in time.

Rafael panted as he glared at the Prince of Hell. And then he vanished into mist.

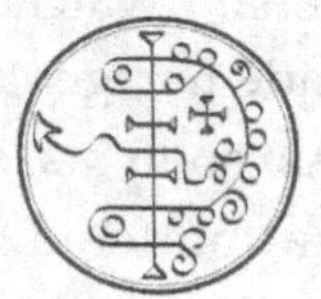

29

"**M**ia!" Az rushed toward me, lifted me into his arms, and then squeezed me so tightly I thought my ribs might shatter. The scent of flames whorled around me as shadows pulsed against my skin. For a moment, I let myself give in to the steady, firm sensation of his body against mine.

He cares, I internally whispered. *He actually cares.*

But then I forced myself to pull back and climb out of his arms. "You can't let him get away. He's going to run straight to Lucifer and tell him everything. This was a test, to prove you're saving souls. Now he knows you've turned your back on Hell."

"Shit." Az ran a hand down his face. "I should have seen this coming. Rafael has always had it out for me."

"He might not have gotten far yet, boss," Phenex said, jogging toward us and hefting his glittering sword onto his shoulder. "We don't know how far he can travel with his vanishing power. It might not be much. We should search the streets. See if we can hunt him down before he leaves for Hell."

Az nodded and gave me one last squeeze. "I agree. You two wait here."

The Legion thundered out of the warehouse, leaving me with Serena. I watched them go and then knelt back down beside her, gently removing the sock from her mouth. As soon as she had use of her tongue, she let out a muttered string of curses that would have made a sailor blush.

"I should have known not to trust a dumbass guy who seemed perfect on paper." She ripped the ropes off her legs and tossed them across the floor. "Cute and nice. Kind to animals. With a ridiculous amount of shared interests. It was all pretend, the whole time. And you want to know why?"

I sat back on my heels and gave her a sad smile. "Why's that?"

"Because I work at the law firm," she spat. "Asmodeus is one of our clients. Noah…Rafael. He thought he could get access to some of Az's private contracts. I caught him looking through my drawers a few times. Thought it was odd, but he always had a good excuse for it." Growling, she shook her head. "I should have known. And dammit, I wish he'd tried this shit during a full moon. The things I could have done…"

"I'm so sorry," I whispered. "At least you're safe now."

The watery look in her eyes shook me to my core. Serena never cried. "You came for me."

I gave her a weak smile. "Of course I did. You think I was going to let him lay a fucking hand on you?"

"But you're human. You could have died."

"I don't care." I threw my arms around her neck and buried my face in her lemon-scented hair. "I would do anything for you, Serena. Anything."

"Well, isn't this a sweet reunion?" Rafael's harsh voice rang out in the silence.

My heart hurtled into my throat. Tensing my entire body, I slowly unwound my arms from Serena's neck and turned to face the fallen angel. This time, he wasn't alone. Another figure stood beside him. Even without the mask, I recognized him in an instant. Tall, muscled, rippling with power. Twin pits of anger stared out of his sleet grey eyes, boring right into my soul. The killer from the alley.

I shivered.

Slowly, Serena rose to her feet and stood beside me. It wasn't a full moon, but she'd still be strong enough to put up a fight now that she knew that we faced danger. Before, Noah-Rafael had likely caught her off guard. She wouldn't make the same mistake of trusting him again.

Still, it wouldn't hurt if a few of my demon friends decided to join the party.

How long would they search the streets before returning to the warehouse? We needed to keep these assholes busy and distracted until the Legion showed.

"I'm *glad* you came back," Serena said with a smile that showed the sharp points of her canines. She rarely liked to flash them around. It made it obvious she was not at all human. "Means you'll get to experience what it's like to face a very angry werewolf."

Rafael rolled his eyes. "We're immortal angels, little wolf. Your scratches will barely harm us, let alone kill us. Nothing can."

I wet my lips and swallowed down the words that threatened to pop from my throat. There was actually *one* thing we could do to stop an angel. Take his heart. Did Serena know?

"Why exactly are you here again? Don't you have something better to do?" I asked with a faux bravado that would make Broadway proud. "I thought you wanted to run to Lucifer with your little news."

Rafael and Michael exchanged grins. "I would never walk away from a chance to sacrifice two corrupt souls to Lucifer."

Corrupt? Excuse me?

"If you think *I'm* corrupt, then maybe you should take a good look in the mirror," I replied, trying not to panic when the two angels began to cross the floor. They pulled matching daggers from their waistbands and grinned. Where the hell were the demons?

I lowered my voice to a tense whisper. "Serena, I know you're angry and you want to destroy Noah, but…do you think maybe we should run?"

"Absolutely."

"Is there a door behind the plastic sheet?"

"Yep."

"Think we'll make it?"

"Nope."

"Oh, good. So….are we going to try anyway?"

She nodded. "Now."

We whirled on our feet and ran. I made it about six steps before a large beefy hand closed around the neckline of my dress. He tugged me back, and I fell onto my ass. I scrabbled back onto my feet and jumped sideways when Rafael swung for me again.

Out of the corner of my eye, Serena threw a punch into Michael's gut. I didn't even try to hold back a smug smile when a groan erupted from his throat. The knife flashed in Rafael's hand again, dragging my attention back onto his twisted face. He looked tormented, broken. As if the world had once crashed down on his head, and this was the only thing he knew how to do.

Not that I could let myself feel sorry for an evil angel who had killed at least a hundred supernaturals in New York City. One who was currently trying to stab me in the heart.

His dagger loomed before my eyes. With a laugh, he slashed it at my face. Terror charged through me, quick and hot like lightning. Az's face flashed in the back of my mind. Those slats of ice in his eyes. The strong, unyielding jaw. The thought of him steeled my nerves and urged me not to give up.

With a sharp cry, I dodged back, but the knife made contact with my arm. It sliced through my skin, almost to the bone.

A *rip* of pure, unadulterated power hurtled from my chest and slammed into the attacking angel. Rafael's eyes widened as the force launched him into the air. He flew across the warehouse and landed by the rolling doors.

Rafael let out a tense laugh as he climbed to his

feet, his eyes unfocused and dazed. "Do you *really* want to fight me, Mia McNally? You're in league with a group of demons who care more about themselves than anything else. Your life will always be in danger as long as you're with Az. Lucifer is going to find out about this, and he'll torture you for eternity. Maybe you should rethink which side you're on."

The rolling doors shuddered up to the ceiling, and Az stepped inside with shadows pulsing around his body. Fury burned in his eyes as he swung his sword at Rafael's neck. The angel rolled to the side, and the sword hit the concrete ground.

Az slowly stalked toward him. "I told you to stay away from Mia."

The danger in his voice sent tremors through my body. Or maybe that was the shock of my wound finally hitting me. My arm burned. Pain flared deep within me, pulsing like a repeated punch against my bones. Slowly, I slid to the floor and caught myself with my palms.

Michael blinked out of the warehouse just as Caim and Phenex rushed inside. Rafael glanced behind him, saw his partner had fled, let out an annoyed growl, and vanished into mist. I sagged toward the ground. The fallen angels were gone. Again. Hopefully, it was for good.

"Ow," I said as Serena fell to my side, wrapping her hand around my wound to staunch the blood. "That really fucking hurt."

"Asmodeus," Serena shouted over her shoulder. "Mia's losing a lot of blood. She needs healing. Can you do the...?"

Dimly, I realized she hadn't finished her question. That was odd. What was that all about? Did it have anything to do with the things Az kept secret? Didn't really make much sense. Why would he want to hide that he could heal people?

Could he heal people?

That would probably be useful right about now. The warehouse began to blur, like grey smudges of paint on a canvas. Darkness hovered in the corners of my eyes. The sound of music filled my head. It was very pretty. So pretty that I didn't feel the pain anymore.

I opened my mouth to tell Az I liked it. And that I liked him. He needed to know. I'd never told him, and I didn't want to walk out of his life before giving him the truth.

I was falling for a Prince of Hell.

The world went black.

30

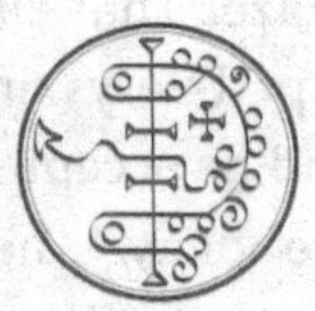

A pigeon cooed in my ear. My eyes flew wide. Heart hammering, I struggled to make sense of my surroundings. Darkness filled a room that smelled achingly familiar, like the scent of fire after a storm. A sense of calm settled over me when I realized where I was.

Az's room.

He'd taken me here after I'd passed out from my stab wound.

I sucked in a sharp breath and flipped back my shirt. My skin was mottled and bruised, but the stab wound was...gone. There wasn't even a scar from where the dagger had sliced through me. Heart thundering, I thought back to what Serena had said just before I'd passed out. Az had healed me, hadn't he? I might feel like shit right now, but I would live.

Groaning, I climbed out of bed and padded into the living room. Az was on the sofa with an open book propped in his lap. The sight of him clenched my belly. He looked so normal like this. So non-threatening. And yet I knew he would rip apart an angel just to keep me safe.

"Az," I said.

He glanced up, and his eyes stormed across me. For a minute, I could do nothing other than stand frozen beneath his gaze. That *zing* went through me again, hot and sharp. Every single part of me felt bared before him. And he accepted it all.

"I'm glad you're okay," he murmured before patting the sofa. "Come sit. We need to talk."

My stomach flipped over. Talk? That sentence never ended in anything good. Especially when it came to relationships. Of course, Az was a demon. He was above the stupid games of mortal men. Probably. Unless I'd read him totally wrong. His fury toward Rafael had made it seem like he cared for me as far more than just a fake girlfriend, but what if I'd jumped to conclusions? Maybe he didn't see me as special at all.

But he ripped up our contract...

I shuffled over to the sofa and settled down beside him. When he stared into my eyes, another shot of that *zing* went through my core. Surely he felt that, too. Didn't he?

What did it mean?

He ground his teeth and glanced away. "Rafael is a bastard, but he was right about one thing. As long as I'm in your life, you'll be in danger."

I stiffened. "He was just saying that to scare me. It didn't work, Az."

"No." He shook his head. "Angels don't lie, not

even fallen ones. Anything he said to you was the truth. Look at what you've been through in the few weeks you've known me. You've almost been killed. More than once."

My heart squeezed tight. Tears filled my eyes, and I glanced away. "Yeah, but as soon as you take care of Noah…Rafael, I mean…all of this will be over. I won't be in danger anymore."

"Mia," he said with a hollow sigh. "Rafael and Michael are on their way to Hell. They'll tell Lucifer about all of this. You can't be near me when he comes to New York."

"You think he'll come here?" I asked in a small voice. Despite everything I'd said, the idea of Lucifer waltzing through New York City made my gut twist into knots. He was, you know, *Satan*. What was to stop him from outright killing people in the streets? As far as I could tell, nothing but that stupid game he was playing for souls.

"Most certainly," Az said, catching my hand in his. Shivers stormed through me. Even while he said I needed to stay away, he pulled me in. "It will take a week for Rafael and Michael to reach Hell, and then another week for them to return. Lucifer will want to see what me and my Legion are up to with his own eyes. And if you are in my life when he gets here, he will want to dissect you. What kind of human would motivate Asmodeus to destroy a soul contract?"

I loosed a shuddering breath. "Okay, well. We'll figure that out when it happens. Two weeks, right? That gives us some time."

"No, Mia." He pulled his hand from mine. "We

have enough time to stop the soul sacrifices, but after that, we need to go our separate ways just as we originally planned. We might even need to draw up a new contract. One I don't destroy. It might trick Lucifer into believing me."

Pain ripped through my heart. "But you said angels don't lie. So anything they tell him, he'll know it's true."

"I might be able to convince him that they were mistaken and nothing more. As long as we have a real contract in place." He closed his eyes. "I didn't want to have to do this again. Another contract. It means your soul will be on the line."

"Not if I fulfill my part of the bargain," I whispered to him. "And I will. I'm not going to walk away from this now. Away from you."

"After the ball, you'll *have* to."

"Why?" I fisted my hands and pushed up from the couch, irritation boiling in my gut. "Because I'm human and too weak? Because you don't think I'm brave enough to face Lucifer? All this time, it seemed like you saw that I'm more than that. After everything I've been through, I have a skin of steel. You said it yourself. And now you want to throw me away like..."

Like it meant nothing.

He stood with flickering eyes. "I think you're brave as hell, Mia, but you don't know what you're asking to face. You know what he will do to you? Do you have any idea? He will peel your skin off your bones and feast on it while your heart still beats. He will find every single soul you love, and he will do the same to them. Right before your eyes. You think you know about demons because of me. Because of Caim and Phenex and the others. But you have *no idea*."

Shuddering, I took a step back. Images flashed in my mind. Tormented souls screaming. Bright gleaming eyes full of hate. Az was right. I kept thinking of Lucifer as someone like him. Dangerous and violent when provoked...but kind and heroic beneath all the shadows.

"But you're nothing like that," I finally said. "None of you are."

His jaw rippled as he glanced away, his eyes lingering on the brilliant city lights beyond the windows. "I used to be more of a demon than I am now. If you knew the things I've done, you would not look at me the way you do."

Taking a deep breath, I took his hand and stepped in so close that he had no choice but to meet my gaze. There was turmoil in his eyes. So much turmoil. "I don't care what's in your past, Az. Whoever you were, it's not who you are now. I will face Lucifer by your side if you'll let me."

For a moment, I thought he'd changed his mind. He dropped his forehead to mine and breathed me in the same way I breathed in him. Our noses barely grazed, just enough for the *zing* to rip through me again. Somehow, this demon had gotten past my walls and into my soul in a way I'd never expected. Meeting Lucifer terrified me. But I'd do it if that was what it took to stay in this life.

He dragged a finger across the edge of my jaw,

and I shuddered against him. Need flickered in my core. I pressed up onto my toes and wound my arms around his neck. His lips met mine for a fleeting second.

And then he pulled away. He stumbled back, eyes wide.

"I can't," he grunted out, twisting away from me and storming over to the windows. His body transformed into a dark silhouette against the city lights. "Mia, I can't. He will destroy you."

I squeezed my eyes shut, but a few tears escaped down my cheeks. Dammit. I couldn't let him see me cry like this. Quickly, I brushed them away.

"You're an asshole," I whispered.

"For keeping you safe?" He whipped back toward me, danger turning his eyes a shade darker than they normally were. "If that makes me an asshole, then so be it."

I glanced away.

"Tomorrow morning, I will start hunting down a job for you," he said bitterly. "Something normal where you sit at a desk and type shit into a computer. I know a few people. My recommendation will be enough to secure you the role. And then I'll find you an apartment. Somewhere safe. Under a different name. That way Lucifer can't track you down when he gets here. Even if we part ways, he'll try to find you." He nodded to himself, as if that confirmed everything. "We'll need to get you some new documents to go along with the name. You won't be Mia McNally for a while."

"You can't be serious," I whispered.

"I've never been more serious about anything in my life," he said. "In fact, I should ship you out of the country. Send you somewhere far away from New York. Hong Kong, perhaps. Rome or Greece."

My mouth dropped open and I squeezed my arms around my chest. "Az, no. Please don't do this. I can't move to a foreign country alone. I don't know the language. Or the culture. Or *anything*."

Tears spilled down my face. It had only been a few hours ago that I'd been imagining a future with both him and everyone at *Infernal*. And now I was being tossed out the door. I knew Az was only doing it to protect me, but it still hurt.

This had been the first time in two years I'd met someone who didn't believe the worst about me. A lot of someones. I'd found somewhere I finally fit in. A place where I didn't have to hide. Now it was being ripped away from me. Because of the King of Hell.

His expression softened, but the determined set of his shoulders didn't flinch. "All right. I'll find you somewhere in New York, but only on one condition. You have to swear to stay away from me. After the ball, we can never see each other again."

We were prisoners trapped inside a gilded cage. Scowling, I strode from one end of Az's ebony penthouse to the other while Serena curled up on the sofa reading a book. Hendrix perched on the table where I'd left him a bowl of breadcrumbs. Az was in his bedroom, making phone calls. And two guards—Valac and Bael—stood on the other side of the single door to prevent any unwanted visitors.

Or a hasty escape by yours truly.

My skin bounced like it wanted to jump off my body and run. We'd been told we couldn't leave unless accompanied. And I hated every minute of it.

Serena sighed and set down her book. She was re-reading *A Dance with Dragons* for the millionth time. The TV show hadn't satisfied her thirst for finding out what had happened to Jon Snow, and so she read the series over and over again, waiting for the next book to come out. Once Serena got her mind on something, she never let it go.

"Can you stop pacing?" she asked in a plaintive voice. "You're making me nervous."

"I hate being trapped in here." I stopped and caught the haunted look in her eyes. "How are you doing? You haven't said much since last night."

She pressed her lips together, hugging the book to her chest. "I feel like an idiot. Noah was using me the whole time. Why didn't I see it sooner? Looking back on our relationship, it makes so much sense. He was always so interested in my job…"

"Serena, you can't blame yourself for this. You weren't being an idiot. He actually seemed like a nice guy for a while." Until he didn't.

She sighed and shook her head. "I knew something was off when he got weird about you and your past. We had a huge fight about it, and then he completely turned it all around and said he'd never once doubted you. That should have been a red flag. Good sex makes my brain fall out of my skull."

"Tell me about it," I muttered.

Serena sat up a little straighter on the sofa. "Um, excuse me? Don't tell me that you and…" She whipped her head toward the closed bedroom door, and heat crept into my cheeks. I hadn't had a chance to tell her about my, erm, *encounter* with Asmodeus. She probably wouldn't approve. I wouldn't if I were her.

She popped up from the couch and pointed a finger at me. "That look. You're embarrassed. I *knew* it. I absolutely knew it. My god, Mia. You had sex with a Prince of Hell."

"To be fair, he isn't one of the *evil* Princes of Hell."

Snorting, she laughed. "So how was it?"

"What do you think?"

"I'm guessing you got an answer about what his dick looks like."

"It definitely does not have a weird spade demon thing on the end of it." I grinned back, relaxing from the familiar banter between us. It had been a terrible past few days, but Serena was alive and I was alive, and that was all that truly mattered.

The door clicked open, and Az stepped into the room. My smile died as the flames in my cheeks grew hotter. I really, *really* hoped he hadn't overheard our conversation. How mortifying.

Serena cleared her throat and plopped back onto the sofa. She grabbed her blanket and hid behind the book, clearly abandoning me in a sea of awkwardness. I shifted from one foot to the other and eventually settled on joining her. There was nothing left to say. Az had made up his mind, and I had too much pride to beg him to reconsider.

"How's Jon doing?" I asked Serena.

"Oh," she said sadly. "He's about to get stabbed. I hate this part."

I shot her a fond smile. "Then why do you keep reading it over and over again?"

"Because your favorite books burrow their way into your heart." Her eyes turned to the page, and awkward silence filled the penthouse. Az still hadn't said a word, and he'd made no indication he'd overheard my conversation with Serena. Of course, that didn't mean he hadn't. Demons had better hearing than humans did.

A heavy knock sounded on the door, rescuing me from humiliation. Az growled and stalked toward it, yanking it open. Phenex stood on the other side with a slip of paper between his fingers. He held it up, waving it in the air.

"Looks like someone got an invitation to the Covenant Ball." He craned his head over Az's shoulders and waggled his eyebrows at me. "Your little date worked."

Relief and panic tangled together in my gut. This was a good thing. It was exactly what we needed. Now we could get inside that ball so Az could do his thing and save some souls. Great, right? Except it was probably going to be pretty dangerous. And it would be the last time we would ever see each other.

Az took the invite and nodded. "Thanks, Phenex, but I'm not sure this is a good thing. I'm having second thoughts about this."

Phenex frowned and ducked inside the penthouse. The door slammed shut behind him. "Second thoughts? But we've been working toward this for weeks."

"It's too dangerous," he said, stalking toward the dining table and tossing the invite on top. "Mia is a human. What if something goes wrong? She needs to go back to normal life before we get her killed."

"Um, excuse me?" I strode over to the table and snatched up the invite. "You honestly can't be backing out of this now. This whole fake relationship was so that you could get inside the Covenant Ball. It's why you hired me. It's why you made that deal."

"I know." He turned to give me a tortured look. "I never should have put you in this position to begin with."

"Nope. Absolutely not. I'm not letting you back out of this now." I waved the invite at him. "There are human souls on the line, and this is your only way in."

"I don't want to put your life in any more danger."

"I don't care," I snapped back. "We said we were going to do this thing, to *save* people, and so we will." With a glare, I whipped toward Phenex. "You agree with me, right?"

"Ah." He shifted uneasily on his feet, running his fingers through his red hair. "I think maybe I don't want to get in the middle of…I, oh hey, Serena, what are you reading there?"

Phenex drifted off, leaving me and Az glaring at each other. Again. We seemed to do this a lot. With a frown, I folded my arms and met his gaze. He could kick me out of his club and his life. He could hide me away with a fake name in an apartment far away from here. But I wasn't going to turn my back on all of this now.

"We have to save them," I said.

"Mia…"

"We'll have the Legion with us. I'll get out of the ball before anything goes down." I took another step closer to him, steeling my nerves. "As soon as we get inside, I'll leave. You'll stop the sacrifices and save a bunch of souls. And then we can part ways, just like you want."

He winced and flicked his gaze away. "You don't know what you're asking to do."

"Yes, I do." My heart pounded as he reached out, and his fingers grazed mine. "It's just one more fake date, Az. One more, and then all of this will be done."

"You'll do everything I ask you to do?" he asked insistently. "You'll listen to me if I tell you to run?"

I nodded. "Of course."

"All right." His brilliant ice-blue eyes slid shut. "We only have a few days until the ball, and you and Serena will stay here until then. It's the best way to keep you safe. The Legion can come here for our meetings. We will develop a fail-safe plan while I find you somewhere else to live. And then we will say goodbye."

32

The week passed in a blur. Az and I never had a moment alone. He'd moved himself out of his bedroom and into the spare, and he'd insisted Serena and I take his. Meanwhile, the living room had been transformed into a frat house for demons. A constant stream of them came and went all throughout the day and meetings lasted well into the night.

Open pizza boxes hunkered on top of the dining table. Crumpled papers spilled out of an overflowing trash can. Cans of beer formed a pyramid on the kitchen counter. Az seemed to grow more agitated by the day. His pristine palace had been overrun.

The door flew open and Phenex stomped inside wearing a wicked smile that would make most girls melt. I felt shockingly immune to it, though. In the past, a guy like Phenex might have caught my attention. A dangerous bad boy with tattoos, a crooked past, and a fondness for knives. But he was nothing compared to Az.

"It's done," he announced as he tossed a white apron into the corner. "Got in and out easy. No one expected a goddamn thing. Idiots."

Az had decided the only way he'd go through with our plan was if we guaranteed my safety. He'd even put the whole plot at risk to give me a way out of the ball. Phenex had posed as a caterer to get inside the building before the party. Once inside, he'd found the bathroom window and made sure it was unlocked.

"Where is it?" I asked from my perch on the edge of the dining table. Hendrix sat on my knee, cooing happily.

Phenex traipsed over to a wall that had been trans-formed into a massive whiteboard. He yanked off the top of a pen with his teeth and then scribbled a drawing of the building's interior. The blue ink showed a maze of corridors. Wherever we were going, it wasn't a little apartment in Hell's Kitchen.

"Here." He stabbed a hole he'd left at the bottom edge of the drawing. "This is the door. You go down this hall, hang a left, and go all the way down here. Bathroom's inside this door. There are four stalls. Wait until it's empty, and then climb out the window here. A fire escape's just outside it. Easy way out. No one will even know you're gone."

I nodded and ignored the tension pounding against my skull. "Yep, no problem at all."

Az frowned. "What if someone sees her going into the bathroom?"

Phenex shrugged. "Humans go to the bathroom all the time. No one will notice."

My brows arched. "*Humans* go to the bathroom all the time? As opposed to supernaturals...?"

From the kitchen, Caim barked out a laugh. "Depends on the supernatural."

Okay, this was weird. And potentially TMI. I didn't really want to think about the bathroom habits of demons. Still, my gaze drifted to where Serena lounged on the sofa with a new book in hand. She'd moved on from brutal stabbings in the dark and was now reading a faerie romance.

She shrugged. "Don't look at me. I'm not a demon."

So werewolves were a yes. Demons...no? What about vampires? Probably also a no. They were the undead after all. Weird.

"Can we please stop talking about toilet habits and get back to the task at hand?" Bael drawled as he stepped up to the whiteboard. He tossed a soccer ball in his hands as he stared at the messily-drawn map.

Phenex nodded. "Mia, are you happy with where the bathroom is? You okay with climbing out onto the fire escape?"

"Probably?" I said, my voice more of a question-mark than a statement. "How many stories up is it? Four? Twelve?"

"Forty-seven," Phenex said evenly.

My mouth dropped open. "*Forty-seven?*"

Shit, oh shit, oh shit. I wasn't afraid of heights per se, but climbing out of a window forty-seven stories high was pure insanity. Fire escapes were wobbly, rusted things. And I'd have to climb down forty-seven ladders to reach the ground.

I needed to sit.

"She looks pale," Valac said from where he perched on a chair in the back corner. He was hidden in the shadows. Pretty typical for him. "Humans do that when they're scared."

"Very pale," Stolas muttered as he strode across the floor to take my elbow and usher me into a seat. "Don't worry, Mia. We'll be right up on the roof waiting for you. As soon as you step inside, we'll fly you to safety."

Fly?

"I don't think that's any better."

"You wanted to do this," Az said, folding his arms. "This is what it entails. If you want to back out, now's your last chance."

I met his gaze. He wanted me to quit because he didn't think I could handle it. "No, I'll do it."

His jaw hardened. "Fine. You better get ready then. We have two hours before we have to leave."

❦

The glittering lobby yawned before us like a monster's massive jaws. Or maybe I was just being dramatic. Az walked by my side, and I had my hand tucked into his arm. The soft material of his fitted black suit slid like silk against my fingers, and the scent of his musky cologne peppered the air.

We followed several other guests to a bank of elevators along the back wall. Men in crisp suits with glamorous women on their arms, a pair of suited women with their hands clasped, and a very obvious vampire who stood alone. His red eyes caught mine, and the hint of a sharp canine snapped out from his top lip. I swallowed hard and glanced away.

Other than that weirdo, it was impossible to tell who was who. Each couple would have a human and a supernatural between them, but none of the supernaturals were being obvious about what they were. None of these humans would know their dates were supernatural Lucifer fans who planned to sacrifice their souls. Only me.

Each couple took a separate elevator until finally it was our turn to join the party. We rode in silence, tension bouncing between us. As the floors rolled by, I couldn't help but wonder if this moment would be the last one we shared. My bags were packed. Az had found me an apartment and a job, and Phenex was assigned to take me to my new home as soon as I was done here.

We'd signed two contracts. One to make Lucifer happy and one meant only for our eyes. Az had insisted, as a way to keep me safe. The deal was this: if I ever showed my face at *Infernal* without an invitation, I'd lose my soul.

"You look very striking tonight, Mia," Az finally said as we rushed past floor twenty-nine. "I wanted to tell you before we go inside."

I cast a glance at my gown. It was a long, flowing number in a deep silky green. The color was the perfect contrast to my flaming red hair that I'd decided to wear in loose waves. Priyanka had come around to help with my makeup, and she'd given me a very distinct swoosh of eyeliner that made my eyes pop. I'd never made this much of an effort for a normal date, let alone a fake one.

"Thanks." I bit my lip and tried not to stare in his direction. He looked as dangerously lethal as he normally did. Shadows curled across his jaw, and his pupils looked like pools of darkness. A sudden *zing* shot through my gut. That stupid thing again. It was starting to piss me off.

He turned to me and took my hand in his. "Mia, I just want you to know that—"

The elevator doors whirred open. His hand tightened around mine, and he pulled me close. Whatever he'd been about to say was lost to the sudden buzz of activity in the loft. Hand in hand, we strode into the ball.

Brilliantly-lit goblets drifted through the air on invisible strings. Intricate designs had been carved into the golden-edged walls, and butlers pranced by with elaborate silver plates topped in miniature food. The sound of harps drifted through the loft, but the thing that caught my eye the most was the far wall.

It was entirely gone.

The room faced the Uptown buildings, and a warm breeze rustled the hair around my shoulders. There wasn't a single pane of glass. Not even a railing. Where the floor ended, it just…dropped off.

My nerves jangled in my belly as I glanced up at Az. His gaze was locked on the pane-less windows, his jaw clenched. "I believe it's time for you to make your exit now."

I gave a nod, my gut twisting. This was goodbye. The end to me and Az, not that there'd ever been anything more than strained lust between us. I tried to tell myself that my life would be better off without demons in it, but my heart didn't believe a word of it.

With a deep breath, I turned to go, just as a glittering Eisheth stepped in front of me. Her gown matched her lip color—deep red fabric that stretched across her curvy frame. She flashed me a painted smile and reached out with long, perfectly-manicured fingernails. They sliced through my hair, tangling in my curled strands.

"Don't you look cute?" she asked in a patronizing tone that made me want to punch her right in her pixie nose. "Here, have a drink."

Eisheth grabbed three champagne flutes from a nearby butler, handed one to me, and then passed another to Az. He took it begrudgingly and gave me a nod to do the same. I needed to play along until we could get rid of her, or she'd realize something was up.

As I took a sip, Eisheth latched her fingers on my arm. "I'd love to show you something, darling Mia."

I opened my mouth to argue and shot a panicked glance toward Az. This wasn't part of our plan. The Legion was waiting for me on the roof, and I needed to get out before things went down. Az would never stop the sacrifice with me here. All these humans—whichever ones they were—would lose their souls if we didn't pull this off.

Still, there was little I could do as Eisheth dragged me over to a painted symbol on the floor. Drawn in bright red paint, it looked a lot like Az's seal, just… different. The circles inside the swirling lines curled left more than right. And the pointed tail was nowhere to be seen. My heart pounded as I stared down at it. It was another demon's seal. *Lucifer's.*

I took a step back as fear transformed my knees into jelly.

"What do you think?" Eisheth asked in a sickly-sweet voice.

"I…" With trembling hands, I downed the rest of my champagne and shoved the glass toward Az. He watched me with pinched brows and flat lips. He couldn't say anything, not without giving us away. I had to do this all on my own.

"I need to go to the bathroom," I blurted out.

Eisheth opened her mouth, but I didn't stick around long enough to hear what she planned to say. With a determination I didn't know I had, I hightailed it out of the room and soared down the quiet hallway. Following Phenex's instructions, I hung a left and practically *ran* to the end door. I flung it open and stumbled inside, lungs aching, heart racing. The door slammed shut behind me and I slumped against the cold, biting metal.

"Thank god," I whispered, wiping the sweat off my forehead. I may have seemed a little frantic, but at least I got out of there. Now Az could save those souls.

After I caught my breath, I pushed away from the door and reached for the window. It was shut. Frowning, I tugged at the bottom, wondering how that had happened. Phenex had said he'd left it open so I could get out as quickly as possible.

The window didn't budge an inch.

Heart racing, I curled my fingers tightly around the wood and pushed with all my might. Nothing happened. The window wouldn't move. It was almost like…it had been nailed shut. With a gasp, I pushed up onto my toes and saw the nails. Six in a row. Ensuring this window would never again open.

I stumbled back just as a wave of nausea rolled through my head. Catching myself on the sink, I tried to think. Someone had nailed the window shut. After Phenex had been here.

Someone must have found out.

Another wave of nausea tore through me. I stumbled to the side and tried to blink the dark spots out of my eyes.

Maybe I could break the window and climb out that way.

Pain flared through my skull. My body buckled beneath me.

The world tipped sideways, and then shadows filled my mind.

33

Cotton balls filled my mouth. Or maybe it was an old dishrag. Whatever it was, it tasted like dirty socks. Sputtering, I sucked in air and flipped open my eyes. Candlelight flickered all around me, circling the bloody demon seal on the floor. My heart flipped over as I glanced around and found half a dozen more bound humans surrounding me.

They'd caught me. Az hadn't been able to stop them. And now, we were all going to be sacrificed to Hell.

Shit!

Frantically, I gazed past the flickering flames to find shadowed faces peering back at us. Eisheth was there in the front. Beside her stood that creepy vampire from the lobby. But on her other side…my stomach twisted as a new wave of pain ripped through me. Asmodeus was there. Alive and well. Doing nothing to stop this.

What?!

My mind raged against me, trying to understand what I saw. It seemed like an impossibility. This couldn't be right. Whatever had knocked me out— poison in the champagne most likely—was playing tricks on my mind. Az couldn't be part of this. He just couldn't.

I'd put my trust in him. He'd tried to protect me from all of this. The new contract. The job, the name, the fake passport, and the secret apartment in Brooklyn. All of that had been his idea. Because he'd wanted to save me from Lucifer.

So why wasn't he doing anything?

This didn't make sense.

I tried to meet his gaze, but he avoided my eyes. His jaw clenched as he stared straight ahead, listening to an intense chant spilling from the mouths of a few robed figures in the crowd.

And then Eisheth stepped out from the shadows, her hooded eyes gleaming in the light. She motioned toward Az, who strode forward with a determined set to his shoulders.

"Asmodeus, Commander of the First Legion of Hell, first Prince in line to the throne." Eisheth smiled. "The fallen angels Rafael and Michael have brought accusations against you. They believe you are working against our King. This is your opportunity to prove they're wrong. Sacrifice this human's soul, and all will be forgiven."

Eyes flying wide, I screamed against the cotton dishrag in my mouth, but only a muffled whimper came out. Heart rattling beneath my ribcage, I tried to scuttle back, but my bound ankles and wrists didn't let me get far. Suddenly, I understood everything. They'd trapped Az in an impossible situation. This was his chance to show them they were wrong, to prevent Lucifer from finding out the truth, and to save his Legion, but...surely he wouldn't go through with it.

Surely he was just playing along until he found an opportunity to rebel against them.

He wouldn't actually sacrifice my soul...

Would he?

His words rang in my ears.

I will do anything to get what I want.

Just because I am helping humans doesn't mean I am good.

I am still a demon, Mia.

The Legion are my family.

But I had seen the good in him. He'd proven it ten times over. He could have been pretending, but what would have been the point of that? If he'd wanted to sacrifice my soul, he didn't need all these games. He could have just done it.

But how could I trust him when I was literally lying bound in the middle of Lucifer's demon seal?

Everyone else in my life had let me down. My parents had abandoned me. My sister had, too, even after everything I'd done for her. My friends. My neighbors. The whole damn world.

Fear thrummed through my veins.

Eisheth took a deep sniff of the air and smiled. "Do you smell that?"

"The delicious scent of fear," Az murmured back.

"Good," Eisheth said. "Very good. Now do it, Az. Stab her right in her pretty fucking heart."

"With pleasure." Az reached behind him and pulled a long gleaming sword from thin air. The blade rippled with flames, splashing orange fragments across the blood-painted floor.

Terror screamed through me as I tried to scrabble back. He was really going to do this. There was no mistaking the viciousness on his face. How could I have been so wrong? A demon loomed before me with eyes the color of ice, and he was going to kill me. My entire body trembled. The fear left nothing behind but a numb heart and a bitter mind. If only I wasn't human. If only I could fight back...

Wait a minute.

I still had his fucking signet ring.

Az strode toward me with his sword held high. Before I could talk myself out of it, I pulled a deep breath in through my flared nostrils and threw all of my emotions toward him. I still didn't know how the hell to use this thing. I just went by instinct. All I thought was *push*.

An invisible force slammed into Az and threw him out the window.

No, not the window.

The blank wall that held no glass.

His eyes widened as he hurtled out into the darkness. My heart stopped beating, and my helpless cry was muffled against the rag. Even though he'd been two seconds away from sacrificing me to his demon overlord, the last thing I wanted was to kill him.

Just as he began to tumble toward the streets, he

pushed his dark feathered wings from his back. In the darkness, I swore I saw the flicker of a smile.

My heart thundered back to life, galloping up into my throat. I'd managed to knock him back, but he'd return with a vengeance now. And I was pretty sure this ring had to recharge before I could use it again. All I'd done was make him angry.

Az flapped his enormous wings, his gaze zeroing in on me. And then two massive figures thundered into the ball, appearing out of nowhere. Their golden feathers gleamed against the candlelight, their shirtless bodies corded with power and rage. Suriel and Gabriel shot toward the cloaked figures with swords bigger than my body.

My mouth dropped open. Or, it would have, if it hadn't been stuffed with a rag that tasted like socks. The angels swung their swords at the figures. Several of the supernaturals screamed and ran, charging toward the elevators. Only a few stuck around to fight.

Blood arced through the air as the swords made contact. Bodies tumbled to the ground. With tears in my eyes, I crawled away from the carnage and pressed my back against the nearest wall. The other human sacrifices joined me and tried to shield their eyes. I hated being helpless like this, unable to do anything other than watch the angels strike down their foes.

If I survive this, I swore to myself, *I'll learn how to fight.*

The battle was over not long after it began. The two fallen angels stood heaving over the supernaturals. The whole thing had been a blur, and it had been next to impossible to follow the fight. All that mattered was that our captors were dead or gone. Glancing around, relief filled my heart.

Az wasn't among the dead.

I frowned at that thought. Why should I even care? He'd tried to sacrifice me.

Suriel strode toward me, knelt, and unbound my wrists. Then I yanked that stupid rag out of my mouth and spit. Not very ladylike, but whatever. That thing was gross.

"Good timing," I told him. He offered a hand, which I reluctantly took. Out of all the supernaturals in the world, why did it have to be this guy?

A smile curled his lips. "You say that like we didn't plan it this way."

Shock flickered through me. "Plan it? How?"

He glanced around us. "It's better if we talk about this somewhere else. Come with me."

He held out his arms, and I gave him a look. "What exactly are you suggesting?"

"I need to take you somewhere. Flying will be quickest."

I folded my arms. "Absolutely not."

"I just saved your goddamn life, Mia." He held his arms wider. "Now stop arguing and hang on."

All I could do was stare at him. Leaving with a fallen angel who had kind of been stalking me…after everything that had happened? Probably not the best idea. He and his friend had cornered me in the dark streets. They'd been snooping around, trying to pry into *Infernal*.

They were against the Legion. But then again, maybe they'd had reason to be. Not ten minutes ago, Az had tried to stab me with a sword. None of the Legion had flown in to help when all hell broke loose. They had tricked me and betrayed me.

So why did I still have any shred of loyalty toward them?

Sighing, I edged in close to Suriel and wrapped my arms around his neck. Heart pounding, I hung on while he soared out into the city skies. The world dropped from beneath me as my legs dangled like puppets on a string. His heavy wings blasted hot air into my face as he rushed across Manhattan.

I realized far too late where he was taking me.

Straight back to *Infernal*.

34

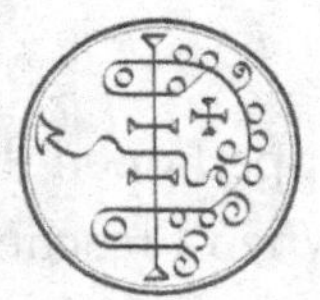

A s soon as my boots hit the sidewalk outside the club, I shoved Suriel's bare chest and stumbled back. "What the hell is this? Why did you bring me here?"

He folded his arms. "There are some pretty anxious demons inside who want to see you."

I shook my head as tears filled my eyes. "Is this some kind of joke? Az just tried to sacrifice my soul to Lucifer. He came at me with a *sword*. He was going to kill me, Suriel. I thought you were saving me from him and instead you drop me right into his lap again?"

"He wasn't going to kill you." The angel pointed at the back door that led into the bowels of the club. "They'll explain everything. You're invited inside. If you don't want to hear their side of the story, then fine. I'll take you to your new apartment in Brooklyn."

For a moment, all I could do was stare at him. I

311

should leave. Go on with my life. But it was a life that Asmodeus had designed for me. Obviously, if he wanted me dead, he wouldn't have to lift a finger to find me. He'd picked out my new name. My new job. Even my new apartment. And if I tried to flee to Canada or something, would I get very far?

Probably not.

Dammit.

With a growl, I ripped open the door and stormed down the corridor. When I reached the meeting room, they were all in there waiting for me. Pinched expressions were carved on every face. I stepped inside, bracing myself for battle. They all leapt from their seats and cheered.

The demons surrounded me in an instant. Arms wound around me, hair and muscled skin slammed into my cheek. I couldn't even breathe for how hard they squeezed me. Caim was there. So was Stolas and Phenex and Bael. Even Valac joined in. The scent of flames roared in my head.

For a moment, panic ripped my heart open wide, but then it slowly ebbed. They weren't trying to crush me. They were…hugging me.

When they all stumbled back, my eyes found Az. He huddled in the back corner, arms folded, eyes downcast. He'd been the only one who hadn't rushed to my side the instant I'd walked through the door.

"You pointed a sword at me," was all I could say.

His mouth tightened as his eyes stayed locked on the floor. "I'm sorry. I never wanted to do any of this, but it was our only choice. I had to make you believe that I'd betrayed you. She isn't a demon, but Eisheth can scent emotions even better than I can."

"Wait." My stomach dropped. "You're saying you *planned* all of that?"

He nodded and finally glanced up. Pain churned in the depths of his eyes. "The plan we told you wasn't the real plan. I hated to lie to you, but if you'd known the truth, Eisheth would have scented it on you. You had to believe you were in actual danger. She had to smell your fear."

I shook my head. "So when Phenex went early to unlock the window…"

"I hammered it shut," he admitted with an uneasy cough. "I'm sorry, Mia."

"Because you wanted me to be scared."

It made sense. Horrible, brutal sense. They'd lied to me about the plan.

"You have to understand," Az said, pushing off the wall. When he stepped into the light, the shadows danced away from his skin. "Rafael told Eisheth everything before he left for Hell. She wanted to test me. She wanted me to prove the angels were wrong. I had to do whatever it took to keep my Legion safe. What I did tonight…it will go a long way toward convincing Lucifer we aren't against him. She thinks I would have sacrificed you if the angels hadn't interfered."

"The angels. Why did they show up?"

"We asked them to fly in to save you and the others since we couldn't do it ourselves," Az said quietly. "I took a chance in trusting they'd be on our side once they understood what we do in here."

Caim gripped my elbow as all the blood rushed from my face. Az had used me. To protect himself. I shouldn't have been surprised but I was. Had he ever really wanted me to back out of the Covenant Ball? Or had his objections been just for show, too? If I'd tried to leave before tonight, would he have let me?

At least he wasn't actually evil, but…he'd still dangled me as bait. Without me knowing.

"You should have told me," I whispered.

"I couldn't."

"That was dangerous, what you just did. What if something had gone wrong?"

"I was right there with you the whole time." His hands fisted. "I'd never let anything happen to you."

I turned away and blew out a hot breath. This hurt far more than it should have. What was worse, I understood why he'd done it. Hell, if I'd known, I would have volunteered myself. But I hated that he hadn't told me. I felt like a pawn.

"What about everything else?" I asked, turning back toward him. "The apartment and the new job. If Eisheth tells Lucifer you tried to sacrifice me, then maybe I don't have to go anywhere else. I can—"

"The job and the apartment are real." His eyes shuttered. "I asked Suriel to bring you here so that we could explain everything to you. But it's time for you to go now. You need to lead a normal human life. Without me or my Legion in it."

35

The one-bedroom apartment in Williamsburg sat in the middle of a tree-lined block. Az and I trailed up the four flights of stairs and pushed inside the steel door. When I closed it behind us, I spotted six different locks, two of which were electric. A number pad had been bolted to the wall beside it.

Hardwood floors gleamed against the sunset streaming in through the small windows that faced the street. Az strode over to them, peered down at the ground, and then nodded to himself.

"You need to keep these windows locked at all times. Never open them." He vanished from the living room to check out the rest of the apartment. With a sigh, I shuffled into the tiny kitchen. Enough room for one. Just me.

Serena had gone back to her own apartment. Az had offered to find us a two-bedroom to share, but she'd have to go into hiding with me to do that and she didn't want to leave her job. Since she was a were-wolf, Az felt satisfied that she could protect herself, but I'd asked his Legion to check in on her from time to time.

Rafael—Noah—would return from Hell soon enough. I hated that he knew where Serena lived.

"All right," Az said when he returned to the living room. "It's all clear."

I nodded, heart twanging. I hated that this was goodbye. But worse than that, our final moments would always be remembered as weird and awkward. I didn't know what to say to him anymore. He didn't seem to know what to say to me, either.

"Thanks," I finally said, hugging my arms to my chest. "It seems like a nice place."

"It's a good building on a good street. I know I don't need to tell you this, but keep your real name to yourself."

"I think I can manage that," I said quietly. "I did that a lot for two years."

His eyes softened. "I know, and I'm sorry. When I first brought you into this, I intended to help you get a job using your own name so you could move on with your life. I hate that it's turned out like this."

I sighed and closed my eyes. "It's okay. You were only trying to do the right thing. It's just that some-times the right thing is more complicated than you think. We saved those souls, Az. That's all that matters."

"That's *not* all that matters, Mia," he said hoarsely.

My eyes flew open. His gaze latched onto mine. Tense heat rippled between us, and a *zing* went through my heart. Az took a step toward me, those shadows rippling across his skin. His hand caught mine. He pulled me to his chest and wound his arms around my back.

My heart thundered against me so hard, I knew he'd feel the rhythm of it in his bones. All my anger toward him melted from that single touch, and a sigh popped from my throat as I leaned against him.

Our foreheads touched.

Az tensed and pulled away. "I'm sorry. I have to go. This is where it ends."

My hands dropped to my sides as I watched him stride through the door and vanish from my life.

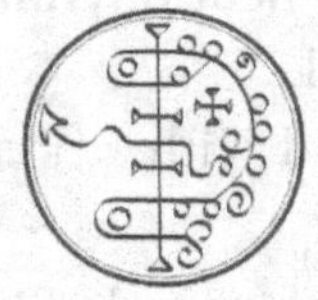

"Mia!" Serena called out as she pushed into my apartment, clad in an all-black suit, with Hendrix on her shoulder. "I have your pigeon, and I have news."

My lips cracked into a grin as I held out a hand toward my pigeon. He cooed, hopped off Serena's shoulder, and landed on my arm. It had been a full week since I'd seen him, and I'd feared the worst. Had he flown off into the great city, never to be seen again?

But no, he was here.

Serena had found him.

"First, thank you," I said as I strode straight toward the kitchen to rustle up some bread for Hendrix. "And two, please give me the news immediately. While I'm grateful for my job, being a receptionist at a publishing company is boring as hell."

She stopped short and arched a brow. "So you

haven't found out anything about Jon Snow's fate yet?"

I laughed. "No, Serena. I'm a receptionist, not an editor. And those books are published by an entirely different house anyway."

"Yeah, yeah." She stabbed her finger into my chest. "But if you do hear anything, I need you to tell me as soon as possible."

"It's a deal," I said with a nod. "Now what's your news?"

"Ah." Her smile dropped. "Big stuff is happening in the supernatural world. My bosses are going crazy. Lucifer arrived in Manhattan yesterday."

All the blood drained from my face. I sat hard on the stool beside my kitchen counter. "Lucifer's here."

Logically, I'd known this was coming. He was always going to leave Hell to investigate Rafael's claims. And there was nothing to worry about. The little parlor trick at the ball had convinced Eisheth that Az hadn't changed sides. She'd pass that on to Lucifer, and he'd go on his merry way back to Hell.

I didn't have anything to worry about. And even if he came looking for me, he'd never find me. I was no longer Mia McNally now. I went by Luna instead.

"He's coming by the offices tomorrow to look around." She grimaced. "Seems he found out we're Az's lawyers, and he wants to review some of his contracts."

"Wait." My stomach dropped. "Can he do that?"

"He can literally do whatever he wants. No one is going to stand up to the King of Hell."

"Right...Az doesn't have any incriminating deals on record with you, does he?"

She shrugged. "Honestly, I have no idea. I've never worked on his contracts, and I don't have access to them. Only the partners do. I tried to have a sneaky look today, but I couldn't get past the login screen. Anyway, it's probably fine. Az is smart. He wouldn't have left behind evidence."

"Right. It's probably fine," I repeated. "If there was anything incriminating there, he would have taken care of it."

"Exactly." She patted me on the knee and pressed her lips together.

I narrowed my eyes. "So then why do you still look so worried?"

"Well, there's another thing. I don't know if it's just a rumor."

My gut twisted. "What is it, Serena?"

"I need you to stay calm, and—"

"Tell me what it is," I said, fisting my hands around the edge of the stool. "Just give it to me straight."

"You'll stay calm?"

"Doubt it."

She tightened her grip on my knee and sighed. "Alright, fine. I guess I can't blame you. I wouldn't be calm either. Lucifer is looking for you."

I nodded, breathing in sharply through my nose. "Right, okay. We saw this coming. It was only a matter of time. That's why Az hid me. It's fine. Totally fine. I'm protected here, right? Fake name, new apartment. No one knows how to find me except for you and Az."

"There's more," she whispered.

My heart rattled. "What more could there possibly be?"

"Lucifer wants to make you his bride."

ALSO BY JENNA WOLFHART

The Mist King

Of Mist and Shadow

Of Ash and Embers

Of Night and Chaos

The Fallen Fae

Court of Ruins

Kingdom in Exile

Keeper of Storms

Tower of Thorns

Realm of Ashes

Prince of Shadows (A Novella)

Demons After Dark: Covenant

Devilish Deal

Infernal Games

Wicked Oath

Demons After Dark: Temptation

Sinful Touch

Darkest Fate

Hellish Night

ABOUT THE AUTHOR

Jenna Wolfhart spends her days tucked away in her writing studio in the countryside. When she's not dreaming up stories about swoony fae men and stabby heroines, you can find her doing CrossFit competitions, rewatching Game of Thrones, and drinking far too much coffee. Born and raised in America, Jenna now lives in England with her husband and her two dogs, Nero and Vesta.

www.jennawolfhart.com
jenna@jennawolfhart.com
tiktok.com/@jennawolfhart